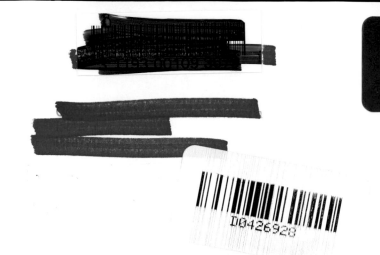

Paper Fish

Paper Fish

Tina De Rosa

Afterword by Edvige Giunta

The Feminist Press
at The City University of New York
New York

Published by The Feminist Press
at the City University of New York
311 East 94th Street, New York, NY 10128-5684.

First Feminist Press edition, 1996

Excerpt from "Mutt Bitch" on page 139 from *Vendetta* by Rose Romano. ©1990 by Rose Romano. Reprinted by permission of the author.

02 01 00 99 98 97 96   9 8 7 6 5 4 3 2

Library of Congress Cataloging-in-Publication Data

De Rosa, Tina.
    Paper fish / by Tina De Rosa : afterword by Edvige Giunta.
      p.   cm.
    Originally published: Chicago : Wine Press, 1980.
    Includes bibliographical references.
    ISBN 1-55861-146-0 (alk. paper). — ISBN 1-55861-145-2 (pbk. : alk. paper).
    I. Title.
PS3554.E1156P36   1996
813.54—dc20   96-19342
                                                              CIP

This publication is made possible, in part, by public funds from the New York State Council on the Arts and the National Endowment for the Arts. The Feminist Press would also like to thank Mariam K. Chamberlain, Marilyn French, Helene D. Goldfarb, Joanne Markell, Caroline Urvater, and Genevieve Vaughan for their generosity.

Printed in the United States of America on acid-free paper by Royal Book Manufacturing Inc., Norwich, CT..

For Bruce,
a friend of mine.

CONTENTS

ACKNOWLEDGEMENTS

It is seventeen years since I completed the final draft of *Paper Fish* at Ragdale in Lake Forest, Illinois.

Time is so mysterious, blessing and robbing. For me, in the seventeen years since I first sat down to begin the many drafts of *Paper Fish,* time has blessed me with many friends: another family. So many that I hope I do not forget anyone as I acknowledge my sister, Fred Gardaphe and Susan, Anthony Tamburri, Paul Giordano, Edvige Giunta, Joshua Fausty, Father Patrick Henry, Gloria Ciucci Leischner and Ralph, Jerre Mangione, Bill Towner, Rona Jaffe, Lynn James, Michael Anania, Patricia Touhy, Judy Polovich, Mary Jo Bona and her parents, Nicole Bensoussan, Bee Grabowski, and all the people at Little Friends, Fred Hang, Bertha at Saint Margaret's, Alice Ryerson Hayes and Albert, Carroll Stuhlmueller, Father James Gleason, Father Emmett Collins, Father Kevin Fraher, Father Gino Dal Piaz, James Serritella, Ralph Mills, Jr., Nancy Cirillo, Fred Stern, Carol Glick and Norman, Jan O'Toole, Connor and Austin and Boo and their parents. I acknowledge Judy Truett, Mary Larkin, Leon and Dan, Lee and Bonnie and Joan, Peggy and Jim Tucci, Michael Maria, Wes Bengston, Susan Collins, Larry Leck, and Marianne Moore. I acknowledge Nora O'Connell, Suzy and Jackie Larkin, Stephanie Fernandez, Stacy Verdone, and Christine. I acknowledge Barry Goodman, Jim Axeman, Julia Sparacino, and Lillian Baldi. I acknowledge the Carmelites in Des Plaines, the Scalabrinians in Stone Park, and the Redemptorists in Chicago. I acknowledge the Illinois Arts Council, the Ragdale Foundation in Lake Forest, and the Rona Jaffe Foundation in New York.

I acknowledge Stephen Pearl, Edward Lazzar, Anthony Grande, Stuart Poticha, Quentin Young, and Birgitta McGuire.

I acknowledge Florence Howe and all the staff at The Feminist Press who have placed so much faith in *Paper Fish*.

Above all I acknowledge Bruce, to whom this book will always be dedicated. Bruce: my mother thanks you, my father thanks you, my sister thanks you. And I thank you.

Tina De Rosa
Park Ridge, Illinois
1996

Our images and our memories
face each other,
bewildered,
in a mirror.
Who is to solve the mystery?

PRELUDE

This is my mother,

washing strawberries, at a sink yellowed by all foods, all liquids, yellowed. This is my mother scalping the green hair of strawberries, scalping them clean, leaving a pink bald spot where the green hair was, and the strawberries grow bumps under cold water, or were they already there, and nobody noticed? These are my mother's hands, skin that has touched thousands of things now touches strawberries, and strawberries are the first thing she has ever touched, but she is not noticing. The sugar will be broken over the strawberries, the strawberries will grow cold in the icebox and she glances at the man outside the window three floors below, who is her husband. When I was little, I did not know the season of strawberries, did not know that my mother and father were married. When I was little, I wanted to pick apples, but it was always too late, the snow fell too soon, chilling the fruit. The man who was my mother's husband and who would become my father experienced great shots of pain when he died. Death comes too slowly, too quickly. He barely had time to finish his work in the garage that afternoon. He would be dead in twenty-one years. What could he accomplish in one hour? My mother's skin brushes strawberries, her skin will brush my father's, that night their skin will make me, but I know none of this. I am less than the strawberries, I am less than the carving my father is making with his hands, less than the brown intent of his eyes over wood, less. I exist with the god of decisions, and he is deciding me. I do not see any of this, do not know any of this, because I am less than a fraction, the smallest fraction of time, of moment, of memory. I sit beside the god of decisions, who is considering me. My sister has already been born. She was born the first child. Over and over the family says: She was broken early in life, a toy that was too beautiful. She frightened my mother, who did not know what to make of her and my father, my father was appalled. No child could be that beautiful. Early in her life something happened, something that went without explanation, and she was broken. It is all leaves, leaves falling out of a tree, with no hands to catch them. No one asked questions. Everyone acted as though none of it were happening. No one recognized her, no one saw beyond the black eyes. No one looked. My sister was a swan, a black swan that flew into the incorrect night, followed the wrong moon, and my family was left with glass eyes.

My father's hands are long, are fine. The fingers are straight, are perfect. They are pianist's fingers, carving wood. They are fingers that were intended to know the skin of the piano. The skin of my father's fingers touching wood will touch the skin of my mother's hands killing strawberries, and I will begin in white waters. My father will never play the piano. She will not give me her blood directly. She will not give me her blood as a free gift. I will steal it from the thin skin of her cells and inside her body I will survive. I will skin the walls of her

2

cells and I will leave no scar. The arm of my father, which is this moment strong, which this moment is strong enough to carve wood, will one day scream with pain, but my father will remain silent, only his eyes will be a curtain of water. That will happen in twenty-one years, so what can he accomplish in one hour? The curtain of his eyes will lift with the last pain and his soul will be a scrim, lifting, and my father's eyes will open and know. His eyes will open and speak; they will say to his death, "I know you. You lied." No one will hear him say this. In the kitchen, by the yellow sink, my mother throws the green hair away and the strawberry scalps glisten.

PART I

THE MEMORY

Marco was a young man, tall and thin, still not comfortable in his policeman's uniform, when he walked into the restaurant where Sarah was a waitress. He was, in the eyes of the department, still a rookie, Italian and stupid. He was treated politely, but with little respect. He felt the hatred of the men he worked with, but he was proud with the pride of a young man who has found his place in life. When he awoke in the morning, it was to put on the uniform of his city, he was allowed to wear a badge, to carry a gun. That was a great trust, his mother and sisters and brother looked at him with silent eyes, served him the best meat in the evenings. His father held a surly silence; he looked at his slim son with anger and with honor, and was silent. Marco sat looking at the shiny gabardine, he removed the cap from his head and rubbed the hard red line it sliced into his forehead. The young waitress asked him what he wanted. On the table she placed a glass of water beside the cap with his number 274 in clean metal. In the supple light of her eyes there flashed a thing that caressed his chest and burned it. In the line of her black hair pulled behind her ears, in the little rhinestones that gemmed her white ears, there flashed this thing. He ordered scrambled eggs, which he did not like. She wore a white waitress dress of crinkled cotton. She disappeared into the kitchen.

Sarah was tired that day, and her tooth hurt. It was abscessed, the dentist said, and must be pulled. Her father said they did not have the money, but they never had the money. She ran her tongue over the hard red lump in her gum and gave her father the order for eggs. It was a hot day, the uniform clung to her under her arms. In the kitchen, the heat was red hot and steam; the pots sweated. The sunlight through the windows banged the pots hard and metallic, the silver light bounced off them and into her eyes. The pain in her mouth reached down her neck, and she licked the sore tooth again. In the corner washing dishes, her mother was already old and shrunken. Her little body was humped and broken and angry with the white suds that rose from the sink and covered her arms to the elbows. Sarah picked up the plate of scrambled eggs and returned to the young policeman sitting at a table that was barely big enough for one. She noticed that the tablecloth was off-center, that the white metal was showing underneath. The young policeman looked up and fell into the sea. He fell beneath the surface

4

of the sea. He floated into the blue water, his head showing like a rose that has a face, like a silent animal filled with anguish, filled with joy, and his heart, his life, was liquid, fluid like a fine fish, and he fell far beneath the sea. He was a marionette without strings, the sea was his string, his ribbon, holding him gently. His life dallied below him, below the water, his life was magnificent and his smile was small, above the liquid line of the sea. He was a doll, floating, with a marvelous secret just under the water. The woman serving him his breakfast looked at him out of feather eyes. The plates hit the table's surface like the bite of a cold tooth. She was confused, she looked away.

Outside the restaurant window, two children looked in; they pressed their faces against the window of the restaurant and they watched. The restaurant filled with light, as though it were at the bottom of the sea. The children filled their hands with the light, they tossed it above their heads, and the light landed on their hands, their faces and noses. The children were delighted, their faces were filled. Marco looked at the eggs, looked at her; everything was in love with him because he was alive and confused. The young man moved his hand toward the silverware, the young woman poured the coffee. The room seemed filled with blue water, until only the heads of the man and woman were floating, confused and blinking, and the children waved and waved. God was delighted.

2.

The room here, with the shades drawn, was a twilight blue that she loved. Sarah heard her husband and mother-in-law talking in the kitchen and wondered, then barely cared. She let her hands fall over her belly, felt the loose skin where the space was baby-shaped, and empty. When she was young, she wore a sequined dress with a green feather in her hair, with a green feather she danced, she danced till the night fell away and her feet ached. She took off her shoes and danced. Men looked at her, looked at her flushed red face, her body alive with the dancing, her face laughing. It was her smile, they all of them always loved her smile, because the smile made her beautiful. After dancing, it was walking in early morning with the vendors in the streets sorting out vegetables and fruits, watering their horses to begin the morning round. They were beginning their day's work in overalls, smelling of potatoes and feeling like potato skin, but she, she had been dancing. She passed them in the streets, the old women with the cloth shopping bags, up before the sun and waiting for the vegetable wagons. She passed them in the streets, the horses standing in their own dung flattened like yellow pancakes and drawing flies, she passed the women with onion-wrinkled faces, the men hauling garbage.

Somewhere in her mind, that was all true, that was all true and she was a young woman in love with her new husband, and all night they spent dancing. Somewhere that was all true.

She was thirsty. Her mouth was shrivelling with thirst but the blue twilight was lovely, and she wanted it alone. She wanted in her mouth the meat of a fat orange, she wanted cherries or grapes, she wanted her new husband beside her in the blue night and herself with a feather in her hair. She wanted nothing in the blue twilight. The milk was building, was hurting, her breasts pounded with it.

The baby slipped out and took the green feather with it.

She closed her eyes, thought of cinnamon and cold water.

3.

Sarah's feet were small, the shoes were thin black leather, and torn. The veins in her legs were bulbous and painful. Doriana sat near the sink and watched the legs with the thin gray skin and the thick veins. Her doll's face smiled at her; the tiny fingers were not separate; the diaper was painted on. The doll was cool and rubber against her face; she watched her mother's feet. They shifted on the thin rug before the sink, and the veins breathed under the skin. The potato water sprinkled down onto the floor, and the thin rug ate the water quickly. The kitchen door opened; large black feet entered.

The man was tall and his face was young and spare. When he removed his policeman's cap, it left a hard red line across his forehead. Near his elbow, a large pot of water was reaching a boil. He removed his jacket, loosened his heavy blue tie. His eyes were still young, still lit up with laughter, though that afternoon he had removed a drowned body from the city's lake. The body smelled green and fell apart in his hands. He told his wife about the body, what it felt like. On the floor, Doriana shut her small ears; she did not move her hands, but her ears were shut. Sarah listened, peeled the brown skin from the potato.

Through the kitchen window Marco saw his mother grabbing clothes from the line on her porch across the alley. Her hair was wet from the rain, she was laughing. Sarah walked to the stove, dropped the naked potatoes into the boiling water. She shook salt into it from the blue box and they sat tightly together at the table.

Beneath her arms, Sarah's cotton dress was wet from the water of her body. She bent her head over the chicken, plucking it clean with her tweezers. She told Marco about the wash, the cleaning. Behind her black eyes, a tiredness was forming. The tiredness welled and she felt the rough skin of her feet pressing against the thin leather. She smelled and she knew it and she wanted a bath.

When Marco lifted the window, flakes of yellow paint fell onto his shirt. Flies screamed past, out of the rain. He called to his mother in English. He told her to get out of the rain. She called back to him in

Italian. He laughed and told her to talk English. She pulled a wooden clothespin out of the rope. They both laughed. Her porch door slammed; he heard it in his kitchen. Marco picked up a newspaper, took out the comics, went into the toilet and locked the door. Sarah sat and pulled the hairs out of the chicken. The skin of the chicken was cold against her hot skin. Behind her, the potatoes began to boil.

Doriana was, as a child, particularly impossible to hold in any one place. She seemed always to be moving towards another place, different from this. She was impatient of the glass bottles which held milk for her, of the toys colored especially to make her smile. She was impatient of it all, the little yellow duck was wrong. Sarah remarked it often, it startled her when she approached the crib, to find the child so taken elsewhere. Doriana was beautiful. Her hair was remarkable, thick and curly like a lamb's, Grandma Doria said. Sarah's own hair had once been splendid, she had been proud of it. But the baby's beauty, her brilliant face, remained a mystery to her; she could not guess the child's origin. Washing dishes in the tiny kitchen, Sarah watched the blue bumps which were veins in her hands, looked at the knotting of the blood in her hands, the stretching of skin over bone. The wall above the kitchen sink had split open, the plaster was coarse and gray underneath. Outside the window, the sounds never ceased, the deathless call of children playing in summer heat, the chew of roller skates against cement, the stink and clatter of the cars. Always when she was off doing a chore in another part of the flat, Doriana cried and the mother wiped her hands on a thin towel before lifting her. Her belly bumped against the chipped sink. The second child inside her stirred.

In his room, Marco smoked cigarettes; he lit paper after endless paper filled with tobacco and filled his lungs with the smoke. The skin inside his chest winced. The bedroom window faced into a world filled with the gray smoke of dead fish being burned at the market. Always in the summertime the fish market across the alley burned the dead fish during the day; the cold-water flat filled with the smell. Sarah went pale from it; she breathed it until she could stand it no longer, then she shut the windows and watched the fish smoke outside, pressed flat against the glass like a soiled bed sheet. Once she vomited silently into the kitchen sink.

There had been a morning between them when they sat over their coffee cups and the coffee was black inside his cup and pale white in hers; his was sweet with anisette. The coffee grew cold. He had come home the night before like the snapped string of some instrument. There was no limit to human depravity, he touched it every day in his uniform of a city policeman. It was more a part of his life than the skin of his own hand. Only because of the crystal did he survive any of it. He preserved in the confusion of his mind a kind of crystal, a small clearing that had solidified itself like stone. In this crystal he often stood and felt himself clean, and thus, clean and new, did he watch the raw world. The crystal seeded his world; it bore fruit. Because of the crystal, he read. Because of the crystal he purchased records of classical music to which he listened repeatedly alone in the living room. Because of the crystal, he could return after a day on the streets in which he had gathered the severed leg of a man or the remains of a suicide and silently sit by the lamp.

But the crystal did not always suffice. This turning to his wife in the night had nothing to do with the crystal, or with him. It was something apart, something which grew out of the green fear which filled his lungs in the dark. Then he needed the touch of her flesh against his, and he took it. He had had to wake her. She had stopped expecting him. In the early days of their marriage, she had spent unmarked hours washing her only white nightgown, maintaining it, immaculate. She scrubbed it at the washboard until her hands were cut, but the gown was white. She had washed and brushed her magnificent hair until it shone blue. She was lovely. He had always found her so. Hers was the beauty of women which he had watched all through his young manhood, and his eyes had grown moist with the contemplation of it. Such a woman should be worshipped, guarded, protected. Then he had married one. Her body overwhelmed him. He did not know what to do with it. Unveiling her large breasts, he was astounded. Pressing his face against them, into her hair, he wanted to weep. He felt feeble in his soul, in his body. He felt his legs had dropped off and he floated in midair. The pits of his arms grew cold, then wet. On the first night, she had stood there in the dark, her hair and her breasts luxuriant, and looked at him. When he did nothing, she took his head in her hands and held him to her. He wept. Then he heard her voice, calling to him sweet as an angel. She rocked him against her body till he suckled her breasts like a child. Later he took down his pajamas and let her touch him. Her fingers were like a little girl's.

Now after he took her in the nights, she fell immediately to sleep, pitched into it as though sleep were a white well filled with silk. He went into the kitchen. He squeezed his eyes shut in the light and stamped dead the cockroaches with his bare feet. The kitchen table was cold; it was the one gift he could give her for the marriage. When she first saw it, she scraped the small price label clean off with a knife and wiped the metal head of the salt cellar before she put it on the table. Across the dark alley he saw the lights still burning in his mother's house. He watched them grow slowly dim in the blue light, and he wept again. He did not think he would weep again. At night, he sat in the window of his kitchen, and the light was electric and yellow behind him. He sat there exhaling blue cigarette smoke into the night; the smoke lifted through the kitchen screen like white snakes, and from the back porch of her home across the alley, Grandma Doria sat in the sleepless nights of old women and watched her fine son alone in the black and yellow night. In the bedroom, Sarah's eyes closed over mercurial dreams and Doriana shut small fists in her sleep.

The rain chased itself through the kitchen window, so quiet one had to look up to see it. Sarah did not look up. She did not know it was raining. The tweezers in her hand was slick with the slickness of chicken flesh; small black hairs clung to it, to her fingers. She sipped from her coffee cup, barely disturbing her rhythm. Behind her, she heard the newspaper pages being slowly turned in the bathroom; she barely listened. She wanted a cigarette; she couldn't have one, now that her husband was home. Wiping one hand clean on her cotton dress, she left black chicken whiskers there. She continued the job; it was something she did every day of her life, something she would do every day for longer into the future than she dare imagine; she prepared the dinner. At the sink she ran cold water over the chicken, washing it much as she washed her own child, her own face, mindlessly, her mind on any place but here, her mind here of all places, from which she could not free it. Doriana looked up at her. The face was extraordinary. The eyes were large and black; they seemed to hold spectacular secrets or no knowledge whatsoever; they looked up from under lids that were tinged almost blue. The face was the soft, fleshy face of a child; it was purer than could be forgiven. Looking down into her own child's face, the mother saw a beauty that she mistrusted. The child would grow to be a graceful woman, and then who would the mother be? She continued washing the chicken. The water was too cold. The child at her feet was a stranger. The water ran over the chicken, a thin film. She would bread it and brown it. She would chop green peppers and onions and mushrooms; she would brown them all until the onions went clear. She would place the vegetables over the chicken like a small blanket, pour tomato sauce over it all, and that would be dinner for her family this Tuesday. She moved over to the icebox for green peppers. The floor beneath the icebox was wet from the dripping iceblock; it formed a small dirty pool on the linoleum. The pool from the melting ice wet her feet through the thin shoes.

Inside her body, the baby that was growing made her profile a strange one. Walking was difficult. She kept her feet slightly separate and looked like a crippled dancer who has forgotten her role. She walked across the kitchen to the dripping icebox and she maintained her balance on the tightrope. Beneath the tightrope of her kitchen was another family, a Mexican family living one floor below them. In that kitchen, the Mexican mother chopped lettuce and shelled beans. Her husband sat in the corner, his skin burned the suede brown of a Mexican living through the summer, and watched his brown-skinned wife. In the kitchen just below Sarah, the Mexican husband was squeezing the large tit of his wife, and the wife was laughing delightedly. When Sarah upstairs was preparing the dinner on her table, the Mexican couple below was tumbling and heaving in their bed, locked wetly together. Upstairs, Sarah was balanced precariously on her tightrope, trying to make it to the icebox on the other side of the room. Had she a balancing stick, she might be the star of a circus. She might be walking the tightrope in a ball of green light. Below her, a small band would play tin music. The drummer would sweat heavily as she shimmied one foot down the rope, as she held the other gracefully to the tune of the little tin band.

As it was, no one watched her cross the floor except the child who lived inside her. The waiting baby was not sure. The mother felt a slap of nausea when she opened the icebox. A curtain of food smells rubbed harshly against her face; she felt the sticky coolness of the box settle into her skin. The green pepper in the corner of the box was greasy in her hand; it perspired a slick white dew. When she reached for the knife to slice it open, the nausea slapped harder. She sat down to rest at the kitchen table. Outside the day's heat jelled at the window. If she touched the summer air, she would leave a fingerprint. She watched the smoke in the alleyway, held her hand up to her face against the smell of dead fish burning. The smoke rested outside the window like a serpent; it stared out of its white eyes.

Sarah touched the slender golden horn at her neck. Her skin was hot; if she could see herself in a mirror, she would grow concerned. Her face was hot and frost-white.

Across the alley, Grandma Doria was spooning tomato sauce over a dish of pasta which curled up like little pig's tails. She was using a wooden spoon and in her mind were happy thoughts of nothing. The sauce spilled down the pasta like a healthy red river; she tasted the sauce and spooned more. Grandma was breaking the lettuce for the salad, was wiping the water from her hot face when she heard the call of her son from his kitchen. His face was a small white circle in the window; she looked at him and remembered how tiny he was as a child, born weeks late. When she untied her apron slowly, she wondered with a quick chirp in her mind if this baby would be a boy, God bless. In her bedroom, Sarah was unsnapping the heavy latches of her bra, to be more comfortable. The Mexican couple was saying in their own rapid language a slow prayer to their God before dinner. Doriana was holding her hand to her diaper crotch and the baby inside Sarah was still, oh was still very unsure.

The cold-water flat was a collection of little squares, the hallways were rectangles which held the squares together. The windows were squares, the walls, floors, ceilings were squares. Marco and Sarah lived in a collection of squares and into the middle of them they placed the new round baby and called her Carmolina.

She was round, her head was round, it resembled a cantaloupe. Her eyes were round as small pennies, her fingers, her fists were round, she was a round little creature. She flapped her tubular arms into space, and the space was vacant and endless. It was not warm. Things moved through the space, things flew through it. Long dark shadows flew up to her and watched. The shadows made sounds, they splintered and jangled against each other and were lost in the vacant air. Bottles flew into her mouth. She sucked at them until someone pulled them out and then she cried.

Light and dark things flew through the air, she never knew what to expect. Light flew in and stayed too long. It had no arms or legs. She squinted her eyes in the light and then the shadows laughed, the hollow air filled with their laughter and hurt her ears. She squinted her eyes and could make a small border around the light.

She was surrounded by bars. She tried to eat them. Someone lived with her, behind the bars. He was soft, he had round eyes; he was round and silent like her. She sucked his nose.

Everything pressed hot against her, the sheets scratched, the dark was falling apart and turning yellow. She searched the air. Her fingers found her toes, she stuffed them into her mouth.

A small sound came into the room. With difficulty she rolled over to watch. In the doorway a small person stood and looked at her. The visitor moved into the room in little jerks, she could fall into the floor easily. The baby in the crib watched, eating her toes.

The little girl walked into the room, the bells on her feet were a gentle sound. The baby listened to the singing feet.

She fell into the small puddle of sunlight, astonished.

The baby watched. Something happened. The small person disappeared, she flew out the window, she was gone. The baby chewed on her toes. The toes were stuck in her mouth.

On the other side of the bars, the small person popped up again.

The little girl pushed herself up as far as she could go; the white shoes squeezed her toes together. She could almost see into the crib.

The baby yanked her toes out of her mouth.

The little girl tried to smile.

They saw each other's eyes.

11

The baby was made of rubber; she twisted herself into a doughnut; her baby eyes watched everything.

The little girl stayed.

A hand fell out of the crib, reached for the little girl through the bars. The little girl wet her pants.

The baby's hand jerked, landed on the little girl's nose.

The little girl disappeared again.

The baby's eyes filled with tears. People were always flying in and out this way.

Now there was a hand on the mattress inside the bars.

The baby looked; her body burped.

The hand sat there. She tried to touch it.

They remained that way a moment, the sun shooting dry yellow rain into the room, shooting the little girl's hair full of burned light, squeezing shut the eyes of the baby who watched the hair go black and light between the bars.

The baby tried to eat her knees.

The little girl stood near the bars of the crib, her hand rubbing the wet crotch of her diapers.

*

There was something wrong in the house, the wife sitting by the kitchen window in the yellow electric light, doing nothing. Grandma Doria's hands sliced into the green pepper, a tired fire burned in her eyes. From the porch, where she sat, she watched the young wife in her kitchen, her face was lovely, was bent over something on her kitchen table. Sarah was a good woman. Doria yanked the stem out of the green pepper, the knife in her hand bit the vegetable in two. From her porch, she could hear the slow voices of the men talking on the street. It was a shame to Doria, that Marco was with them. With her fingernails she scratched the seeds out of the pepper.

Marco sat in the night. He was now twice a father. He sat with the other men where it was alive with quiet; he sat in the silk-backed night air broken by the men's serious Italian, and the baby's face bobbed before him like a flower in black water. She was a mystery to him; he looked down at Carmolina's face in the crib and she was his secret mystery. He had no idea where she came from. She dropped out of his wife's body like a little doll. She lay there and looked at him out of her eyes, and he thought she wanted to say something. She opened her infant mouth and he was certain; she had something to say. It was the secret. He bent his tired head over the crib; he strained to hear. His face was wet with perspiration as he watched her, unblinking, unsmiling, staring from her crib out of eyes round like pearl onions. He listened hard; there was quiet; the angels moved their silken wings and flew away.

Carmolina's face followed him everywhere; it looked up at him from out of his own mirror where he covered his face with soap in the mornings and scraped his whiskers away. It looked at him from out of his eyes and stopped him dead in the day's light, so that he stood with the clean razor like a knife in the air between his face and the water. His sadness began to accumulate, like sand. The man became almost silent; he sat in blue rings of cigarette smoke with his friends in the evenings, he sat on the stoop where men in undershirts too small to cover their bellies bit into stumps of cigars, and he saw the small pink face of his second daughter with the liquid eyes. She was born with sad eyes. He would give her everything. He would die, he swore, before anything hurt her, because her legs were so small; it was difficult to believe she would ever walk or run on them, where was the guarantee? Her body was so small, it was like a pigeon's. When he was a boy, he had searched for the gate, for the key, for the door which would lead to everything. The baby Carmolina lying in the crib, she would find it, she would give it to him. She would find the door and point to it for him. Somehow he would squeeze through.

In the streets, the night grew darker; the lights were dim blue. The peanut vendor passed by, the slow smell was of peanuts in the air, peanuts inside their warm shells, in the vendor's bright green wagon. Down the street, the watermelon stand shone like a white jewel in the night. The slices of watermelon rested on fine shavings of ice like diamonds; the watermelons were sweet red mouths open on the diamonds. From his seat on the cement stoop, Marco watched the light of the watermelon stand, how it was white in the night and the man inside was a black spot of ink, spreading.

Smoking his cigarette, he watched the world through the fine blue film. On the back porch a half-block behind him, his mother was a purple mark in high relief against the summer sky.

It was a brick building, not tall, three stories. It was of brick, square and solid, with a cement stoop in the front and a long gray gangway at its right side, with little sun. In the middle of the gangway, a wooden door opened into the building's deep green interior, a hallway that had been painted green so often, even the old layers beneath the fresh paint were another shade of green. The hallway always smelled, of green and of not-quite wet wood. The wood was the stairs, which had always been just washed or needing to be washed. In either case the stairs smelled and were a wonderful smell to anyone who lived there and recognized the smell of old wood and of home.

The stairs were a wonderful place to step on, when Carmolina was young, when her feet were young and she was running up the stairs to home again. The stairs wound marvelously, turning where she least expected it, presenting surprises at corners and landings. As she ran up the stairs, her feet were bare and rubbing against almost-wet wood, and the doorway at the top was charmed, behind it lay everything.

The door was old and too big. Carmolina had to stand on her toes to reach the knob, and got splinters in her toes when she did it. Or she just knocked, lightly, with her sunburned hands and the door flew open by magic. Or she called, called for her mother, and then there was the kitchen. The kitchen was as yellow as the light she left outside, and now she had to believe in the light, because it didn't fit in here through the skinny windows, it might as well be a cat trying to crawl up the side of the building. The kitchen was filled with the thick feelings of food; she walked in and the food touched her face. The soup was steam and blushed her skin. Baked apples twitched her nose; she knew it was baked apples if her nose did a small jerky thing. Apple sauce touched her skin, nose, mouth and made Carmolina feel that this room was like no other room in the world.

The lady in the kitchen was her mother. Daddy called her Sarah. She called Daddy Marco. She had black eyes and black hair, and always wore a cotton apron over her cotton dresses. The apron was filled with wrinkles, was as warm as the food. It made Carmolina's face warm, when she hugged her mother and she smelled the baked-down apple smell in the apron; little chicken whiskers stuck to her face. Mama laughed, if she noticed them, and she wiped Carmolina's face with a damp rag and then Carmolina blew her nose into it. The skin of Mama's hands was rough; they were like the sandpaper in Daddy's garage. The food that turned by magic into dinner was in the icebox. The icebox door was taller than Carmolina, but she was big enough to change the pan under the box. Outside the windows the summer air was so hot, it wrinkled. It was stapled to the screens at the windows like sheets of strong paper. Flies flew against the sheets and got stuck on the screens where they were smashed. Doriana ate the flies. Carmolina squinted her eyes, blinked. No one noticed Doriana eating the flies.

Painted onto the blue paper was the world. Grandma's house was just across the alley from the kitchen, Carmolina could watch Grandma out there, sweating circles into her dress, stringing red peppers onto the clothesline, to dry. Grandma looked like a funny fat balloon, standing on the porch that way, and her mouth was singing. Carmolina was too far away to hear the song, but she knew it was Italian, something Grandma learned in Italy where Grandma was born and Carmolina had never been. The red peppers looked like skinny balloons that needed to be blown up; then they would sail away across the sky, and everyone would laugh at Grandma's red peppers floating across all the streets.

14

But they were not balloons, they were red peppers and Grandma was hanging them out to dry in the sun, between the bedsheets. The sheets always smelled like red peppers, and in the wintertime when Grandma got sick and Carmolina spent the night with her to be sure she never died in her sleep, she rubbed her small nose into the pillowcase and smelled the red peppers and remembered Grandma in the summertime, hanging them on the clothesline to dry like tiny shrunken heads.

When the peppers dried and were like paper, so that they fell to pieces in your hands, then they were ready. Then Grandma would ask Carmolina to sit with her on the back porch and crush the red peppers with her, and the two of them would sit there, crushing the peppers like dust or like nothing between their fingers, letting the red pepper stuff fall into the Mason jars on their laps. And they would both laugh, and sit there in the sunshine and listen to the children screaming and playing in the streets. The children's voices reached them like voices in somebody else's dream, because the children were not sitting on the porch with Grandma and breaking red peppers. The peppers were for sausages, they peeked out at Carmolina like a funny face or a joke and made her laugh, when she ate the sausages. And Grandma was making the world for her, between her shabby old fingers. She was telling Carmolina about Italy, about the land that got lost across the sea, the land that was hidden on the other side of the world. When Grandma said how beautiful Italy was—how it was near blue waters which were always still and how she could watch wooden sailing ships coming so close to her house that one day she jumped on one and sailed away— Carmolina wondered, why did Grandma do that?, but she was glad Grandma did, because otherwise she wouldn't know Grandma, and that would be strange. Sitting on Grandma's porch, Carmolina could see her own kitchen window, and sometimes she could see her mother at the kitchen sink, washing a chicken under cold water. And Carmolina would laugh, how she would laugh, because that's where *she* was sometimes, on the other side, in the kitchen, watching Grandma on the porch, only now she was on this side and she was lucky, because she could see both sides. And Carmolina would wonder, sometimes, if she were really in the kitchen and watching two people on the porch. If she were, if she were really in the kitchen, then she could look out the window with its blue paper stapled against the screens, and see a little girl with brown eyes looking up at her Grandma, laughing.

*

The light is dim, the light is gray coming through the heavy curtains, the Venetian blinds. Light barely enters this room. Grandma's eyes are weak. She takes the sun only when she is ready for it, all at once, opening the back porch door where she knows the sun is waiting for her and she can not avoid it. But here, in her parlor, she draws the drapes to protect her weak eyes. They are watery, they are blue. Behind the glasses, they are small pools of water which might break at any instant. Her sight is fragile, her heart is fragile; she is the strongest woman in the world.

When the wrappings around her feet come off, she can smell it, the smell of the swollen purple flesh which is her feet. The wrappings are heavy brown cotton; they are held together with a safety pin. Beside the wrappings are her shoes, black, so old, she will not let anyone buy her a new pair because her ugly feet will split them open. Sitting by the wrappings is Carmolina. She is small, she is removing the wrappings. In this dim light, with these dim eyes, Doria can see that the child is plain, that she does not possess her sister's beauty. Her hair is thin, is brown. It is parted in the center and falling into her eyes as she bends over the feet. Carmolina's face changes; the smell is making her stomach sick. In this spare light, the grandmother can watch the change in the face of the child. Her hands are five years old; they are careful. They unwind the bandages and the five-year-old skin touches the green medication, the white drippings which grow out of the feet. The carpet is worn, like the light. Beside Carmolina is a porcelain basin of hot water. The little girl dips a white clean cloth into the hot basin, washes the feet. The old woman's eyes watch the ceiling where the sunlight is gentle, a mere stroke. The sores are touched by warm water, the old woman closes her eyes. In her kitchen there stand three Madonnas. In her kitchen there stand brown bags of brown sugar. On the back porch, she keeps the olive oil. Her own mother kept the oil in wood, she poured it from a wooden spoon. When Doria was a child, she sat on the dirt floor of her mother's kitchen and watched. Now she watched the picture of her mother hanging in the bedroom. It showed a beautiful woman, whose proud face was yellowed and blackened from the wood behind the photograph. It showed a very old woman; Doria can not look at the picture anymore. Her mother is bones in Italy. The mice chew at her.

Doria squints her eyes to the sunlight and tries to remember Brazil. It is a sun country, white, clean. She did not understand the language. There was confusion; she came to America instead. In the sea crossing, there was confusion. The sea coughed and spit and screamed at the boat that carried her, it spit up cruel black waves. The sea rankled; it could stop nothing. A young man was tossed over the side and churned down to dust on the floor of the sea.

Carmolina looks up at her and smiles. She rubs Vaseline into Grandma's feet and the purple flesh grows warm.

At the time of the sea crossing, she had young breasts, a mystery Doria tries to imagine, but can not. She squints her eyes and tries to see the Brazilian sand, like crushed pearls. She tries to remember the young man she met and loved and married. It is pictures floating under water.

She believes most of all in Italy, watches it disappear and reappear in the water.

In the pantry, Carmolina touches the cans of olive oil. They are warm with the life of Grandma's hands. She walks back into the parlor with the pain pills, sits beside her grandmother.

The pain in Grandma's feet makes her cry herself to sleep.

The hushed sun falls on them both.

The soup was barley, rice with a quick brown cut in it, like a dent. It was thick, because of the barley, and the feeling was of goodness, of body, of someone having cooked it. The medicine left an ugly taste on her tongue, a strange aftertaste as though it had kicked her on its way down, but the soup was barley, and good. Carmolina believed she was sick because she had barley soup. The tomato was cooked down to a pulp and the onion was clear, on the barley. If she finished this cup and asked for another, there would be more barley because it always settled in the pot. and the second cup was better. It was thick and good and warm, and it was soup, made by the mother for the sick child. The hem of the blanket was blue taffeta and frayed, she picked the taffeta threads off in her small fingers and blew gently at the threads on her flesh, so that they would float. And when she was sick and a child, the rough-skinned mother was always there to feed her, to tell her the soup was good for her, would make her better, so that she began to believe the soup was magical. And when she was sick, the rough-skinned mother with the thick fingernails and the dry purple patches of skin at the elbows was always there to smooth the hot-child skin, to run her rough hand across the forehead, to make it better, so that when the child grew to be a woman, she never let herself get sick, but stayed enormously healthy even though she smoked the cigarettes which had killed her father, because the mother was no longer there to comfort her. The mother would never again walk through the bedroom door in her wonderful black hair and her cotton dress, the mother would never again turn oh so quietly the knob of the door and step into the room to calm, because that mother would die when the child grew up, that magical lady with the wonderful hair who cared so much would die when the child grew to be an adult and a strange old woman would take her place, a woman with white hair and falling flesh on her face and with deflated breasts and a rasp in her voice, with spittle on her lips when she talked, a strange old lady who had mysterious pains and mysterious old eyes would kill the young mother with the wonderful black hair and the child would never see its mother again, its mother would never again tiptoe oh so softly into the bedroom with the magical barley soup to make her well again and the little girl, oh how the little girl would miss her all of her life.

4.

The family plot was purchased as soon as they had any money, before any of them had decent clothes. It is big enough for all of them, they will be buried on top of each other like layers of a wedding cake. The family name is carved into the stone, and the negro grave attendants can not pronounce it. The stone is so large, it is visible a good distance away, so that any living member of the family who visits it never gets lost. On Sundays, they pack a picnic lunch and go to take care of the grave. On the way to the cemetery, in the summertime, they stop at a specialty store that sells monuments and wreaths and small plants for the gravesite. Inside the store, stone angels with blank eyes and a look so forlorn it will tear your heart out if you are five years old are lined elbow to elbow on the wall. The angels sit with their legs crossed, their eyes have no pupils. They sit with their heads in their hands. There the family buys plants green as artichokes, flowers red as blood. In the wintertime, they buy an artificial black wreath and set it in the snow. But in the summertime, the entire living family spends Sunday afternoon at the gravesite.

Marco and Sarah help Grandma Doria out of the blue sedan. Grandma is wearing her old straw hat to protect herself from the sun; stuffed under her arms are the long loaves of Italian bread. Aunt Katerina, Aunt Josephina, Aust Rosa carry straw picnic baskets filled with tomato, with onion. Uncle Salvatore stuffs into his large pockets the bottles of wine. The blue sedan pulls up silently to the curb by the gravesite, the sun shines on them as they all tumble out of the old blue car, tumble out onto the gravesite, telling each other to keep quiet, helping Grandma and her proud old hat, settling Doriana to sleep in the car's back seat, striating the vigorous cemetery grass with their baskets, their wine, their own healthy bodies.

Set into the stone are the small framed pictures of the dead; their faces are set so that they always look directly into the eyes of anyone who looks into theirs.

Carmolina is five years old. She sits and eats tomato sandwiches with Grandma Doria while the family laughs and talks and digs little holes into the face of the grave to plant the flowers. Grandpa is under the flowers; he does not eat tomato sandwiches. Carmolina runs, when she is asked, to fetch water from the pump at the corner to water the new plants. She is careful not to step on any graves when she does this. She stands, holding the heavy watercan over the family grave and watches the cool water spill out over her tennis shoes, wetting them, watches the holes just dug by Mama for the plants eat the water up. Inside the grave Grandpa listens to them sing, but he does not get water on his face. Inside the grave Grandpa Dominic is glad they are there, is glad the old woman Doria his wife and his children are there with the tomato sandwiches. Grandpa had a white mustache; it's with him in the grave. Carmolina sings the Italian love songs which Grandma taught her, *O rosa! O rosa! O rosa gentillina!* her small mouth opens and sings, and Grandma looks up at her from where she is slicing the onions.

The skin of the onion squeaks in Doria's hand when she pulls it away from the white body. The thin yellow paper of the onion makes no sound, but the first layer of skin squeaks. She watches Carmolina singing in her small broken Italian; she is growing up with the music tooled inside her brain. The sound of Carmolina's growing is filled with music in her head, of the laughter and quick tears of her large family around her. The sound of Doria's time was quiet, was patient, the sound of her growing up was slow and deliberate. The time of Doria's growing was marked by usual, small events, but her people had their own way of remembering. They sat in the dusk of Italy and they made their lives slowly, measuring out the days like milk or salt. They kept picturebooks of their lives, and in them they pasted likenesses of themselves. The pictures were bound in corners of black paper. The people in the pictures had skin the color of onion; they were dressed in shades of brown. Their smiles were fixed and faced forward toward the man under the black hood who with his great funny puff of white smoke would seize them. Their skins were not truly the color of onion; their clothes were not really shades of brown.

On the day that the first family picture was made, Doria wore a white dress which was made for her by her mother Carmella from the wool of sheep. It was a heavy dress, much too heavy to wear in the sun that day, but it was her best dress and her mother insisted. After the picture was taken, Doria wiggled out of it and gave it to her sister Sabatina who immediately undressed and got into it while the family looked on. On the day the first picture was made, Doria was eight years old. She lived with her family on a small hill in a town near the city of Naples which they visited on holidays if the year was good. Their town was a small one; the furthest border was a graveyard whose markers went back to the sixteenth century. The white stucco house was Doria's house. It was buffed white by the sun of Italy; there was no glass in the windows. In the summer the glad weather washed through the windows; the trees became part of the family. In the wet season the rain washed into the house; it dripped down the walls. Then Doria's mother set out after the great black waterbugs with her straw broom. Sometimes Doria and Sabatina found a waterbug in their bed and they snapped it open between their fingernails. Outside was a small garden; this garden was the joy of Doria and her mother. The two of them, dressed in black dresses, sat under straw hats and weeded the grasses away from the small green plants. The mother spat into her hands for luck before she began the work. From the garden came sharp white radishes and lettuces for the salad. Sabatina did not like the garden; it dirtied her hands. The mother said that Sabatina was the child of royalty, that she was kidnapped by gypsies who wore golden earrings and stole children. She said she found Sabatina in a basket in the garden, and that Sabatina was a princess who would never do a lump of work in her life. Doria laughed when her mother said this, because in her heart she knew it was true that Sabatina was lazy as the sun and would never amount to anything if she did not wake up soon. It was true that there were gypsies. They roamed the countryside and played music on their dulcimers, they shook tambourines in the dark. The cries of the strings and of the little silver bells enchanted the children. Doria had seen them, the black eyes and black souls of them. The breasts of the women were large, like the udders of cows; they swung under bright red dresses. Their bodies were dressed in golden jewelry; they wore silver combs in their hair. They were beautiful; they were terrifying. They frightened goats in the night so that their milk turned sour; they terrified the chickens so that they went barren. Whenever Doria and Sabatina passed the gypsies on the dirt roads, they crossed themselves and called upon the Madonna for protection from the evil eye. At night the two little girls lay in their white bedroom, on the clean sheets beaten white in the river. Outside the moon was a blue hole in the sky, washing the world blue-black, making the trees black as ash or as death, making the trees stick all out of the world like the broken brooms of witches. Outside the world turned blue from the moon, its enchanted light made the bedroom blue, and the sheets and their toes sticking out from under the sheets turned blue along with the world. It was then that Doria and Sabatina heard the singing of the gypsies, heard the cry of the dulcimers and the strangled chatter of bells, heard the laughter and songs of the gypsies reaching up out of the ground. The gypsies ride black horses, Doria said, and Sabatina curled into her side of the bed, pulled her feet away from the pitiless blue light, hid her face in the pillow. The gypsies ride black horses that once were devils, the devils grew tired of hell and changed themselves into horses. The gypsies find them and ride them, and the horses run faster than the horses made by God. The teeth of the horses are like knives, they can bite through the walls, Doria said. Sabatina buried her pretty brown face in the bedclothes and her legs were stiff. The horses run faster than the wind, faster than the rain, and if a gypsy wanted to catch you, you could never run fast enough, Doria whispered. Outside their windows the trees were black as matchsticks; a gypsy could set them on fire with his curse. Outside the window the trees looked into the bedroom with twisted faces. The voices of the gypsies travel through the ground, Doria said. The gypsies can reach up out of the ground and grab you with their teeth. The devil gave them special power. Sabatina screamed into the pillow and Doria scared herself. The sound of the dulcimer and of the thin tambourines travelled through the night hills. It was magic music, and sad. The gypsies were sad because they had been cursed by God to wander the world; they must live forever in tents, pitched by lonely fires. They sat round the fires dressed in their devil's gold, with gold at their ears and at their breasts, with gold at their waists and in small beautiful rings round their toes. The gypsy women sat with their long black hair and sang out of throats which burned. The men with their hard gypsy muscles listened and wept and grew angry. They revenged themselves. They stole children. They twisted the life of the animals so that goats vomited and chickens gagged. Sabatina rushed to the window, slammed the wooden shutters shut. She slapped out the blue light of the moon and the evil arms of the trees. Under the sheets, she still heard the music and Doria laughed at the way she scared little princess Sabatina. In the dark room, Doria watched the small slip of blue light under the shutters, clean and swift as a fish. She watched the shadows, stuffed like thick milk into the corners. The shadows only seemed to move. When she grew up, Doria would run away to the circus. With her blue eyes and black hair, she saw the circus and loved it. She loved the humped little dwarf with the yellow teeth, she loved the old wagons. There were green babies, flat and floating in bottles. The people of the circus dressed in clothes like jewels; Doria with her laughing blue eyes would be a part of them. The people in all the towns the circus passed would call out, there is Doria run away. Sabatina would grow old and fat; she would be forced to make large dresses to wear; no bracelets would fit her fat arms. But Doria would be beautiful, with slim ankles. She would lead the elephants, smiling.

In their small bedroom, his children were still asleep. Pasquale glanced for a moment at his daughters. He was a rough man. He had learned all he knew at the side of his father now rotting in the graveyard. The skin of his hands was almost as thick as the wood he worked; his eyes and the world they saw were the same. He wrestled with the world and forced it to yield to him all he demanded. He spat in the face of anyone who would steal from him that which was his. Carmella his wife was his; she had been given in proper ceremony. He had taken her properly in bed. She had yielded him two children though neither, curse God, was a son. He hammered and nailed and chiseled the wooden world into place. What would not yield he placed in a vise and then shaved off or sawed off what would not submit. His hands were black from his work; the palms were scarred by small tears in the skin which would not heal and by slivers of wood which were fixed parts of his flesh. His eyes were not the eyes of his brothers the farmers. His eyes were not marked by days spent under the yellow sun. His eyes followed the narrow grain of wood, followed it closely so that it would not deceive him and crack at a vital point. His eyes watched the fine shavings give way to correct proportions. His eyes ran over countless beams, ferreting out failure. The earth and its rooms, its fields and gardens, its houses and sheds, smelled of varnish and turpentine. He had long since lost the smells of his wife's kitchen, of the dishes set before him. Long ago he surrendered the delicate feast of anise in his coffee, the smell of honey in his cakes. The world smelled of turpentine and of sharp black varnish. His hands he had trained to know a slab of wood as a lover's hands know a woman's sex. They were hands fine in their work, and from them came the cabinets, tables and chairs which enabled him to marry Carmella his wife. His work had given him his family and this small house. He would not, like his father, become a broken doll, lose his trained eyes. He had taken care of these his eyes and hands, the tools given him by God to make his way on the earth a man and not a shrivelled worm.

He did not know if his children were beautiful. He knew that they were his. He had made them, he continued making them the way he made a ladder or stool. When he walked into his daughters' bedroom on the morning when the pictures were taken, he noticed only that they were asleep. His eyes were trained to see the joints and pinnings of the world, and not its luster. Behind him, the black hills of Italy were filled with spectacular creatures, with creatures of myth, of legend, of dreams and nightmares, squirming out of the people's minds, leaping out of their souls. The restless people looked up from their cooking, from their seeding, working the pulp of fig against the soft skin of their mouths like squirrels, looked out from their eyes and seduced from the humps of stone images which nourished them as the earth could not. They supplemented what the earth failed them. They provided the mysteries which God in his haste had overlooked. Thus the hills were peopled by bandits who slit human throats with the ease with which mothers slaughtered chickens; who slit open and spilled human life while glancing at the stars. Their taste was for swift and splendid death, their hands were bruised with blood, and they licked them clean. Headless bodies floated in the streams, suspended astonished in the water. The air was rich with the smell of their blood. Travelling through the hills was never an unconscious act. The people's eyes filled with what they expected to see; their irises were moist with the blood they might shed. Waiting, the people believed their bones lacked marrow, like birds. But more than the thieves filled the heavy pockets of the hills. The unborn, the never-seen, populated the trees, the small stone paths, and the stories of these astounded Doria. Creatures which had never existed lurked in the tales of her mother, Carmella, lurked in her words, in the catches of her voice. They peered out of their red eyes at the small child listening. The mother stirred beans in the pot on her stove, shredded the cheese and told Doria of these, the unseen creatures. The mother's face was deeply olive and her eyes sought the truths outside her kitchen window, as she prepared the meal. The souls of the unforgiven dead walked the hills at night. They held their hands before their faces, hiding their rotted features. They marched in a hard blue line and the sight of their faces could shoot you into madness, could spit you into hell. On a hill outside the town they gathered in a blue-black circle and chanted their prayers for forgiveness. They set their faces towards the stars, searching out the fingers of God which would hold them safely once again. They dressed themselves in leaves and danced. In the rain, they turned silver as pond scum, in the rain their secrets were revealed. It was true according to Doria's mother that each man is given a secret when he is born. He is meant by God to protect his secret, to hide it like a jewel throughout life. Each secret is different, and only God knows them all. The telling of secrets is forbidden. They must be held close to the body all through life, because they are the only treasure. Without them, a man is a snail. You must never, Doria, squander the secret. You must, Sabatina, be careful. Do not tell.

Sabatina is one of the faces on the family stone. Her eyes look out from behind her glasses; her smile is quiet on the stone where Carmolina is watering the grave. Her quiet dead eyes smile at her sister Doria. She looks like Doria who is slicing the tomatoes open so that the seeds will spill into her hands, but Sabatina is slimmer, and she is dead. She does not have little whiskers on her chin.

Because Grandma Doria is the only member of the family who has little whiskers on her chin, like a goat. The whiskers float in the air when she talks to Carmolina, Carmolina stares at the whiskers, they are like the antennae of a gentle insect. She laughs from her stomach; Grandma's laugh has a wheeze in it. It is as though she uses up too much breath, laughing, and Carmolina is frightened of the wheeze, let God never take Grandma's breath away. Her skin and her teeth are yellow. When Grandma makes lunch, it is cheese on Italian bread, or tomatoes on Italian bread, or just Italian bread. They sit together at the Formica table in the kitchen, the whole world is burning from the heat of the summer, but coolness is on the table and Carmolina and Grandma talk:

When Great-Grandma Carmella died, she was sick a long time. Then Grandma was just a little girl and she sat with Great-Grandma who was dying, and everyone else was asleep. Deep in the night, Great-Grandma screamed and sat up in bed. Grandma saw a woman dressed in white crawl out from under the bed; she was a skeleton; she was Death; only Grandma saw it. Grandma screamed and ran out of the room;

Great-Grandma died instantly. There is a mountain in Italy filled with candles. Some of the candles are tall and white. Some are short and sputter with the blue flame. Each person has his own candle. When he is born, the candle is lit; when the candle goes out, he dies. You can see this mountain, Carmolina, only in your dreams, but God will not let you see your own candle, even in a dream. If there is a mistake, and you see your own candle, you will die. This is how people die in their sleep. Great-Grandma, knock wood, did not die in her sleep.

Grandma keeps food on the back porch. She hangs long red peppers from the line with wooden clothespins. She keeps white lima beans in jars of salted water; she keeps them there until they grow juicy and bloated; then she salts them more and feeds them to Carmolina, who loves them. Grandma keeps trays of seeds from the pumpkin to dry in the window. When they dry, she salts them and cooks them in the oven until they are brown.

Grandma stands by the window on a hot summer day; the air is yellow outside. She is laughing, she is fat in her black cotton dress. The sun makes her little whiskers precise and obvious; they are white. She is smiling at the little girl called Carmolina and lifting the screen from the window. The sill is cement and the birds are nowhere to be seen, but Grandma breaks the day-old bread and places it on the cement sill. The sun is making her face beautiful. It is doing magic to her face, and here, in the corner where Carmolina sits, the shade is gray and peaceful and Grandma is standing in the spotlight of sun that someone is shining on her because she is feeding the birds. The old woman laughs, she throws bread out the window. The little girl Carmolina can not reach, the grandmother picks her up, holds her high against the sun so that she can feed the birds too. The circle of sun shines on the little girl, she is laughing, her grandmother owns the sun and is calling the birds:

In the sun the sand was hot like nothing else could be hot under her feet, so that her body did little jumping motions when she walked and she looked like she was flying, but she wasn't, she was walking on the hot sand that sent her up and jumping into the world. In the shade the sand turned cool. It was gray there and small things grew with quiet rocks and red lady bugs that flew in the air and landed on her skin, and all that made it cool. Carmolina left the land and went walking off into the water, and before the water began, the sand was ripples, it was rippled by the wind and was packed hard, like a bed sheet, and she went walking into the water, which was blue like an egg, which made long soft breaking sounds out there where it struck against the world, and spilled over. Standing in the sand, she could hear the water breaking from far away, it sounded like thunder only it was sweet and she wanted to go out into it and she did, she ran out, she ran into the blue water and it was cold around her feet and the water was eating her body up, like a little rock or a fish, and she jumped up and down in it, she put her feet into the bottom of the water and she stood on the world and laughed. When she looked back at the sand, she could not find the blanket with her family on it, she could not see her grandmother with the lunch basket filled with sandwiches, she could not find the right colors in the sand, none of the colors were hers. She splashed her hands in the water and her toes dug themselves into the sand, it was packed hard, with little rocks in it, the rocks bit her feet, they were small mean bites under the water, like angry fish. Then a voice called her from the sand, one of the colors was moving, she watched the color float across the sand, it had no feet, but moved towards the water and was calling a sound like her name. Her toes dug into the water, something was coming to get her. The color came into the water, it was big like a tree, it called her name but she could not find its face and the water no longer was cold, the warm skin lifted down for her, in its hands she was warm, and she was lifted from the water and carried back to the sand. Then she rode the horses of the merry-go-round. The horses were painted red and gold and green and black, they had separate saddles and the reins were real leather, the bit was metal. She climbed up on the horses and she was as far above the ground as she would be on the second level of the monkey bars. The merry-go-round started slowly, it made slow circles of light in the hot summer air, and slowly she moved past her mother and father behind the mesh fences. They were small figures, smiling, and she smiled back at them as the horses moved past. Then they turned into quick little blurs of colors, whisked by air into pure colors which were smiling at her. And her horse rode up and down, it carried her up closer to the top of the merry-go-round where she could see the fantastic iron works which made the horse move, the iron bars pumping steadily up and down, making the horse dance. And the music of the merry-go-round was sad, it was the sound of the ball park where people stood straight and sang to the flag, where the wind was so gentle it was like a hand on your face, and sometimes you saw the moon over the grass until someone moved it and you had to watch the game instead. It was the sound of the men at the ball park whose voices called coke and hot dogs and beer and peanuts, it was the sound of the men running out there. The feel of the wooden horses between her legs was cool like the sand on the beach when the sun is going down and it's time to go home. It was the feeling of the fun house where everything happened and moved and exploded and disappeared in the half-light; it was the sound of her mother calling, calling to her where she drew chalk pictures into the bricks of the alley to come home, because the sun was going down and dinner was ready but she never wanted to leave because she loved it and this was the last day of summer before school started because tomorrow was September. And the music of the merry-go-round slowed down and the funny fat colors turned into her mother and father, and they were smiling because she was laughing so hard on the horses, and when she got off the ride, she couldn't find them for a minute because she was so dizzy and everyone looked like maybe they could be her mother and father and she looked back at the merry-go-round, at the horses, at the man who stood by the lever, the giant metal lever that made the horses move, and he was lighting a cigarette and his face was sweating, he was wearing a dirty t-shirt and one of his front teeth was missing. And the horses were hard like wood, like all the other rides in the amusement park, like the wood of the roller coaster where they strapped you in so you wouldn't fly out and bump into the clouds or blow across the ocean to the other side of the world. And the music of the merry-go-round was the sound of young voices calling at the beach to pick up the blankets and wrap up the sandwiches, to shake the sand out of your clothes and the rocks out of your shoes, to run to the water to wash the sand off, to splash your feet in the water, to watch a bird fly away, to do everything quickly.

PART II

SUMMER, 1949
LATE JULY

The sound of the skooters hit the street like broken teeth on a plate. Carmolina felt the sound through her feet, through her red tennis shoes.

Someone touched her on the shoulder; she jumped a little and turned.

Three boys stood behind her. They all had blue eyes like ice.

The fat one wore a yellow shirt and a tweed cap that came down over his head, that hid his eyes from her.

"You the dago kid come and dirty up our street?" he said.

The smoke from his cigarette made her eyes tear.

The apple man glanced at Carmolina out of the side of his eye.

Carmolina rubbed at her eyes with her wrist, but the cigarette smoke was too close. She looked up at the light of the streetlamps. Her eyes turned white with street light.

They moved into a circle around her. Someone shoved her from behind.

She bumped into the fat one.

"You sure look like a dago kid to me," the one in the blue shirt said.

Carmolina squeezed her eyes. The street was a straight line that ran up to where they stood.

It was a thin blank line, with the lights burning white as the stars.

Somewhere on the other side of the city, at the other end of the streetcar line, Mama was behind the kitchen window, doing something that Carmolina couldn't see. That was where the stars stopped.

The headlights of his car cut sharp white disks into the falling sky of summer. He drove with his hands gripped tight and blanched against the plastic steering wheel; the veins in his hands bulged. The summer heat pushed in against him; his skin buckled in discomfort. He shoved his policeman's cap back on his head, reached into his blue shirt pocket for a cigarette. He was driving a blue sedan and the lights were searching, fighting the quick fall of the night. The soft package of Pall Mall's dropped into the seat beside him, out of his hands. With one hand on the wheel, he used the other to tap the package against his thigh, cursed because his hand was shaking, isolated a cigarette. He spit the tobacco shreds out of his mouth, lit it. His mother would say that God will punish him for the cursing. You swear, Marco, she would say, and that little girl, she be lost forever. Maybe Ma was right. The cigarette package landed on the seat beside him, next to the billy club. In his car's rearview mirror, he watched the flash of endless houses passing him; his eyes blinked at the reversal of images; the houses staggered past him broken and backward in his eyes. He cleared his throat, blinked, made an effort to keep them open. In his mouth, there was the taste for sleep. The summer heat pressed in on him. Sweat dropped from his hair, down the sides of his face. She could be anywhere. Somewhere on this street, hiding in a gangway, trying to cross a street she had never crossed before, where there were trucks, Carmolina his daughter was running in this same night. She understood traffic lights, that was good. Good God, but she had never been more than five blocks from home before. Not alone. What kind of father would let an eight-year-old walk more than five blocks alone? He spat the tobacco out of his mouth. She could not have gone far. She knew the way to school, to church, to the market street. She had crossed maybe a dozen streets in her life, and every person on every street knew her, could tell her the day she was born. In the small rearview mirror were the silver images of the houses, the bricked houses with cement stoops, the wooden slat houses with fallen faces, the houses with clotheslines at the back porches hung with the clothes of the families inside, houses with small gardens in boxes at the windows, because there was no room for real gardens when families lived six to a house divided into cold-water flats. When Carmolina was seven years old, she read about Leonardo da Vinci, how he wrote everything backwards. No one knew why he did that, she said. One Saturday, she locked herself up in the bedroom with Doriana and her three-ring binder. Sarah could barely get her out for meals. They were afraid, Marco remembered, that she was spending too much time with her sister, that the disease would spread. On Sunday afternoon, after Mass, Carmolina came back from the bakery with the fresh loaf still hot. The center of it was missing. Look what the little mouse brought home, Marco said, but Sarah slapped her on the ass for ruining the loaf; it would go stale faster. Carmolina smiled and wrote something on the white paper bag. No one could read it. You have to use a mirror, she told them, and when they read the message, This bread brought to you courtesy of Carmolina BellaCasa, their smiles were uneasy, and Carmolina told them the story of Leonardo which she had read in a book, then went off singing to herself into the bedroom to tell the story to Doriana, who was sleeping. The talk began then in the family of keeping the two sisters somehow apart. There was only one bedroom for the children, Marco said, what else could be done? Doriana slept most of the time and could not harm Carmolina. Carmolina they kept to themselves, Marco spent all the time he had with her, telling her stories, listening to her stories, protecting her. Let Carmolina live with me, his mother had said, and Sarah cried. Give Carmolina away to the grandmother? Too bright. The littlest one was too bright. She had stolen the brains of her sister. Marco shook his head.

At some of the windows, women watered flowers from Mason jars, in the mirror. Behind him, the streets passed him slowly; he squinted the lids of his dark eyes when he passed an alley, a darkened gangway. He was a policeman; could he not find his own daughter? At first he had walked, looking on foot for her, shining his large flashlight into every alley, every passage between houses, calling out her name, lighting up the bare skeletons of wooden back porches so that neighbors sitting in the quiet of their own evenings started and said, Marco, what are you doing?, and he would be forced to admit that Carmolina had run away from home, no one had seen her since this morning, she had only seventy-eight cents, have you seen her? He shined the light into their faces; familiar eyes stared back frightened and dismayed; the faces were full of questions; they whispered to each other that the gypsies had taken her; he was only a policeman and helpless in the face of black magic. He walked blocks that way, in his city uniform, calling up to his own brain all the cunning his department had taught him about searching out the joinings of the world for a human being in hiding. There were too many gangways here, too many hallways, the eyes of his flashlight were weak. And so he rode now in his car and felt the impotence of his uniform.

"Carmolina," he shouted into the night, and neighbors turned their slow summer faces towards him, women dressed in black cotton with saints' medallions at their throats shook their heads, men in white shirts and black slacks turned their eyes in perplexity away from him, who was looking for his daughter in the dark.

The circles of his car's lights grew stronger; they were engorged white eyes in the blue night now gone completely black. He drove slowly, the sweat running down his neck into the hair of his chest; the shirt was matted against his skin; the package of cigarettes was almost gone. The moving car's mirror passed the bricks and cement and stillness that only a night set like a jewel into the summer can bring. Behind him a fire hydrant cleared its vigorous throat of water, emptied it into the street. Half-naked, a handful of children dashed in and out of it like puppies, pulling at their own clothes, dunking their own heads under the hydrant into the full thrust of the water, stupified as they drew them back, amazed at the power of the water slamming against their own heads. The water gathered at the curbstone, floated over the gutters stuffed shut with newspapers and refuse, ice-cream-bar wrappers, coke bottles, horse dung. Half-naked, they were laughing.

With their black hair pasted wet against their skulls, they played in the water. A small boy in a wet t-shirt shoved a board against the open mouth of the hydrant; the water sprayed out in a clean white arc across the street. Marco blinked. In the spray was the small form of his daughter, laughing, dripping in her dress, waving at him from behind her dark eyes. She was talking backwards to him in the mirror, he could not understand the words, she was talking backwards and laughing because he could not understand. He blinked again, cursed the blue ghost, asked God to forgive all curses, cursed again.

All the families went to sleep. Behind the dark windows, they slept in their beds and thanked heaven for their children safe beside them.

Marco stopped the car, stood on the corner beside the wooden hot dog stand. On all sides of him, the city stretched out, street after street. He was a point drawn on the city's grid, and the grid was infinite.

"Carmolina," he shouted. His own voice returned to its home in his throat, made of glass.

Gustavo the ragpicker led his blind horse down the alley. The large metal garbage drum was stuffed like a dirty ear with newspapers and bottles. He sniffed at the garbage drum; his nose moved, his mustache moved. The blind horse stood with patience beside him; he knew Gustavo well; his long lashes blinked away the flies. Gustavo's trained fingers picked at the treasures and the refuse; his fingers selected from the overflow those bits of rag which would turn themselves quite simply into paper and into money in his hands. From under his straw hat, the horse stared at nothing. Gustavo shoved the rags into the wagon; in front of the wagon, the rump of the blind horse contracted and let out its yellow dung. Gustavo picked up a newspaper, wet from last night's rain. Small paragraphs of newsprint adhered to his fingertips. He held them close to his eyes, examined farsightedly some of the words which he didn't understand because he couldn't read, peeled them off slowly. He lifted the wooden handles of the wagon, worked it down the bricks of the alley.

"Carmolina?" he whispered ahead of himself into the alley.

"*Bambina?*" he called.

The horse turned its head, its ear stood up.

"So that you name?" he said to the horse.

From a clothesline one story above him, a bed sheet flapped.

The face of the church seems scraped off, shaved away, as though the church had lived a difficult life, a lonely one, and this loneliness and difficulty shows on its face. The cement face of the church is wearing away; children who pass the church on their way to play softball in the streets run their hands along the face of the church and the cement rubs off on their fingers. The face of the church is brutally old.

Ah, but this is all so serious, so serious, Father Anthony would say to the children running by, who will not come in anyway. Go ahead, little boys. Rub. You have the dust of God on you hands. This is so serious, no?, the church falling down around our heads, he would say to the women in black who were in church all the time anyway. The church, ah, she is a geode. The face, she is too serious, eh? Come in, come in. You, Mrs. Esperanza, you think the face is everything? Look at you own face. Ha! That make you smile. We all beautiful inside, no? Why you all so serious? Because you poor? Nothing more poor than this church, God bless her old face. Nothing more beautiful than the inside this church. She a geode. That's right. Come in.

Inside, the church is cared for by nuns in black habits who flit back and forth across the altar, dusting the faces of the saints, arranging the white cloth at the communion rail, polishing the wings of all the angels who kneel in all the corners of the church. They whisk up the three flights of stairs to the shell of the organ in the second balcony at the back of the church. There they all raise their small black heads in wonder and then bow their heads for faded glory, *sic transit gloria mundi* they all say to themselves, they look at the spot where the organ stood until it was sold to pay for the ceiling which was falling down and *sic transit gloria mundi* they whisper again, and then they leap up and polish the six-foot pipes of the organ, dozens of them all at the same time and they don't make a sound.

Father Anthony lit the final candle at the altar.

Soon the women would file in for the first Mass of the morning.

This would be his only time alone with his God.

He felt in his stomach the soft gray spot which was his cancer, growing.

His face was thin, white, the bones of his face stood out like a structure of abandoned architecture, and set into these bones were his eyes. He genuflected before the tabernacle, a mighty cough seized him, he pulled a handkerchief out of his cassock sleeve, spit the blood into it, looked around the church to be certain he was alone. No women yet. The nuns were praying in their chapel. Bless them, God, but they like little spiders. You and me, we keep our secret, eh?

Before him, the altar rose three stories. The angel bearing the cross at the top nearly touched the ceiling. Thousands of gas jets burned out of the altar, into the church. They surrounded the niches which held the statues of the saints, all of them reaching down their plaster hands in blessing, looking out of plaster eyes with their simple stares of holiness. The lights of the jets reflected off the white-bone face of Father Anthony, who stared back at them like a child. Behind the altar and its hundreds of lights, the walls of the church were peeling, like the skin of an old woman's hands.

Well and so how are all of you this morning? Father Anthony whispered to the statues.

He was a young priest, he had not expected to die so quickly. There would be no time, he thought, for him to wear out the fine leather slippers sent to him by his parents in Italy. So maybe I send them back? he said to the tabernacle.

He had wanted to give all his life to his God, this God behind the wonderful altar, but God did not want much time from him.

Even now, priest that he was and allowed to enter into God's holy places, he looked up into the face of the altar and there was a contraction in his heart he did not notice.

His eyes filled with the reflection of the gas jets. The altar reminded him always of a ferris wheel at a carnival, the lights so many and intense, the determined carved faces of the saints staring down at him from their set places. He looked at the stone angel stooped in prayer at the side of the altar and thought perhaps the angel was too serious.

It was as though one night when no one was looking, the entire altar could begin turning slowly and the saints would maintain their set faces, and the wheel would move more quickly and the lights would spin, and Saint Patrick would hold onto his miter and Saint Theresa, God bless her, would hold down her skirts, and the saints would chatter and wave, and the entire altar of saints and candles would go spinning off into the lap of a trickster God, who would gather them all up like toys.

He blessed himself. There was in his throat the deep velvet syllables of the Latin, syllables which he said to himself as he fell into sleep on his pallet at night where in his dreams he considered his own death, the surprise of it. The Latin was a lush ornament in his mind; he touched it with care. But there was on the other side of the Latin the God who smiled, who could, when He chose, lean against the lever of the ferris wheel and ask someone please, now, to get off.

He opened the door of the confessional, slid back the wooden partition. On the other side of the grid was a raisin-black shadow.

"Bless me, Father. . ."

Father Anthony cleared his throat, coughed into his handkerchief.

". . .for I have sinned. My last confession. . ."

Father Anthony waved his hand in front of his eyes, to wipe away the confusion. A black line shot across the horizon of his pain.

". . .was two days ago."

Something moved in his mind. He waved his hand before his eyes again.

"Carmolina?" he whispered.

There was an uneasy shuffle on the other side of the grid.

He had broken the holy silence of confession.

"No, Father. It's Maria."

"Maria. Oh, child. Forgive me. And how is you mother?"

"She's fine, Father."

"Forgive me. Continue."

The small voice whispered through the grid.

The priest fingered the wooden beads of the rosary, cupped one hand like a shell at his ear.

At the back of the church, the blessed water in the holy water font was still as the skin of a cell.

Some of the women hold hands as they walk down the street. Dressed in black cotton dresses, their eyes are swift shots of light in their dust-gray faces. They all wear black shawls over their black dresses. Some walk with their arms around each other. They are a long black line moving down the street. Each woman is a perfect black image of the woman walking next to her, except for one. She carries a thick tapestry bag with leather handles attached. The bag is filled with potatoes and is too heavy for her thin arms. If the bag were to hang dead weight from her arms, she would sink into the cement. She holds the bag close to her breasts.

They are looking for Carmolina.

They have just returned from church, where they nodded their bone heads over their skinny necks, where they beat their flattened breasts with their fish-boned hands, and did not listen to one word the priest said. Their minds are wires attached to their memories. One of the memories wakes up, pulls on the wire, and the women's heads jerk back and listen. While the priest prays the Introit, they remember the death of the first child, buried beneath an olive tree in Lucca. Now her fingers are part of the leaves. The birds pick at them. While the priest reads the Gospel, they remember the spit of blood escaping out of the mouths of their late husbands, how they rubbed the bedclothes against the washboard after the burial to remove the blood and the final green stain. The priest holds up the host for consecration and they pray in their separate dialects the prayers of the rosary and beg the Madonna to take them all quickly too, they are ready, the stoves were cleaned this morning.

They know the gypsies have taken Carmolina.

They know how to get her back.

One lights a church candle and the others nod their heads. They rub their hands together over the candle. No one can fool with black magic. The gypsies send a cat into the house where a mother has rocked to sleep a newborn baby. The cat crawls into the crib. It stands over the baby and breathes its soul away. One breath, and the cat has inhaled the soul of the baby.

The women touch the golden medals around their necks.

They leave the church with the blessing of Father Anthony on their heads. He tries to speak with them before they leave. He can not stop them. Now he must pray for their souls.

They walk down the street and one holds a tapestry bag filled with potatoes and the rest hold hands.

One woman's yellow fingers reach into the cloth bag and pull out a raw potato. She sinks the stumps of her teeth into it. Now they are ready.

They walk toward the street corner. They have reached the corner where she disappeared. They nod to each other.

Now they are a silent dark line of women who separate like beads of black mercury at the street corner, each murmuring in her own thin or wrinkled voice: Carmolina, Carmolina, Carmolina.

The horse, with great effort, lifted his iron foot from the rough tooth of brick, held it a moment up to the flies, then set it deliberately down again, as though in pain, when actually it was only slow and lazy. The white wagon the horse pulled was full of tomatoes like lusty mouths in the sun, the corn was taut under its green skin and silly yellow hair, the onions were sweet enough to be eaten raw. In the early sun, the children ran like little animals, they ran and swiped and chewed at each other, nibbling one another like members of a frayed litter, hitting themselves in the backs of their own heads, delighting and frightening themselves they ran with their hair black and clean in the sun, their necks red where they had struck themselves or where their mothers had scrubbed them clean with yellow soap bending their heads over kitchen sinks like dead chickens, they ran and the air filled with the balloons of their voices, these balloons the children swatted back and forth at each other, and all this the horse watched out of his eye, while he was stopped and the vegetables were sold.

The great horse of the vegetable wagon turned slowly his torn head to one side, whisked his tail at the angry flies, and in his eye was the small round picture of the women's faces, their features stuck like fruit inside the round bowls of kerchief. The men stumbled sleepy and fed out of the houses and landed in small circles where they faced each other. From the windows of the houses, rugs were hanging out like great tongues to dry in the sun; the mouths of the windows were open and the rugs panted out of the clutter of the tight rooms into the sunshine above the head of the horse who watched the children. From behind the rugs, the mothers looked out on the morning, listened for the sounds of the children murdering each other in the streets and alleys below.

Mrs. Consuelo walked up to the vegetable wagon, sniffed her brown nose in the baskets. She felt the heavy weight of the onion in her hand.

Giupetto stood inside his wagon, behind his watermelon belly. Between his teeth, he chewed at the remains of a tomato; his elbow rested lightly on the white metal scale behind him. The scale shone white as the single tooth of an infant. There was a dimple in his elbow.

Mrs. Consuelo hefted the onion in her hand. "You no see her?" She considered the green pepper, ran her fingers over it; it left a slight film of grease on her skin. "And where the red peppers? Why you bring only green, you old fat turkey?"

"I look for her from the market," Giupetto said, "you skinny old duck. All the way from Climpton Street." He spat out the tomato's green head. "No Carmolina. Whisk. She gone. I look for her between the bushel baskets at the market." He leaned over his belly. His eyes were jet-black marbles. "She gone like the head of a dandelion."

Mrs. Consuelo stood with her hands resting on her skinny hips. She threw the onion at Giupetto. He ducked. "You know what it like to lose a child?" she screeched. She threw a pepper at him, smashed a tomato against his belly, volleyed a potato past his ears. She whipped an ear of corn over her head. "You *know*, you fat old turkey with paper in you head?"

Giupetto bent over his belly; he disappeared inside his wagon.

He unfolded himself; his red face appeared. His hands were stuffing the smashed produce into a paper sack.

"That be fourteen cents, dear Mrs. Consuelo," he said. "With one skinny corn, that make sixteen."

The seedman pushes his green cart down the summer evening street. In the dozens of boxes on his cart are the pistachio nuts, blushed soft red, white chi-chi nuts, bloated yellow lima beans. He blows on his metal horn; it sounds like a conch shell down the empty streets. From doorways and windows, from gangways and from porches, the scratched and scabby heads of children appear.

He blows on the thin horn; it is shaped like a paper cone and the sound it makes is spare and melancholy. The sound runs down the street for blocks ahead of him, like a small animal on a very long chain.

It is a thin sound, the call of the seedman's horn. It is melancholy because it means the summer evening is almost finished, and the last thing to do before being hauled off to bed by weary mothers is to run out into the street with a nickel and buy pistachio nuts, buy lubeans, and eat them slowly, as slowly as possible so that it is impossible to go to bed, because who would waste a nickel?

The children tumble down the stairs on top of each other to reach the seedman.

He blows the horn.

"Luuuuu-beeeeens," he calls out. His front teeth are missing.

The children are frantic, and fathers stuff their tobacco-stained hands into torn pockets, stuff fat hands into baggy pants, looking for the nickel.

The horn sounds.

"Peeeee-staaaaa-sheee-ooo."

Mothers are digging into the bottoms of Mason jars which once held pasta and now hold pennies.

"Pummmm-kinnnnnn."

The seedman looks at the children spilling out of gangways, the little boys straightening the small caps on their heads, the little girls pulling down their skirts and pushing past the little boys who shove past the little girls. The dark heads of women poke out of kitchen windows and smile at the seedman, like black flowers growing in trees.

He blows the horn again.

"Carrrr-mo-leeee-naaaaa."

Outside, it begins to rain.

"This is a night filled with black swans," Grandma Doria said. She pulled a rosary out of her bra, crossed herself with its crucifix. The beads of the rosary were the wrinkled pits of green olives, knotted together on a string. With the rosary draped over her fingers, Doria already had the look of a dead person, Sarah thought.

"Ma, have some coffee," Sarah said.

"No good for the heart. Sarah, you drink too much coffee," Doria said. "The coffee beans, they strangle you heart, you no can breathe, you face it turn the color of the coffee."

She looked at her own hands, their brown patches. "You see," Doria said, and raised her shaking fingers, held them in the air like the hands of an angel in church. "They make you skin brown, old like mine."

The line of tears in her eyes was like a separate skin, a skin of water. She blinked behind her glasses so that the skin would not break. Marco put his hands over hers.

Sarah switched on the small blue flame under the glass coffee pot. The flame was so purely blue, she was afraid to watch it. Her eyes were hypnotized by the blue flame, became a part of it.

"Black swans," Doria said. "See, the tears of the black swans fall outside you window. It a sign."

Marco pulled the kitchen chair next to hers, put his arm around her.

"Ma, it's just raining."

"In Italy, when we see the tears of the black swans, we know," she blessed herself again. "Oh God, my Carmolina." The skin of water in her eyes broke.

The flock of her children turned towards her.

"Grandpa Dominic, he no sit at this table, he no rest his hands on this cloth," Doria cupped her hands in front of her as though the air were a fruit that she held. "Sabatina, she no here. She no laugh with us. Doriana she have an empty head. The black swans pick her brains away. If Grandpa Dominic be here, he say, 'Doriana?' and she no answer. Carmolina no one know where she is. We sit at an empty table. The black swans eat the family up." She looked around Sarah's kitchen, in her hands the fruit of air was heavy.

"Ma, she'll be all right," Katerina said. "Marco's a policeman. Today he filed a special report."

Doria waved her hands in front of her eyes, as though she were dealing with flies. "The police. What they know? The people they murder in their beds every day. What the police know?" She turned towards her oldest son. "Why you a policeman? Why you no run you father's store like he want? Dominic, he turn in his grave." She wiped angrily at her own tears, as though they were the tears of a stranger. "Then you be home more. You take care you children right. You bring home good food from you own store. Red meat. You little girl, she no run."

Salvatore stood behind his mother's chair, looked at Marco like a puzzled child.

"Eh, Marco?" he said. "The report will work, right?"

At the sink, Sarah ran hot water over the coffee cups.

"It's because we never bought her blue shoes," she said to herself. "She always wanted blue shoes."

Rosa shoved herself next to Salvatore, began to massage the skin of her mother's neck.

"When my sister Sabatina die, the day she die, the black swans, they were there," Doria said. "They cry. They cry their voices in the sky. Just like this."

She waved her fist toward the rain slamming against the windows.

Rosa pulled the shade down.

"You think that stop anything?" Doria said.

Marco put a shawl over her shoulders.

"I had blue shoes when I was little," Sarah thought. "I wonder what happened to them? I kept them in my closet. Maybe they would fit Carmolina."

She rubbed hard at the coffee cup with the dishrag, scraped with her fingernails at the sugar hardened against the bottom.

"It's just that I can't find them," Sarah said to herself.

"I no want to go to my own granddaughter's funeral," Doria

screamed.

"Someone get her heart pills," Marco said.

Sarah glanced over her shoulder at her husband, did not recognize his face. Marco wore a mask; only his eyes were vaguely familiar.

"It's a mistake," Sarah thought, "to think you can lose your own child. I have pictures of her. In my wallet."

"Sarah, get the pills," Rosa said.

"I just don't know where the blue shoes are," she said to herself. She rummaged through Doria's purse. It smelled of wet cloth. She pulled out a brown scapular, stuffed into a corner of the purse. She smiled.

"She no take care my grandchildren," Sarah heard Doria say in the other room. "She no take care my son." Doria touched Marco's face. "Look, how skinny. I can see you bones. And the other one, her little brain is broke like a top. God, he punish us." Doria raised her hands towards the naked light bulb in the ceiling, squinted through her glasses. "What we do wrong? What?"

"Sarah!" someone yelled.

Sarah brought the small bottle of white pills into the kitchen.

Doria looked at her. "Why you no take more care? You first daughter, her brain is gone. You give her to the black swans. You little one, she disappear like a penny. You the wife. Why you no take care?"

Sarah looked at the faces around the table. Doria's children looked back at her. The silence was a thin sheet of glass.

Sarah looked into Doria's eyes.

"You gave her the money," Sarah said.

Doria looked up. "Disrespect?" she whispered. Sarah could barely hear her. "You give me disrespect?"

"She didn't mean it, Ma," Marco said. He glanced quickly at his wife. "She's tired. She cooked for all of us tonight. Look at all the food she made. No one gives you disrespect if they feed you." He looked at Sarah again. "You didn't mean it, did you, Sarah?"

"Sarah would never give you disrespect," Katerina said.

"She loves you," Salvatore said.

"She didn't mean it, did she," Marco said.

Sarah looked at the scales of dry skin on her hands. I'm still such a young woman, she thought. "I didn't mean it, Ma," she whispered. "I'm sorry."

She kissed Doria's hand. "Forgive me."

In the living room, Sarah sat and looked at the statue of the Virgin Mother on the bookcase. The vigil candle burned up into the Virgin's porcelain face. It had been burning the three days since Carmolina ran away. In the wall of her chest, her heart was a hole; a cold wind blew through it.

"They no even sleep together," Doria was saying in the kitchen. "They no even hold each other at night. Marco he sit all night and smoke cigarettes. He kill himself." She looked at him. "You think I no see. I see. I see everything. From my back porch." She nodded her head. "You think you little girls no see?"

The cold wind behind the rain blew at the window shade; it flapped whitely into the room.

Doria shivered.

Her children shrank back.

"Death, she just pass me by," Doria said. "She whistle through my bones." She held her hands to her head. "God forgive me. I disgrace myself. I hurt my own family."

She cried out loud into her own hands, *umiliante*.

Her children sat like water glasses around the table.

Sarah listened from the living room. Again that silence, that silence which fell out of their hearts and cut the words cold in their mouths.

"Forgive me," Doria said. "Forgive me. I hurt you. I say things I no should say. I swear on Grandpa Dominic's grave, my heart is sorry. May God strike me dead if I lie."

The children shuffled in their seats.

Salvatore glanced at Katerina.

Doria cleared her throat.

"Marco, you smoke a cigarette front of me. It all right."

"All right, Ma."

"Sarah?" Doria called. "Sarah, come back? Where is Sarah? I ask her forgiveness."

"Now," Doria said, "Now what we do to find my *bambina?*"

The children looked up at her.

"Somebody go, go get Sarah," Doria said.

In the living room, Sarah blew out the candle in front of the Virgin, sat alone in the dark.

PART III

THE FAMILY

1.

Like a peach the sun rises over the street.

The street is called Berrywood. It is narrow as a single bone in a skeleton finger. The sun rises sweet and languid over the crowded life of the narrow street, and the voices of the people rise, are like thin strands of glass and only the people know how to spin them. The people know what they are talking about, they are talking excitedly or sleepily in the jigsaw puzzle of their Italian dialects, and somehow they understand each other. All along the street, rich dirt runs beside the curbstones. This dirt reminds some of the men, when they drink too much wine, of Italy, and then they go down on their knees in the dirt and dig their hands into it. They find no olives, only chips of glass. Then their sober wives run out of the house with their hair bound up in cloth rags to curl it, and they haul the men off their knees and into bed, where they slap ice bags onto their heads. All along the street, the light poles are rusted to a deep red. They were once silver.

When the poles were silver, it was the turn of the century. Then Carmolina's grandmother was a young woman. She arrived with other immigrants to settle in the midwestern city that was eating them up like a giant The silver light poles caused a flurry of wonder, bringing as they did light into the dark quarter where astonished Italians found themselves living on top of each other. One night the gas lamps flickered on, illuminating the streets. Grandma Doria opened her mouth in surprise and dropped the wooden spoon into the sauce pot. She picked up her skirts and went running into the street where she bumped into other Italian matrons who were not yet accustomed to the light; they could not see by it. They stared at the new light as though somehow God had smiled on them all, then went back to serve their large families beans and pasta. Now when they smashed the cockroaches dead with their brooms, they could see.

It took a long time for the poles to rust red. By then, the men whose brains were sometimes soaked with wine knew there were no olives by the curbstones.

The street runs rapidly to the church at the corner. The church was built to house the God of the immigrants who threatened to burst open the street like a grape. Always it seemed the street would spill open with their laughter, their bodies, their children, but always the street expanded, breathed them in, breathed with them, and the dark-skinned Italians moved slowly down the quick little street to kneel in the church. The street never got too small for them. There was always another corner for the new baby, move the laundry basket. The church never got too small for them, because only the women attended.

The women dressed on Sundays in black, on Tuesdays in black, and during the rest of the week, they wore black. Their bodies were always too fat or too thin. The veins in their legs were bloated and purple. Such legs were created by children. Such legs followed the bearing of too many children, babies born not in the Italy of the white hot sun, children conceived not among the sweet smell of olive trees and figs, the smell of soot and stucco, the smell of earth rich as a dipper of cream, children whose eyes filled not with the yellow square of sun set into the window with white curtains, but children instead stowed into this tiny closet of a street with pinched back porches, the sky folded and pinned like fabric between the buildings.

These children slept late in the mornings, when it was possible.

In the mornings the women covered their heads with cotton scarves and began their walk alone down the street to the church. Never did one take more than a step from her front door than another woman said *buona mattina*. They chatted in their half-sleep. Into the brown cotton brassieres under their dresses were stuffed small leather purses filled with coins to buy the produce. Into the armpits of their dresses were stuffed handkerchiefs to wipe the sweat from their faces. In the yellow light, their mouths moved slowly. Behind the doors of the houses were the sleeping husbands, whose breakfasts they would return to prepare. Behind the doors of the houses the children began to toss toward wakefulness, toward the whiteness of day, their eyes half-closed to the fig of the world coming to life, their eyes half-open to their dreams. With brown legs and arms tossed across white pillows, their black hair blown across brown faces, the white sheets kicked away by feet in the midst of sleep, the children slept, and rumpled bedclothes uncovered hairless genitals.

Doria was not with the women this morning. Some mornings she could not be with them. Her feet were turning into purple growths, soft as moss, at the ends of her legs. Sometimes she could not walk with the other women to pray in the church. They missed her; she missed them. From her bedroom window where the early light turned the paper shade gray, Doria heard the women chatter, some of them with rosaries hanging from their necks. In her bedroom, she lit a small candle before the Madonna, she lifted the brown scapular to her mouth and kissed it, and she began her prayers alone.

The women entered the church slowly, on small quiet feet, whispering the last gossip quickly before making the Sign of the Cross with the holy water, feeling the water cool their skin, then separating to sit in isolated pews in the church. The priest spread wide his arms open toward the pews, flecked with women like pigeons. He greeted them in Italian, his voice strong as the bells which rang over his altar. The women beat their breasts; the small coins jingled in their leather purses.

The priest turned his back, began the Mass. At his side two small altar boys struggled to remember the prayers. They were slightly sick to their stomachs from lack of sleep. The women could hear nothing. The priest swept his purple garments up and down the stairs of the altar. The eyes of the women examined the woolen cloak over Saint Joseph, squinted at it through their thick glasses. Their small round backs hunched over their rosaries, they counted with their lips the number of dollar bills fastened with safety pins to the saint's cloak. The golden bell rang. The women knelt on the wooden kneelers, covered their faces; in their minds they watched the pictures of their families sleeping. The bell rang again, the women formed a black line down the aisle. Between their brown teeth the priest placed the white host.

Outside the open doors of the church, the wooden wheels of the vegetable wagon turned the corner.

In the air was the sweet smell of corn.

The women rolled their tongues against the roofs of their mouths, made a little ball of the host, swallowed it.

Mrs. Consuelo shook awake Mrs. SantaMaria, who had fallen asleep beside her.

When the women left the church, it was full and yellow daylight.

They pulled the scarves from their heads, smelled the yellow dung of the horses, fresh and steaming on the street.

The priest locked the door of the tabernacle.

Grandma Doria snuffed out the candle, opened her bedroom window.

This is a summer morning, and the sun has risen like a peach.

In Grandma Doria's kitchen was an old steel radio; the knobs were oversized and moved the needle easily from station to station. Her children gave it to her to keep her company. She talked to it. Confused by its English, she told it in Italian to make some sense or shut up, but she loved it. Standing by the sink in her light cotton housedress, she wiped clean the metal colander with the warm dishcloth, felt the water warm the cold fingers of her hands, listened to the announcer's voice coming out of the steel box, and gently wiped the radio clean. His English words and the English words of her children mingled in her morning mind. It was information, information about the world outside her kitchen. In her mind she felt the soft pressure of Dominic's voice, the heavy Italian coming slowly out from under his thick mustache, telling her his plans for her, for his children, now that life was settled in America. Beneath their own feet, beneath the floor of the kitchen was the grocery store he had created out of his own hands, with the small money he had brought from Italy. It had been enough, and the store slowly filled with wooden barrels of olives, with yellow baskets packed with live snails; sawdust was soft and fuzzy on the floor. On ropes in the windows, fat cheeses hung in their wax skins. Behind the counter the man Dominic stood cutting with a heavy knife the meat, grinding it fine in the machine, stuffing hogs' intestines with the sweet mixture of meat and spices, making the sausages. Sometimes Dominic could not stand the ice-cold of the meat and drew back from the bowl hands red in pain. The sun rose and shined its light into his store, warming his skin, touching the ebony-black of his heavy hair, burnishing his dark skin when he stood proudly before his store, talking with his neighbors. Always his white apron was stained with bits of meat, the green juice of the olives. The sun set on the man wiping clean his wooden counter, polishing the metal scoop of his scale like a shovel, until it turned silver. Then Dominic would lock tight the front door, glance out into the street where the horde of children played. Five of the children were his: There were Marco and Salvatore, skipping rocks down the street. There were Katerina, Rosa, Josephina with their small faces. Then he walked silently, the smoke of his pipe ascending white into the sweet air of his grocery store, and his black shoes made clean marks in the new sawdust, until he found his way to the back door, unlocked it, and walked up the stairs into Doria's kitchen. At night when the children were asleep in the small house, he and Doria sat on the back porch above the garden, and his voice which never learned English spoke to her mind which knew only Italian. They sat there together, in evening's long blue spell. Sometimes their hands touched. They laughed. They went to bed. They slept among their children like parent cats among kittens, their bodies knew that their children were near and sleeping. Then one day the hair on both their heads turned white, their children were gone, adults took their places and Dominic no longer descended the stairs to raise the green shade in the grocery store windows, to heave a giant cheese from its hook and stab a slice clean. The store was boarded up, women on the street who remembered the day Doria was dressed as a bride wept into their hands, and his children took the money from the selling of the store to buy the family's burying place, with its stone, and Dominic entered it, first and alone.

Now Doria stood in her kitchen with her silver radio, the announcer made no sense, she moved the dial to music and prepared the pastina for her children's breakfast. In one pot the small pasta thickened in the boiling water; in another, the tomatoes turned to sauce.

The kitchen table was spotless. She wiped it clean. Through the curtains, the sun was yellow. It was almost seven o'clock; she would soon wake them. She opened the back door onto her porch.

In the sun were the clothes on the line, the sweet red peppers were on the line, everything was drying in the sun. She squinted her blue eyes. In the distance, down the long street, the black cross of the church paled.

The sun blew into Doria's face.

The vegetable wagon stopped below her porch.

She moved to the porch railing, bent over it.

The sun rushed to the spot where she had been standing, blew into it, filled it up.

"The tomatoes, they good?" Doria called down into the street.

The horse that pulled the wagon lifted its lashless eye.

Mrs. Consuelo stood on the other side of the wagon, arguing over the price of onions. Doria called out to her. Mrs. Consuelo ran around the wagon, her small yellow hands filled with tomatoes. Doria laughed; Mrs. Consuelo looked like a chicken, doing the shopping.

"*Good?*" Mrs. Consuelo smiled, her weak little head bobbed. "These tomatoes so small, they get lost in the bowl."

"The lettuce, she cover them," Doria laughed. "The children, they say, 'What, no tomatoes?' "

"Children," Mrs. Consuelo said. "What children? You Marco, he getting married. That no children anymore. Look this tomato, she jump out my hand."

"They so ashamed themselves, they run away to hide," Doria said.

"You bruise da fruit!" Giupetto yelled and rushed around the corner of his wagon.

He tried to bend down, his belly slipped out over his belt and stopped him. Doria covered her mouth. Giupetto squatted in his baggy black pants, his fat fingers chased the tomato across the cement.

"My sweet little babies," he whispered to the tomatoes. "You hurt, yes? I kiss you up to heaven." He yanked the cigar out of his mouth, kissed the tomatoes, rubbed them on his white shirt.

"Ah! *Gentildonna* BellaCasa!" He swept his hat off his head, made a bow to Doria on the porch. "How Marco? His stomach jump into his mouth yet? I come to the wedding, no?"

Doria's eyes shined. "*Buon giorno, signore.* You drop the tomato again. Everyone they come to the wedding. There she go."

Giupetto watched the tomatoes spill and flatten themselves against the cement.

"God, he hungry too," Giupetto said.

"God, he like a good joke," Doria said.

"Eh, I bring you some onion," Mrs. Consuelo said. "You make the salad with onion."

Inside her kitchen, the pasta was white and thick inside the pot, the sauce was covered in bubbles.

The music on the radio changed itself into English.

Doria switched it off.

"And now, Dominic, it time for the children breakfast, God bless." She crossed herself and moved on her soft purple feet toward the bedrooms.

2.

"Katerina! Quick!" Josephina's voice punched out round and big, like her body. Katerina ran into the bedroom where Josephina squatted on her legs, fat like sausages, where her thick fingers were busy with straight pins and the hem of Rosa's bridesmaid dress. "We'll never have the time," Josephina said. "The blue thread, where is it?" The thread was in the catch-all drawer, but even this space was tidy, with Katerina in command of the household now. She ran her fine fingers over the threads, scissors, tape measures in the drawer, her fingers loving the order, the solitude of things set in their correct places. The blue hems of the bridesmaids' dresses, all three of them for Josephina and Rosa and herself, would be finished. The sisters would be dressed on time.

On the other side of the city, the south side, Sarah too was letting her young hands explore. Her small soft body, covered usually in the rough cotton of a waitress's uniform, was held in tight and lovely now by white satin; her body changed under the satin, became fuller, stronger in the world. Seed pearls ran in whoops and swirls across her breasts, her firm belly, the fine satin reached down to a point on the backs of her hands; she had seen pictures of such wedding dresses in storybooks, when she was a child. The dress blazed on her like fire; her face floated above it, young and astonished. She turned her back to the mirror.

On the bed, Sarah's mother sat. Behind her the white satin train covered the pillows and mattress of Sarah's bed. It was a white swan on the sensible blue bedspread, it would be attached at her waist, this lovely white swan with its wings folded now.

The veil hung on the closet door, something like a fine mist of rain. This would cover her face until the ceremony ended, then her Marco would lift it, would look into the bewildered face and kiss its mouth.

Her mother's hands shook; behind her glasses her blue eyes filled with her daughter's white dress. Sarah could see in the glasses only her white dress, as though her mother had white eyes.

"Mama, tell me I look beautiful," Sarah said.

In the mirror the white dress reflected its row of infinite buttons, closed into the satin loops. The back of Sarah's neck was cleared of its heavy black hair, piled high on her head in complicated curls. The veil would be attached to the crown. In the mirror, her hand sought the few stray hairs whisked down from the tight bundles. The small diamond on her finger reflected blue in the sunlight, in the mirror's own strange light. It had belonged to Marco's mother. Her small short body barely filled the glass; the mirror with no words reflected back the common-sense bed, the white organdy curtains, the water glass filled with daisies on the dresser. The dark cut of a man in a dress suit shot across the clean reflection in the mirror.

Sarah turned to her brother.

"Eddie, do I look beautiful?"

Her brother smiled slightly, looked away.

Sarah bent carefully over the bed.

Her mother's back was a stiff blue line.

"Mama?" Sarah said.

The old woman watched her own small body in the mirror, dressed in a violet dress, a small violet box of a hat with gray feathers on her head. She tugged the violet veil over her glasses; it covered half her face.

"You look like a bride," she said. There were small felt butterflies in the veil.

Blocks away, Katerina put the final stitch into Rosa's dress while Josephina struggled to get her zipper up. There would be little time for Katerina to finish her own dress, to brush her hair still wet from wash-ing, to pinch her cheeks to make them red. Her dress still hung in the closet, needing ironing.

On the back porch, Doria sat in the late June sun, her blue eyes soft, sadness moving through them like white birds. Her fallen breasts, belly were zippered into a dark blue dress; her feet were quiet and proper in their black shoes. Under it all, the June sky and the blue dress and the intent gaze of her son, her heart was minute by minute failing. She held Marco's hand in hers. They both sat on small wooden chairs and faced the garden. In the soft summer air, bees were moving from flower to flower. Doria watched the sunflowers, still in the blue air.

"So that be her kitchen, eh Marco?"

Marco looked at the window in the building across the alley.

His profile was a striking one, not handsome, but one that made the eyes look twice. His nose was long and straight, except for the small bump near the bridge where he had broken it as a small boy. His black eyes were his father's eyes, his sister Katerina's eyes. His smile he shared with his mother, a smile with the kind of gentleness that con-fuses, that brings sadness with the smile.

When he had the money, he would bring his wife to live behind that kitchen window, in a cold-water flat in five small rooms with a back porch. There would be no garden. He did not have the money for that.

There would be white curtains at the window.

He bought her a kitchen table.

His hands fell long and slender into the slim black slacks of his rented tuxedo, they fell long and slender into the pocket where he was searching for roses.

"I wish you father be alive," his mother said, "even though she not Italian."

Below, in the garden, the sunflowers were soundless.

*

In the confessional in back of the church, the red pillow on the wooden kneeler was wearing thin in the center. The threads had separated themselves from each other; underneath the white stuffing poked through like the inside of an overboiled egg. The candles on the altar at the front of the church were naked and unlit. From the sanctuary, an altar boy peeked out, genuflected before the tabernacle, reached the long golden rod up to the altar, to the candles, to catch them with flame. The door at the back of the church opened slowly, white light rushed like a cat into the lobby; the small boy at the altar turned his head, saw the small procession of people around the woman, saw them helping her into the church.

She was a small woman and walked with difficulty. On both sides of her, men maintained her balance on her small feet; they seemed barely able to reach the floor. The men's faces were stern and clean as stone; their eyes looked directly ahead. The woman stumbled. Her feet, in their small shoes, were thin, filled with large veins; they pained her. The shoes lost their balance, tripped over each other, and the men caught her, light as a leaf falling from a tree, in their strong hands. At the altar the boy reached meticulously for the last candle, the flame caught gently; out of his eye's corner, he watched them enter the church. Behind the old woman two young girls followed, her daughters; they moved as slowly as she did. Like snow, the church filled with accumulated people.

Sarah's eyes sought out the hollow stone holes in the angels' faces at the altar; they stared back, startled and silent. The vault of the church filled with the slow calling of the bells, their fat round tones rolled out like glass balls and thinned themselves slowly into nothing in the blue air.

Sarah did not know what to do with the picture. It was a small picture, oval the way pictures were once oval, framed in a gold oval frame. In the picture Marco stared out of his six-year-old eyes. His hair was cut short and straight across his forehead, making a little box around his head. He was dressed in a long sailor jacket with a bow at the collar. He wore short pants and button shoes, his eyes looked small and did not blink. Salvatore was five years old, sitting next to him, wearing a jacket with gold buttons. His fingers touched each other tentatively, his feet did not reach the floor. Their hair was identical, their clothes were identical, the eyes in both their faces were small and round like buttons and absolutely set. They stared out of the sepia picture, towards their own futures, their own uncertain endings. In the picture they did not blink in the face of their own endings but held their eyes absolutely still and open. The buttons on their shoes remained forever buttoned, the slightly opened mouths never reached a smile, their skin remained pale brown and paper, Salvatore's feet never reached the floor.

Carmolina they had had to sedate. She could not stop crying over her father's death. She called out for Grandma Doria, but Grandma was already sleeping beside Grandpa, her tired feet finally resting, in the womb of a grave where they would now place Marco. Sarah held Carmolina in her arms, twenty-one-years old and Carmolina was held in her mother's arms as though she were a child, she cradled her and sang to her while her own eyes were steel, but the girl could not stop crying. The doctor said it was time for the pills, they gave them, Carmolina cried in her sleep for her father, her grandmother.

From the sanctuary, the altar boy watched Sarah. Her hair was ice-white, her skin even whiter under the hat's black veil, watching the coffin, a smile around her mouth.

Sarah could not face Marco at her side.

He was chiseled as of stone, complete and gentle.

They had joined their lives together, they had made promises forever.

In a small room in the back of Sarah's mind was the picture of herself, dressed in her mother's wedding gown, the picture of her dressed with white satin buttons like pearls. There was a picture of her somewhere as lovely as that; maybe it was in a movie she once saw. Her mother had told her she looked beautiful. The wedding day stopped and fixed itself like a butterfly under glass.

Sarah did not find it easy, at first, living with the old mother and three sisters and brother. The house was set on a corner in the Italian neighborhood on the other side of the city from where her own family lived, from where her mother spoke in Lithuanian over the sweet blue bed sheets and the crocuses to her neighbors who laughed and responded in Lithuanian. That to Sarah had been a small backyard world, where her father owned a restaurant and her mother cooked meals for strangers in large metal pots, washed the strangers' dirty dishes and she, dressed in white, took orders and served them on Buffalo china. Always she gently pulled the white stuff of the waitress apron over her full breasts and cast shyly her black eyes down while they ordered steak and eggs. Like a mouse she ran into the kitchen with their orders written down and watched her mother's small bent form cracking clear eggs onto the grill where they solidified, spooning large measures of black coffee into the giant pots. At night she walked the three blocks home past small quiet houses behind the hollyhocks, the lights already out in the living rooms and the bedroom lights hissing soft and blue. Then she would stop and remove her shoes, her young feet swollen and turned black from the leather and the sweat and she would cut across the gardens in her tired bare feet, the sweet earth touching them in the night. Then would she glance out of her young black eyes at the white shades drawn down over bedroom windows, and glance up into the trees, the stars. At home, her father sat behind his small thick glasses, going over the books. The light from the lamp reflected gold in the glasses, she could not see his eyes and as she passed him on her way to the bedroom, he said nothing. In her bed her hair was dark against the blue pillowcase which her mother had dried in the sun of the back-yard, and she watched the blue signs of the night outside her window and fell asleep into the next day. When the young policeman walked into the restaurant one morning and ordered breakfast she had been aware of little other than her tooth, which hurt, and of his skin, which was darker than hers. On a summer night one year later, when they sat in his blue sedan near the planetarium, he asked her to marry him. The city's skyline was there, with its abrupt ascendings and descendings of buildings in black and gray, with its thousands of lights against the dark sky like the brilliant eye of a fly. She felt sleepy that night, it was so warm, and he said, "Well, when do you want to marry me?" When she turned, his profile was a sketch against the lights of the city; beyond his face, the lake stretched out entirely black. His hair was parted precisely down the center of his head, thick and black, black as hers, black as his eyes, as her own eyes, black as the earth which touched her bare feet when she walked home alone at night from the restaurant. She asked herself if she wanted to sleep in the same bed with him, right beside him where his hair was messed and tossed on the pillow, above his dreaming eyes. She asked herself if she wanted to have his children. There was his smile, the smile that made her soul go wrong, that blurred her mind like music. They were married.

Now she had left behind her the small white houses of the south side of the city, the picket fences between the yards; the gutteral and minced Lithuanian in the throats of her family, her neighbors, was stilled.

Lying beside her husband in this house filled with his family, she no longer walked barefooted down the sidewalks. His father's house, pur-chased with pride and with his father's dollars from twenty-five years in the grocery store, was set into a night where the language spoken was Italian, sweet and musical like the quick ringing of many deep-toned bells. Here were no white picket fences, no small houses separated by gardens, but rows of buildings three stories high, bricked and set up against each other, each building separated into tiny flats of four and five rooms, and the clothes were dried on wooden back porches that faced alleys and the smell of alleys, where the sun never reached. Here there were lines of wet clothes hung on ropes between the buildings; the wash water dripped on the heads of children playing in the gangways. There was no light in the buildings; in the rooms, it seemed always gray. She and Marco would live in one of the flats across the alley from his family, as soon as he could afford one. Now she slept beside him in his parents' bedroom. Grandma Doria slept in the closed inner porch, near the pantry with its jars of lima beans and olives. Josephina and Rosa slept in the spare bedroom, Katerina on the couch in the living room. In the mornings it was pushing and shoving for the bathroom, for the food in the icebox, it was touching the naked flesh of the family tumbling out of beds, still warm from sleep in the small rooms. Sarah and the baby living inside her were dropped into the middle of the family like extra groceries at the top of a bag.

In the mornings they exchanged slow Italian over cups of thick black coffee. Sarah could never quite catch up and wondered which language the baby would speak. In silence she sat at the breakfasts where large bowls of pastina and butter were passed and felt the cold hand creeping up from her chest into her throat, where it snapped her words in two. Doria was large, larger than any woman Sarah had ever seen; her hands were fat and firm; she swept them through the air in large circles while out of her happy smiling mouth the meaningless Italian fell. Always she was telling Sarah to eat more pastina, it was good for the baby and from around her old neck she removed the golden horn on its chain and snapped it shut around Sarah's slender throat. Because of the horn, the baby would be born with all its fingers, its sight would be perfect.

Katerina was a stenographer for a large stationery company nearby; Marco drove her to her office on his way to police headquarters and in the mornings, Katerina, her hair pinned into a bun, would stand in her black slip and pound on the bathroom door where Marco was taking too long to shave. Laughing, Marco yelled at her through the door and Katerina laughed too, her firm body rocking gently and Josephina and Rosa silently filled their mouths with pastina when Marco emerged from the bathroom, his slim body red from the steam, a white towel wrapped around his small waist. Then he would pinch Katerina's chin and kiss her, telling her if she was not ready in five minutes he would leave without her and all the family would laugh while Doria passed to the young pregnant Sarah another bowl of pastina.

One night the fire surprised them all. The fire began in the kitchen walls, in the wires. For days the fire was coiled, hidden in the plaster, like a thousand snakes. They spit themselves out, they ate their way through the plaster, the wood, slithered out in pure hungry flame and chewed at the air. The white tablecloth was devoured in an instant. The wires exploded and ate through the walls, miraculously reducing the elements of the room to ash. The sleeping family dreamed white dreams and did not hear the flames which were cunningly and silently eating the house. Beneath her blue blanket, Sarah's body was large and ripe and naked under its nightgown; in her sleep, the flesh of her body breathed and caressed the life it protected. Under her skin, the unborn baby slept; its perfect fists closed over its new-formed eyes. The baby's eyes looked in on nothing. Marco slept straight as a stick beside her, his long clean body jerking momentarily in the black eyes of the night, then resting again. The fire hissed out white smoke; the light bulb above the kitchen table exploded; there was a moment of blue light, then the ceiling was a mouth of flames. A flame fell from the kitchen ceiling onto the dining room rug. In an instant the flames twisted past the dining table, licked up the heavy drapes, settled outside Sarah and Marco's door. Salvatore shoved it open.

He shook Marco like a madman. He could not wake him up. Beside him, her large round body barely covered by her nightgown, Sarah sat stone upright in the strange light of the fire. The skin of her face was hot; the smoke strangled her throat. She screamed and scratched at Marco with her nails. He sank deeper into his sleep, then sat up like one who wakes from the dead. It was too late to get to the door, the living room was gone behind flames. He pulled his wife out of the bed, slammed the room's door shut. Outside the world was covered in ice; when Marco forced the bedroom window open, the ice clung to it like the teeth of a mad animal. With his fist filled with sleep and with anger, he punched away the ice and glass, ripped the rotting wood away from the frame. Sarah's black hair gleamed in the white air, transparent as a cobweb. She looked like a madwoman, her eyes two completely black holes. On the other side of the bedroom door, the fire cracked and spit and lunged like a beast. The door leaned with the fire's weight.

Sarah felt the ice on the windowsill touch her feet's bare skin. On her back, Marco's warm hands held her gently a minute, then shoved her out the window. She landed two floors below like a cat, on her feet. Years later, all she remembered of those moments was that her nightgown flew up over her head and she stood naked on the blue ice in front of all her neighbors, staring at her bleeding feet.

When the fire was finally killed, the kitchen was ashes. Most of the small house was gone. Doria always kept a memento of the fire, a wooden statue of the Sacred Heart. She had brought it with her from the old country. The fire licked the painted figure clean; the face was scarred down one side.

A month later, Sarah's first baby was born. Marco named her Doriana after his mother and moved his small family into the flat across the alley. For months, Sarah sat at her new kitchen window with Doriana and watched the workmen crawl over the black skeleton which was the back of Doria's house to measure and rebuild it. For months, the house was like a black spider on the other side of Sarah's window. The family covered part of the house in plastic and at night they all shoved into Sarah's little kitchen, where she prepared and served the meals until Doria's house could be rebuilt.

Years later, Grandma Doria still blamed the fire for what happened to Doriana, and cried out to God during the nights when she was without sleep, why did the fire have to come when Sarah was pregnant, why did He have to make her jump two stories to the ground and ruin the beautiful baby that way? In the night, Grandma Doria crossed herself and cursed God, then begged His forgiveness. Sarah blamed it on the fever, in her heart she knew they should have done something before the fever grew so hot it turned the skin of the baby's face blue, they should have done something more than hold the burning baby under the cold water of the tap, watching the night pass, praying when the sun rose that the worst was over, that the baby would now be all right. In her heart she knew, when the color of the baby's face changed, that they had waited too long.

Still now, sitting in the church with her daughters beside her, Sarah knew it was the fever. She watched her hands. When the baby yelled its green yells into the night, when Doriana curled her small fists around the heat of the fever, when the young mother Sarah felt the skin of her first baby burning in her hands she screamed and pulled at her own hair. Marco said, put her under cold water. Doriana beat her fists into the night, she would not stop screaming. Marco yelled to his mother across the alley, what should they do?, lights turned on in Grandma Doria's house, in the houses of the neighbors, and they all said, put her under cold water. Sarah held Doriana under the ice water until her own hands turned red, then wrapped her in small dishtowels and held her under the water again. When Doriana turned finally blue, when the skin of her face tinged and the small eyes rolled inwards, they wrapped her in all the towels, packed her into ice and drove to the doctor. Sarah's hands were red for a day, from the ice water. Later, when Doriana passed the time when she should be talking, when Carmolina was already chirping like a little bird, they couldn't shut her up, Doriana remained silent behind her black eyes. Sarah couldn't stand the silence and took her to see doctors, who could find nothing wrong with her. When Carmolina went three years old and singing into the house, and poking her nose into books, and making up stories about the pictures in the books, Doriana smashed dishes against the walls and then tried to eat the broken pieces. The neighbors said Carmolina had stolen the brains of her sister, who ever heard of a four-year-old girl making up stories the way she did. Grandma Doria, God rest her soul, always said it was the fire. Sarah knew they should have done something different.

The skin of Sarah's hands was dry, puckered and scaly like a fish flat and dead on a beach where the ocean tossed it away. On her right hand the diamond ring caught the light of the altar candles; the light in the diamond was chiseled and shrill. Long ago the ring had eaten its way into her flesh, embedded itself there; it was as though the diamond grew out of the skin. Sarah stared at the priest at the altar; Doriana glanced at her eyes. They would scream, Mama's eyes. They would scream and fall out of her head, bounce onto the church floor. Mama's eyes would scream and Daddy would get out of the coffin and ask her please to shut up, like he always did when Mama screamed. Inside the coffin Daddy smelled sweet, it made her sick to her stomach. When the box was open at the funeral parlor and the family marched in to slap Daddy good-bye, to knock him for good over there to the place where he was dead, they all made a long black line, like ants on the sidewalk, to wait to see him, and he smelled sweet. Everyone was too quiet and you could smell him, more than the flowers; he made you sick to your stomach. When you got to the front of the line like on the street for the seedman a long time ago when you were still Doriana and a little girl instead of 23 years old like now, you bent over to shove him hard and make sure he was dead. You were supposed to kiss him when you did that but his skin was all white on his face, he was wearing lipstick, and under your mouth his head was so hard you thought his face would snap up over his bones like a window shade and you were supposed to kiss him. That was Daddy lying there and when you put your face close to him, his skin smelled like oranges and inside you there was this hot ball of water, it was in your stomach and coming up into your mouth and you tried to swallow it but you saw the black pencil on Daddy's eyebrows and felt how cold his hands were under your hands. He wouldn't wave to you anymore Good-bye Doriana on his way to work and the smell was making you sick to your stomach and this hot water was coming up because those were the hands that touched the doorknob to shut the door good-bye and then the hot water came out and everybody was looking at you and trying to make you move away so the other ants could come up in line and chew at him but you were bigger than all of them and you were shaking the casket between your arms. Daddy's head moved a little on the white pillow and his mouth stuck open like a puppet's, you thought for a minute that he was going to say something Hello Doriana and somewhere a million miles away you heard your voice screaming. Then someone spilled hot water all over Daddy, there were little spots in his makeup like rain and you listened to your own voice screaming at you and wondered how it got so far away. Now Mama would do it, her eyeballs were going to fall out of her head and of course Daddy wouldn't pick them up, they all made sure he was dead, they cried so much. If you picked them up and put them back in Mama's white-doll face, she would smile and say, Thank you, Doriana.

*

They sat together on the back porch. The mother had now placed a large straw hat on her head, to save herself from the sunlight, hard and hot like iron, and Marco laughed a minute. "You look like you're going to pick dandelions, Ma," Marco said. Doria cupped the air in her fat hands, holding it like the soft ass of a baby, rocked it a little. "I go to a wedding, young man. You wedding. No dandelion." They both laughed. Marco was leaning against the porch railing. Little buttons of water sat on his forehead, his upper lip.

"Hey, Ma, this is my wedding day."

"So?" She looked up at him from under her straw hat, like a peculiar cat.

Again she waved her hands.

"Go ahead, Marco. Just today."

He reached into his jacket pocket, pulled out a package of cigarettes.

"No disrespect, Ma?"

The old woman looked past him, to the impossible yellow sunflowers in the garden.

"No disrespect."

He lit one, smashed the match dead with his patent leather shoes.

Katerina stood in the doorway, behind her the cool house was black; so that he could not see past her.

"You look beautiful, Katie. You'll be a beautiful bridesmaid."

Katerina hesitated in the doorway.

"Come on out. Let Ma see you."

"I need to dry my hair," Katerina said.

She stepped out into the sunshine, wearing the identical blue dress her sisters were struggling into.

"Ma?" she said.

Doria looked at her youngest daughter.

"*Faccia bella*," she said, and watched Katerina leaning over the porch railing, her long black hair drying in the sun, and canaries flew into her hair.

54

PART IV

SUMMER, 1949
EARLY JUNE

1.

The gypsies moved into empty storefronts on the market street, moved in next to the butcher shops where live chickens were decapitated by toothless old women, where chickens gave a gutteral cry out of their long skinny necks before their goofy fuzzy heads were whacked off; the gypsies moved in, hung colored cloth in the naked windows of an empty storefront and settled like black tents into the crazy colors of Quincy Street.

The merchants never knew when they arrived, how in the whisper of the night the gypsies were spoken like a secret word. One morning Augie the grocer showed up with the sun rising at his back, his head scrubbed clean at his small bathroom sink, his short teeth brown with tobacco, the metallic store keys in his warm hands. The sun was an orange circle smudged around his small square body, moving in the last stages of sleep down the street. He whistled to himself a little tune he had made up while shaving that morning.

As always he was the first to arrive on Quincy. The iron grate was still pulled tight, a clenched fist, across the glass window which said in yellow letters, Butcher. The chickens were silent inside, in their wooden crates; they looked sideways at each other out of their slightly crossed eyes. The hot air slipped over the doorsill of the shut butchershop, whirred languidly inside it, lazily blew the sawdust out from under the door and into the street where it landed between the toes of Augie's feet in their leather sandals. Between his brushed teeth, he felt the yellow stuff settle; it settled into his body, against his skin. By the end of the day he would be gritty with it, the hair in his armpits would itch, he would carry Quincy Street home with him, stuck to the heavy hair of his arms.

He squatted at the doorway of his grocery store, his brown eyes squinting down the half-empty street, awaiting the arrival of the produce wagons, the horses. Behind him the bells of the church rolled out, Mass was over, the women would soon arrive, or send their children. Between his fat lips he stuck the butt-end of his black cigar, his teeth closed down hard over the familiar greasy plug. His wife Serafina hated it.

The small hairs in his ears buzzed; his nose flinched at the new smell.

The store next to his which had been vacant since the death of old Luigi who gagged one night at the dinner table on a chicken bone and whose sons the next day locked up the old sausage shop, the store which had been vacant the night before was now filled with gypsies. He whacked himself on the ass for not noticing it sooner. The smell was there; they were like cats. Near the doorway a gypsy woman and her large bosom leaned towards the light. Augie could smell her from his stoop. With the sun rising behind her, he could see the round swells of her body under the thin dress. At her ears she wore the large golden hoops; the fabric of her dress glistened. It was run through with fine silver threads, the work of spiders, a wide band of silver ran round the hem.

Augie broke his squat, shoved his hands into his pockets, straddled the curbstone.

The wagons were close. His fine ear isolated the soft clop of the horse's foot against the cement, his fine ear selected from the soft skein of the sounds of Quincy Street coming to life the threads of the women's voices finding their way to his store.

He rubbed his nose, wiped his hand against his pants leg. The gypsy woman ran long fingers through her black hair; the light glanced like silver water off the fine curve of her neck, off her head thrown back. Her hair drying in the sun smelled sweet. With her teeth she pulled the thin meat off the bone of a chicken wing. Augie smelled her. They were wisps of smoke; they slipped into empty places and settled there, then slipped out through the cracks in the walls. He crossed the street to the baker's.

With his tobacco mouth he broke the brown crust of the bread. Old La Scala the baker went back into his store to dust with flour the flat wooden bread boards. Augie watched the windows of Luigi's store. It was as though the building breathed with them. The cloth over the gypsy doorway moved slightly; the woman was inside; she was gone.

Augie crossed the street to unlock his store.

Augie the grocer liked the BellaCasa family. It was the largest in the neighborhood and always getting larger. He watched Doria BellaCasa's young sons and daughters marrying and richly breeding. Each child was more beautiful than the last; he wondered where it would end. The black eyes, the hair black as blue water, was passed from parent to child like jewels in the hands of thieves. When little Carmolina showed up with her grandmother's list, Augie's fat mouth smiled at her. He touched the soft chin of the child's face.

"Eh, how Marco?" he smiled again and placed the heavy sweet tomatoes in the white scale; the tomato weight pulled on the chain, the iron arrow pointed its head past one pound. He removed one large tomato, placed a smaller one in the scale. "Eh, *bambina,* how's you father?"

Carmolina dropped her dark eyes, studied the floor. The skin of the lids was tinged faintly blue; God blessed her eyes just before she was born. He said, "Carmolina, these are your eyes. Go with them into your family." Her thin dark hair fell into her face, across the brown skin of her cheeks. She would be a beauty, this one. Marco would have to watch her. She had the face of her Aunt Katerina.

"Gypsies?" Carmolina asked. She half-lifted her eyes toward the doorway.

Augie spit out the stone of an apricot.

"You be careful," he said. "They like to steal little ones, especially if they pretty, like you."

Carmolina ran over to the doorway. In the sun her dress was bright red and she stretched her small legs, standing on tiptoe. Bracing her arms in the doorway, she lifted herself from the floor, swung her legs free in the air. Her face turned; it was lit up with the full light of the sun, her hair shone like the bottom of a copper pot. For a moment, her eyes were confused.

Augie looked at her, shook his head.

She laughed.

"Maybe I'll run away with them," she said, and laughed again.

Augie reached down, placed the brown bag of fruits and vegetables in her arms. For a second he saw again the troubled look in her eyes, a look he wished he could take away. It should not be there, in the eyes of an eight-year-old.

"You go straight home," he said.

The lettuce in the bag blocked her vision.

She shoved it down with her chin.

"Ugh," she said. "A mealybug."

They both laughed, and the look went away.

Her tennis shoes squeaked against the moist floor as she left. Augie relit the dead cigar, chewed on it slowly. It was the other one who would break all their hearts. Maybe she had already done it. He turned his hose on the bushel of apples. Nine-years-old, and Doriana had done it already. He thanked God for his own healthy sons, listened to the soft hiss of water on apples. Marco had the look in his eyes, but he was a man and ready for it. Carmolina should play instead, should throw the look away into the face of the devil, where it came from. Sarah, her eyes were glass.

He picked up an apple, rubbed it dry against his shirt, bit into it.

It was too early for apples.

Carmolina walked past the butcher shop. Inside, Mrs. Schiavone whacked the heads off chickens when they weren't looking. The chickens had long fuzzy necks with old flat feathers; their bodies looked like the stuffings inside toys. From the sidewalk, Carmolina looked at her through the length of the butcher shop to the doorway at the back. Mrs. Schiavone stood in the black doorway and the day was a white square behind her. Carmolina squinted. Mrs. Schiavone wore a white apron covered with chicken guts and feathers, purple chicken guts were sticky on her hands and wedged under her fingernails. She stood like that, in the doorway, and a silver hatchet like a square with a thick line of blood along its edge hung from her arm. Mrs. Schiavone reached her other arm inside a wooden crate filled with terrified chickens, with the edge of the hatchet she adjusted the hairnet that was slipping down over her eyes.

"Eh, Carmolina," she laughed. "*Buon giorno.*"

Her laugh had a broken breath in it, as though laughing choked her. She yanked the chicken out of its cage, it screamed like an old woman and stared sideways out of its helpless eyes. Its feet kicked the air violently; Mrs. Schiavone's arms had long red marks scratched into them by the desperate feet of trapped chickens.

"Grandma want some legs today, yes?" the old woman said.

She held the screeching chicken at a small distance from her, considered its yellow claws clenched in terror. "This one a beauty," she smiled. "The feet good for soup. Such a beauty, this chicken. Come, little duck, you watch."

Carmolina said no, not today, but her two feet stood still and flat against the cement.

The old woman moved to the heavy block in the alley outside the doorway. In the white light of the alley, she was as skinny as the chicken in her hands.

She slammed the chicken down against the block, lifted the hatchet. Her face turned towards Carmolina; her mouth was a black slit, smiling. There were no teeth in the slit, only slick thin gums. When the hatchet whacked down, the chicken's entire body jerked, like a man at the end of a hangman's noose; then the headless chicken jumped off the block, its neck pumping red blood like a fountain straight upwards into the summer's white air.

Mrs. Schiavone's arms were covered in chicken blood; she swore at the chicken head on the block; the lifeless head stared out of its baffled eyes.

Carmolina shifted the heavy bundles of groceries in her arms. She squinted through the long black tunnel of the butcher shop; there was the chicken head, like a doll with eyes of glass.

In the alley, Mrs. Schiavone chased the headless chicken, swearing at it in Italian. She waved her hatchet around her head in circles, telling the chicken to stop. Covered in its own blood, the headless chicken ran like a mad child.

*

The late sunlight glanced gold off the large hooped earrings. It was a perfect summer evening. With the earrings scrubbing at her neck, Carmolina watched the blue light that seemed like a curtain blowing behind the world. No one noticed yet that she was wearing Mama's earrings. Her mother sat across the street on a bench; she was sitting in the perfect blue light hunched over, her hands over her bare knees, her cotton dress was pulled up over her knees. The skin on her knees was dry and red. Mama ran her hand through her thick hair. She wore no nylons. Her legs looked thick and worn. She let her hands fall again between her knees, her back was a slope. She brushed dirt off one knee.

Carmolina unclipped one earring and held it up to her eye. Through the golden hoop she watched Mama sitting next to Grandma. She squinted where the sunlight sliced sharp off the golden edge. Inside the earring, Mama and Grandma were small. They were talking, but she could not hear them. She could turn the earring any way she wanted; she could make them bigger or smaller.

Inside the earring, Mama and Grandma fanned themselves; Grandma with a newspaper, Mama with the skirt of her dress. It was too hot, even for summer, they would say.

Their mouths moved; Carmolina watched the quiet mouths through the earring.

"So the doctor say she should go away, eh?"

Sarah shook her head. The hair was tied at the back of her head and pulled. "We can't afford it, Ma," she said.

Through her old eyes, Grandma Doria squinted into the blue light. She saw something moving across the street. She could not see that it was her granddaughter.

"And if you have the money, what then?" She shifted her feet in the enamel pan of water. "You send her away if you can pay? You lock her up like a little animal? Give me some more water, eh?"

"The water is hot, Ma."

"Doriana is beautiful. She like a flower. The water is cold."

"Ma, the water is hot."

Doria saw out of the sides of her eyes the tight pull of hair at the base of Sarah's neck.

"She have the perfect face. Like the angels. You look at you own daughter's face?"

"Ma, I know Doriana is beautiful." The ache at the back of her head was a splinter of wood under her skin.

"You pray to God," Grandma Doria said. "You pray to God and she be all right."

Sarah took the white pan out from under Grandma Doria's feet. Upstairs, in Doria's kitchen, she ran the hot water from the tap and lit a cigarette. She looked out the kitchen window, saw Carmolina playing across the street. She drew on the cigarette, shoved the window open, shouted to her daughter. Carmolina would not listen. Sarah screamed at her to get back across the street, what did she think she was doing? When she filled the pan, the steam turned her hands red. Sarah opened the window wide to let the cigarette smoke out, blew at the smoke to force it out the window.

Close up like this, Mama's eyes were set in cobwebs. Carmolina reached one hand down and scratched her leg. Her skirt hitched up. Mama slid her hands up her dress, adjusted the underpants.

"Take those earrings off and put them away," Mama said.

"I'm playing gypsy."

"I said take them off."

"How will I get into the house?"

"How did you get out?"

Carmolina looked at Grandma, who squeezed her face. "Go find you Papa," she said.

Sarah settled Doria's purple feet into the water.

Halfway down the street a small group of men stood in the asphalt alleyway. Small blue rings of cigarette smoke settled above their heads, thinned out into the azure air. Carmolina heard her father laugh, rubbed up against his pants leg. She held one thumb between her teeth and forgot about the earrings. The bottom of Daddy's chin was stubbled with small black hairs; the chin bobbed up and down when he laughed. She rubbed against the fabric of his pants.

He carried her upstairs like a giant, slung her over his shoulder and laughed and spanked her for stealing the earrings and called her his little kitten. The air of the hallway was dark and smelled. Behind the door of one of the flats, a baby cried. A woman said something in Spanish. The slap of skin was heard. The lights in the hall were dim, like fireflies. Behind all the doors, all the people were moving; through the doors she could hear people coughing and putting away dishes, running water over their hands.

Through his shirt, she smelled how clean her father was. He slapped her again, over and over, she laughed, she reached down to pull up her underpants and laughed more.

Upstairs the yellow kitchen sat in the blue light. The white sink gleamed.

She ran into the bathroom and lifted the latch, locking herself in, still laughing.

In the bedroom, Doriana heard the laughter, as a sound is heard by the rider of a train, so distant, somewhere in the night, meaningless, quickly dismissed. She turned in her sleep. It could have been the barking of a dog.

Out of her black eyes in her face on the pillow, Doriana looked up at the ceiling of the room. Her head hurt; inside her heavy skull it was as though people were trying to kick their way out. She yanked the doll closer to her, held the doll's head close to her own. The doll bit her. She threw it at the wall. Mama walked in. The warm washcloth was over her eyes. There were spiders in the closet. Doriana found one that morning when she was crawling under the dead dresses, looking for her shoes. She snatched one. In her fingers the spider had a fuzzy back like hair. It was soft. She looked for the spider's eyes and then she ate the furry nest. There were dead ants in the nest. Mama came in and took the spider away. With the nails of her fingers, Mama scraped the spider legs off Doriana's hands and when Doriana put the spider's face into her mouth, Mama cried and went to look for Daddy. Daddy had hot skin and his eyes burned at her. He had fires in his head. Doriana tied the laces on one shoe, put it on her foot, but it didn't fit with the laces tied. She sat on the bed. Daddy took her shoe off and opened her mouth. He washed her tongue with a toothbrush. Small hairs grew out of Daddy's face and nose. Doriana put his nose in her mouth.

"I have a pain in my heart," Mama said.

Daddy packed her into the bed.

Doriana bit the doll.

Carmolina pulled her hair.

"Dorr-eee-aaa-nnaaa," Carmolina whispered. She used her hand to make Doriana's stomach tingle. "How do spiders taste? Are they good?"

Doriana blinked her black eyes.

Carmolina sat on the edge of the bed and smoothed her dress all neat around her like a doily on the couch. Then she made a little ball of herself and curled up in the bed on top of the blankets. She put her hands around Doriana's ear. Her hands were soft like milk. "I saw gypsies," Carmolina whispered.

Doriana's eyelashes went up and down. Her head turned towards Carmolina. There was a star in Carmolina's eyes.

Doriana touched Carmolina's face. She was brown and warm.

"Pretty," Doriana said.

Carmolina smiled, she made a little ball and rolled out of the bed. The room was empty again.

Carmolina's head floated above her. It was there all alone. One of Carmolina's fingers touched her nose. Doriana's mouth smiled. "Last night I was a gypsy," Carmolina's head whispered.

Carmolina's mouth kissed her nose. "Oh, Doriana."

The room was empty like a block of ice.

Doriana's eyes wanted to go to sleep. Her eyelids got fat and heavy; they kept closing over her eyeballs. Doriana pushed her eyelids up over her eyes with her fingers. She tried to touch one eyeball with her finger. Her eyes felt like fried eggs when she rubbed them with her fingers in the mornings and smashed them and put them into her mouth. The eggs slid off her fingers and felt like her eye with her finger on it.

Mama came in and took her fingers away.

The washcloth was over her eyes again.

"Sleep, baby," Mama said, and held her hands over Doriana's eyes.

Under the washcloth, Doriana opened her eyes. She blew spit bubbles. She pulled at the skin on her cheeks but Mama's hand was still there. Mama put her hand over Doriana's mouth. Doriana blew spit into it.

"Please stop it," Mama said. "Please stop."

Doriana slapped the hand and kicked her feet under the blankets. Her legs were tied down under the sheets.

"No dream," she screamed.

Mama put the pill into her mouth.

Doriana screamed again. She spit the pill out.

It landed in Mama's hand and made it red.

Mama shoved it back into her mouth, held her mouth shut.

The pill fell down her throat under the water.

"No dream," Doriana said in her small voice.

"Please baby," Mama said.

Everything went away.

"The sugar she make you head dizzy," Grandma Doria said. "Dizzy like circles."

"I know, Ma," Sarah said. She turned the coffee cup in her hand; the coffee was cold already.

The street noises below were muted; the day was too hot for anything. Even the ragpickers were silent and did their work without singing their melancholy Italian songs.

"So you no use it," Grandma Doria said.

"No, Ma. I won't use it."

Grandma Doria held her fat hands together in her lap, squeezed her own fingers gently. "Marco, his eyes look tired."

The cup was ice cold in her hand.

"Excuse me, Ma," Sarah said. She spilled the coffee down the throat of the sink, poured another cup from the glass pot.

"At you wedding, we all so happy." Doria pulled a handkerchief out of her brassiere, removed her glasses, cleaned them. "We sing like birds. Remember?"

"Please, Ma."

Doria reached over the kitchen table, covered Sarah's hands with hers.

"It because I care, Sarah," Grandma Doria said. "I care so much. Every morning with the candles I pray."

"Ma, please go sit with her," Sarah said.

The old woman got up, bent over and kissed her on the forehead.

"I love you," Grandma Doria said. "I love my Marco. I love this little family." She held Sarah's face in her hands. "But this family is like little pieces."

She walked slowly down the hallway towards the children's bedroom, leaning heavily on an old black cane.

Sarah went into the bathroom, turned on the light, waited for the cockroaches to run back to their places behind the tub, under the toilet tank.

"No disrespect, Ma," she said to herself.

She locked the door with the tiny latch, sat on the toilet seat, lit a cigarette. The window didn't need a curtain because there was no light. She looked at the sink, the tub, the white smoke in the mirror.

*

The grandmother's eyes closed over this, her first grandchild. Her face was like porcelain, like the face of a porcelain Madonna. Doriana's face was the ivory-white face of the Virgin Mother, praise God. Grandma Doria watched the sleeping face of the child on the pillow. The eyelids closed perfectly, like the lines in a saint's statue; the eyelids seemed carved by the hands of a saint-maker. Doriana's lashes were black and wet; she had cried herself to sleep. The grandmother moved the blanket. The small hands were clasped tight together, they held each other fiercely. She fought with lions in her sleep, Mother Mary help her. Her small body was rigid under the blanket, her toes curled under her feet as though she dreamed she stood on the edge of a cliff.

The grandmother pulled a chair beside the bed, draped her shawl over the chair's wooden back, rested her cane against the bed. She pulled from her brassiere the black rosary beads. Her mouth began the prayers in small whispers, the room filled with the soft hiss of the grandmother's prayers and the troubled breathing of the child tangled in its sleep.

This was the room where the two children slept, in the midst of the marriage made by the priest. In Italy, it would be different. In Italy little Doriana would run in green fields under the healthy sun, would play in the white sunlight, would reach up and receive from the hands of the sky, from the blessed guardian angels, her own healthy mind, glory be to God, her own words which would help her make the right sounds, to speak to the open eyes of Sarah and Marco what was on her mind. Grandma Doria nodded her head, yes; her eyes closed for a moment. Doriana would run free, she would touch the bark of the olive trees and receive her health. She would then turn in the sunlight towards her smiling parents, would sing songs to them, would call them Mama and Papa. Everyone would smile. Doriana would smile. She would look through her own eyes and always know the names and faces of her family, would know her Grandma and smile at her, instead of stumbling in this small confusion. It was the city that did this to her. It was the fire, first. But then it was the city, it was the empty gray light like a spider sucking the blood of the wonderful child, the child bled out her brains, her smiles, her own words into the empty gray light of the city and there was nothing to feed her. The buildings of the city were bones crushing against little Doriana, giving her pain. Marco, he was never home; he wore everyday the police uniform and went out where people were murdered, were butchered like pigs in the sties. He did not gather olives, sit in the sun, but was instead white like a sheet with his eyes watching the guns, the shooting, the chopping of people in their own beds. Sarah she was pale, nervous, locked up in these small rooms with two children. The food she made was thin, they were poor, but where in the stores of her life, God forgive her, did Doria have the treasure to help them. Her pockets were empty. At night the husband and wife, they faced each other over thin coffee and outside their windows the eyes of the city were a fly, staring at them.

Behind her glasses, the grandmother's eyes grew weak. She drew the shade of the window, cut in two the limp light of the sun, settled down again with the prayer beads in her lap.

Now, in this light, the gray light falling slim through the paper shade, it was as though the child had stopped breathing, her small mind came buzzing to a stop like a broken toy. Her features were too perfect, her mouth was like a chiseled line, like the mouths of the angels at the graves of the dead.

A thin skim of water covered the grandmother's eyes. She squinted hard at the child, tried to detect her breathing.

"Doriana?" she whispered.

The room was soundless.

Slowly Grandma Doria let fall from her hands the wooden beads, bent closer to the child's face. Her skin was pure white, it could be plaster.

"*Doriana mia?*"

If she were dead, what? They would lock the perfect face into a white box and bury it beside the grandfather, and Dominic would have the company of a child whose brain made a dream of the world. The family would be smaller, but the pain in the heart of the family would be, finally, stilled.

Grandma Doria bent over her large belly, reached over to the child. She placed one finger under Doriana's nose and waited.

The paper shade flapped.

Again the room stilled itself.

The grandmother waited.

Doriana's breath fell on her finger.

The grandmother settled back, arranged the shawl around her shoulders.

"God forgive me," she whispered.

The prayers began again.

Carmolina sat on her back porch and watched the alley. Her small brown legs swung free over the gray paint of the railing. Behind her, the porch was strung with a heavy clothesline; the family's clothes were hung out to dry in the sun and patched the gray porch with squares of red, yellow, white, Daddy's undershirts blew out white from the rope like the sails of a ship. The water from the clothes dripped onto the porch, a scrub bucket, an ironing board, a washboard. Carmolina wrapped her thin arms around the porch bannister and watched the alley three floors below her.

Stephanzo the fish man darted like a small mouse out the back door of his market, dumped the fish heads, dim-eyed and dead into the metal garbage drums. Carmolina saw the sun glint silver on the fish heads, smelled the dead fish flesh. Fish tails and innards landed on the bricks of the alleyway, small circles of blood formed around them, the flies darted blue and black over them. Carmolina sucked on her blue popsicle. She wished she could tell Doriana about the gypsies. The blue water ran down her chin, down her arm. She kept her eyes on Stephanzo, watched him dump a slippery pan of fish heads into the garbage drum where he would light fire to them, ran her tongue down her arm and caught the popsicle water at her elbow.

Augie came out of his store, emptied a bushel of bruised lettuce leaves into the alley drum. Carmolina bit the top off her popsicle.

The glass at the gypsy door had been cold against Carmolina's skin. On the other side was the curtain, the long catch of fabric which hid them from her. They were magic. She pressed her face against the glass, listened for the gypsy sounds inside.

They should be different sounds, gypsy sounds, the sound of gold or stolen babies. The glass was hard against her small ears; there were soft noises inside. She heard bodies moving, bare feet moved slowly over the old sawdust. She heard a cough. The door was cracked open.

Inside the room was hung blue like a peacock. Bolts of cloth covered the walls of old Luigi's sausage shop. Over the glass counters where he once kept hogs' intestines were thrown sheets of blue fabric, the hems were gold.

A pigeon flew by the porch, flapped by Carmolina's legs, she reached out for it.

In one corner an old gypsy woman sat in a wooden chair. The back of the chair was torn away. The gypsy sat with her body erect, balanced on the old chair like a grasshopper. Carmolina could see the pink patches of her skull gleaming like the insides of a shell. Her eyes and mouth were enormous. The mouth was as black as the eyes, like a hole in her face. Carmolina saw that she was laughing, but no sound came out. She sat there with her old hands shrunken together in her lap like dead flowers, her bald head was thrown back and her black old mouth was laughing and silent.

The old gypsy woman's eyes darted straight ahead across the room to where a half-naked gypsy man leaned over the body of another woman in bed. His skin was brown and taut, like the skin of a sausage. Through one ear he wore a small gold ring, his eyebrows and eyes were completely black. The woman on the bed moved slightly, the bed made a sound. The gypsy man slid a hand into her open dress. Carmolina looked at the old woman sitting on the chair. She was still laughing; what the gypsy man was doing to the woman on the bed was funny. The woman on the bed moaned a little in her sleep; on her upper lip a small line of perspiration looked like a silverfish. The hands of the gypsy man had long brown fingers. He used them to open the woman's dress. They were large and brown, one fell out of the dress. The gypsy man used two hands to squeeze it.

Grandma said there were mealybugs on the lettuce.

When she ate the popsicle down to the stick, the riddle was there. It was printed in little brown letters, under the popsicle. It said, "How can a match burn twice?"

Carmolina dropped the stick between her red tennis shoes. It floated in the air like a dead leaf. It hit the alley bricks.

Stephanzo set fire to the fish heads. The smoke curled up gray and thick. Inside, Mama was shutting the windows. She saw Mama's face behind her, in the bedroom, shoving the old window down hard against the stink of the burning fish.

Carmolina went to the clothesline, to pull down the clothes. Now the undershirts would smell like dead fish.

She stood on her toes, the muscles of her legs stretched tight, but the clothespins were too far away.

*

It was a family meeting, called by Grandma.

A family meeting means everyone is there, sitting in chairs around the kitchen table, and the night is outside where it can't reach the family. A family meeting is the family together, tight like a fist. It is a record of music playing into the night. Carmolina did not need to be in the room where the music was playing. She heard it from two rooms away, through the dining room and into the bedroom. The hands of the night did not dare touch the family; the family would burn the hands off. She wished she could turn the music off, but what would the silence sound like? A family meeting was the grownups; they came to this meeting because Grandma called it, and they were sitting with the music playing over and over, playing it into the street, and no one on the street listened to it because it would never go away.

Only Grandma could call a meeting in Mama's kitchen.

The kitchen was lit bright yellow, from the paint on the walls. Outside the night was so black, no one could see past the screens.

The flies hit the screens and bounced off. The sound they made was a sharp zip. Then they were gone; the family would not allow them. Behind the sound of the flies was the sound of water rushing out of the hydrant, cold and white. It spat out into the street, like the tongue of a water fish. The sound of the water turned soft; it was too late for the children to play in it, all the children were in bed like Carmolina, but the water made a soft sound so that they could sleep. Somewhere the moon was milky and white with the planet Venus close to it, like an angel. Carmolina read about that in her star books. Her star books were her favorite books; she kept them next to her orange history books which told the lives of famous people. Her favorite famous person was Amelia Earhart. They never found her body.

If she closed her eyes she could see them all there in the kitchen, even though she was in the bedroom where she couldn't sleep next to Doriana who was already sleeping.

Doriana fell asleep because of the pills. Carmolina wandered through her mind holding Doriana by the hand and wished she could sleep. There was no one to talk to. She wanted to talk to herself, to tell herself the stories her mind made up. Her mind made stories like toys, she could wind them up and watch them, they buzzed and jerked and made music. She didn't talk to anyone about the stories. She didn't talk to the stories anymore. If she talked to herself, the family would look at her out of all their eyes and then they would ask questions. Then Carmolina would turn into a skeleton.

She never talked to herself out loud. She stopped talking to her dolls. She was afraid that if she talked to herself, the whole family would walk into the room, or maybe just Mama, and then they would give her the pills that they gave Doriana. Her cousin Phyllis talked to her dolls all the time, but Phyllis didn't allow Carmolina to tell anyone that.

She looked at Doriana. Everyone always said how beautiful Doriana was. Carmolina thought Doriana was pretty, she was probably the prettiest little girl on the block. She was pretty even though she never went outside. On the wall in the living room there was a small oval picture taken of Doriana when she was two years old and perfect. She had happy black eyes and curly black hair. She was really Doriana in that picture.

She touched Doriana's head. She touched her own. She could rub her fingers through Doriana's hair, and Doriana would keep sleeping. She could even pull Doriana's hair and she would keep sleeping. She was the prettiest little girl on the block and her head felt just like Carmolina's.

If she tried hard, if she used her brain and all the pictures inside it and squeezed the pictures as hard as she could and watched them all together, she couldn't remember a time when she could talk to Doriana. She wished she could, but there was no picture in her head of Doriana talking to her. There were a lot of pictures of Doriana sleeping.

The light through the window shade was pink from the streetlamp. The family was still talking.

"The two of you look sick most of the time." Aunt Josephina's voice was loud no matter how soft she tried to make it. It fit her body.

Aunt Katerina asked if there was any anisette for the coffee.

Daddy said, in the cabinet by the sink.

Doriana kept sleeping. Her pajamas went up and down slowly. You could have grown up to look like Aunt Katerina, Carmolina whispered in her ear. You even look like the angels, Grandma says.

Daddy sounded tired.

He wanted to go to bed, but the whole family was there. They were sitting in the yellow kitchen with the black night outside, it was so hot and quiet and she could hear the flies hit the screen.

The bedroom felt small. Outside the window the black night beat like a heart, the curtains at the windows breathed in and out like Doriana's pajamas. On the toychest Carmolina's stuffed brown rabbit sat with its plastic eyes staring. One ear was broken. Doriana's black lamb sat next to it. The lamb was perfect. Doriana never played with it.

Every night Doriana petted the lamb and kissed its face. Its ears were still stuffed with tissue paper.

Then Uncle Salvatore said, what did the doctor say?

The coffee cups were white, Mama always scrubbed them. She could hear the cups being picked up, put down, everybody was sipping, the coffee had anisette in it. The cake was yellow, with almonds. Nobody was smoking, even though everybody smoked, out of respect to Grandma.

Mama said they couldn't afford to send Doriana away.

Grandma baked the cake because she called the family meeting.

Someone told Mama to stop crying.

Now Grandma was crying too, but she was quiet about it.

Carmolina wished she could take Doriana away, to the moon, to the angel Venus next to the moon. She wished she could do that.

Grandma said the family was talked about, everybody they talk about Doriana.

So you want us to lock her up, Mama said, you want us to lock her up to save the family's face?

Maybe the nuns could take her, Aunt Katerina said. The nuns are gentle.

She might be happier, Daddy said.

She need an angel to watch over her, Grandma said.

They all turned to look at her when she walked into the kitchen.

I told you you would wake Carmolina up, Mama said.

Even the linoleum on the floor was hot. Her feet stuck to it.

Mama's face looked like a tomato.

"I have to go to the bathroom," Carmolina said.

She stood on her toes to lock the bathroom door, switched on the light.

The roaches ran away before she could count them.

In the kitchen everyone was silent. They couldn't talk, now that they knew she could hear them. The music stopped. The fist got small.

The coffee cups clicked. She heard them slice a piece of cake. The coffee cups were white.

Did you fall in, Daddy said, and he knocked on the bathroom door.

"I think I'm sick," Carmolina said. Now let them talk about sending Doriana away, when she was right there being sick in the bathroom.

Daddy said, unlock the door.

Madonna mia, Grandma said. She was making the Sign of the Cross in the yellow kitchen. The world was crooked.

Daddy said, I said unlock this door.

"I can't," Carmolina said. "I'm throwing up."

Someone said, poor Sarah.

Grandma started to clear away the dishes. Aunt Katerina said where was her shawl.

Carmolina stuck her finger down her throat.

Mama was saying something on the other side of the door.

The front door opened; someone was leaving. Carmolina broke the family meeting up into little pieces.

Open this door this minute, Daddy said.

Carmolina turned on the water in the sink, she made it run full blast like horses, then she knelt down with her head over the toilet and beat her fists against the toilet seat.

PART V
SUMMER, 1949
LATE JULY

1.

Grandma's house was covered in shingles. They looked loose, as though a strong wind could blow them away across the world like bird feathers.

Grandma owned the entire house. Everything belonged to her, the building, the back porch, the garden, the dishes and spoons. She inherited it from Grandpa's will, when he died. Carmolina did not remember Grandpa because he died before she was born. Carmolina looked at tiny pictures of her grandfather. He was a man with white hair and gray skin. He looked out of the pictures from behind his glasses. Grandparents always wore glasses. Carmolina bent over the picture album, squeezed her eyes hard over Grandpa. Grandpa had no smell, he had no voice. There was no picture of Carmolina sitting on his lap. He was dead.

Now Grandma was the Grandpa of the family. Her building was narrow slats of dry wood, with a door in the side for the storage room. That was the side on Berrywood Street, where Carmolina lived just down the block. In front, on Mallard Street, Grandpa's old store was still boarded up. There were no noises inside the store.

Carmolina remembered when they added the shingles. Men with dirt on their skin stood on the streets around the house with pots of tar. The pots were as big as she was. Inside the tar smelled. The men spilled tar and stepped in it and made tar marks on the sidewalks in the shape of shoes. No one took a picture of the men doing this. The tar smelled; all the windows in Grandma's house were locked shut for a long time. The tar men made some mistakes and even now, a long time later, Carmolina could see fat globules of tar between the fake shingles, where the tar people were sloppy. She could see them from the street where she stood beneath Grandma's window, waiting for her to throw the money down. What she was about to do was a sin. In the summer, the tar globules got soft all over again and flies flew to them and got trapped. Grandma was putting it all down on a list; she told Aunt Katerina what she wanted from the stores. Aunt Katerina wrote it down in neat handwriting because Grandma couldn't write.

From the street, Grandma's windows looked closed, but Carmolina knew they were open. They were always open in the summertime. The sun shined onto the glass and you couldn't tell if the windows were open or shut unless you were a part of the family, and knew. She wondered if she would go to hell. She would have to die first. Grandma's head came poking out of her house, between the open window and the screen. She almost couldn't fit. One time Grandma knocked the screen out of the window when she threw the money down, tied into a handkerchief. The handkerchief landed at Carmolina's feet. There was a small hole starting in the toe of her red tennis shoe. The hole had little white threads around it. Grandma's handkerchief was tied into a knot around the money. Inside was the list for Augie and Mrs. Schiavone. Grandma's arm dangled over the screen from where she threw it; the white curtain blew at the back of her head. If it looked like she was going to die, Carmolina would say an Act of Contrition very quickly and really mean it.

She waved. Good-bye, Grandma.

She skipped to the corner of Mallard and Berrywood, up to the boarded-up store. Grandpa's body was in the cemetery with his eyes closed. He slept the sleep of the dead, Grandma said, and rested in the lap of God. But God let his soul visit the store. His soul moved sometimes; it had white hair and an apron. He watched over the family and stood between them and the angels. The white rim around her tennis shoes was turning black; the shoestrings were gray, like a picture of shoestrings.

When she got to the corner she turned and listened to Grandma one more time. Then she ran around the corner.

The streetcar stopped two blocks away. She would have to stand on the corner and wave to it. The conductor would see her, he would stop for her and pick her up and she would go flying off alone. She wiped her hands on the skirt of her dress; her head was dizzy. Doriana was packed into bed again with the pill in her mouth. This morning at breakfast, Doriana smashed a fried egg with her fist. When Mama yelled, Doriana picked up a fork and stabbed Mama's hand with it. Then she held the fork in front of her own eyes. Carmolina drank the glass of milk with her eyes on Doriana's eyes. From behind the glass she watched to see what Doriana would do. Mama sat down at the kitchen table and cried. She didn't make any noise when she cried; her shoulders just shook a little, like Jello, and tears ran down her face, out of her eyes. Carmolina blinked and her lashes brushed against the rim of the milk glass. Mama's hands were set still in her lap and the tears landed on them. Carmolina watched through the bottom of the milk glass. Doriana looked far away and small; the bottom of the glass was white. At the sink, the water dripped from the faucet in separate drops. Carmolina listened to them fall; they hit the frying pan in the sink. The water heater hissed. Doriana put the fork down.

In the bedroom, Carmolina sat on the toychest and tied her tennis shoes. The window shade was pulled down in this room already even though it was still the beginning of morning and there was no sun yet. Doriana was stuffed in under all the sheets and blankets like a dead fish. The pillowcase was wet from how hard Doriana was sweating. She opened her eyes for a minute and looked at Carmolina.

"I wish I could have told you about the gypsies," Carmolina said. She tucked Doriana's doll into the bed. It was right beside the blue pillow where Doriana could see it when she woke up again. She kissed Doriana above the eyes. "They were magic," Carmolina said. "You would have liked them." She put on two pairs of underpants.

The streetcar came shaking down the street. The bell rang loud. The conductor was hanging like a balloon onto the side of the car. He waved when Carmolina waved to him. It was a sunny summer morning. Her stomach was sick. Down the street Augie was hosing down the sidewalk in front of his store. His cigar was stuck in his mouth. Under his t-shirt, his body was sweating.

The streetcar stopped. A lady wearing a yellow straw hat with a yellow feather stuck into it got off. She was wearing high-heeled shoes. Carmolina had never seen anyone wear high-heeled shoes during the day before. The lady smiled at her; inside her straw purse was a long white bag with bread in it. Carmolina gave the streetcar conductor one of the coins from Grandma's handkerchief. He said good morning in English.

The streetcar was painted red with big yellow letters on the side that said City of Chicago in letters that looked like the stencils in Carmolina's pencil box. Overhead, the blue light of the electric connection sparked, then died. As soon as she got onto the car, she could smell the odor of bodies on the straw seats; her stomach pitched. It was as though someone soaked the straw in old water and salt. Outside the streetcar window, the whole world was hidden in glass. The people looked different, they had stiff faces. They made no sounds when they talked, like goldfish. They were still like that. The straw seat was warm against Carmolina's legs. She put Grandma's money into her shoe, folded the handkerchief into her lap. She leaned one hand against the brass rail, then squeezed her nose shut with her fingers so she wouldn't throw up from the smell.

Doriana might be waking up now. Mama might be folding Doriana's clothes, to send her away. She didn't have many; Mama could put them all inside a cardboard box and write her name on the side. Then they would look around to send Carmolina away, but she would be gone already. Carmolina said a Hail Mary for Doriana and an Act of Contrition for stealing the money.

The conductor yanked at the heavy rope on the bell; the streetcar lurched like a drunken man and began to roll slowly down the rails. Even when the car was still, it shook slightly.

Carmolina looked out the window.

The old train rattled down the tracks, shaking its sides, shaking Carmolina at the back of the car. The car was hooked into the electric line above it through a steel cable; the train shook its windows in their frames and rattled down the street with its steel finger curved up, as though it stole its energy from the sun. Carmolina peeked out the window from behind the steel grating. The grating covered half the window so people wouldn't break into the train at night and steal the seats. She could not see above it. It crisscrossed the world with mesh and the sun shining into the car fell in shredded patches on her head, face, lap. Everything shook quickly in Carmolina's eyes, stopped, then shook again. When the car was hailed by someone in the street, the conductor threw his weight on the heavy steel lever and the car clutched and shrieked to a halt. The lever was as tall as Carmolina. The noise was like the edge of a steel knife; the blade of it hurt Carmolina's ears. No one knew she was in the car. She passed them all, the neighbors, the people who knew her, and they were out there behind the glass and the grating on the street and she was behind the grate and the noise with her fingers in her ears, running away.

Outside the window was old Gustavo and his blind horse. Outside the window was Tony the barber with his bald head shining in the sunlight, and the dizzy barber pole going red white and snakey in its glass tube. There was Anna, Pasquale's Indian wife, with her long hair and black gums. She smiled at Tony. Anna's daughter zipped by on roller skates, her black pigtails flying behind her in the wind. The vegetable wagon was coming around the corner; old Giupetto stopped at the lemonade stand for a paper cup of lemon ice before he started his work with the old women. There was the white shaking head of Giovanni the watermelon man, his hands and his head moving so slightly, it was as though he held the palsy with love. Outside their kitchen windows, the brown faces of all the mothers bobbed like burned apples to the surface, letting the sun shine on them and make them browner while they called out to each other across clotheslines and flowerboxes.

The car stopped by Gustavo. Carmolina slipped down in her seat, watched out of saucer eyes the face of Gustavo. When Gustavo came to America, Grandma said, he brought with him his wife Maria. They crossed the ocean together and tossed in the ship's belly with the kerosene lamp above them. Terrified of fire, of one flame turning the ship of immigrants into a holocaust on the sea, they held each other's shoulders and with their eyes closed prayed one hundred and nine novenas. Maria carried within her their first child; they had been very

74

young then. When Gustavo and Maria reached Chicago, the baby tried
to come out. Maria died with the baby stuck between her legs, and it
took all the money Gustavo had to bury her with a decent gravemarker.
Because he was so poor, he decided to become a ragpicker, to pull a
cart through the streets with his horse, to pick rags and sell them for
pennies. He could afford only to buy a blind horse and so he spent
long slow days leading the horse through the alleys, waving the dogs
away with a rolled-up newspaper, flapping his arms wildly at the dogs
who would spook his blind horse. He lived in a small wooden house
three streets away from Carmolina. The house had two rooms. He
hung yellow curtains in the front window, placed a green plant on his
table and pulled the curtains in the morning so that the plant would
get sun. Beside his bed was a brown picture of Maria who died when she
was still beautiful. He ate soft cheese for breakfast. In the back room
he kept his blind horse. In the mornings he fed his horse straw and sugar
water. On Sundays he visited the grave of his wife and left daisies.

Carmolina watched his face on the other side of the streetcar
window. She wished she had talked to him more. The skin of his face
was drawn with deep lines, like the lines children leave in wet cement.
He wore an old gray hat always; under his hat his eyes looked blind,
as though he had spent too much time with his horse. The car lurched,
grunted, began to move. Gustavo bent over a garbage can; he did not
know Carmolina was running away.

The car slipped along. She would never see Gustavo again. In her
mind's picture, she saw his old hand hover over the metal garbage drum,
the blue flies around his eyes and mouth, around the blind eyes and wet
mouth of his horse.

Always the dogs barked at them in the alleys.

Everything turned into pictures.

The train screamed to a halt. The sound was like teeth on ice. Her
eyes opened, her eyes closed. Carmolina squeezed her sight through the
thin flesh of her lids, her hands waved gently as though the sleep
were water she was pushing aside. Outside the world was so black it
seemed purple. Streetlamps shined fiercely, with precise balls of silver
light around their faces. The car felt empty and cold. A hand was on
her shoulder, the conductor in his blue uniform was shaking her awake
with his warm hands.

She folded her grandmother's handkerchief into four squares,
stuffed it into her tennis shoe with the money. "I know perfectly well
where I am," she said to the conductor.

Behind her the train sat silent as though about to sleep in its depot.
Overhead the long steel finger which had pointed its way through the
city rested against the cable line; it pointed to the night sky. This was

the end of the line and the cars buckled up against each other like metal cows, their glass eyes darkened and unblinking. The smell was of hot steel cooling, of straw seats moist with human perspiration; the smell of the straw was lodged in her nose; her stomach heaved; she swallowed hard and counted.

This part of the city was brand new; it had never been in Carmolina's eyes before. Augie the grocer was not around the corner. No one that she knew was behind any of the windows. It was like being locked up in a stranger's house, in one room, and you weren't allowed to leave the room. The money in her shoe hurt. The bound-up hankie made the shoe too tight; the skin of her feet rubbed against the shoe, a blister was growing.

She walked down the street. The windows of all the houses were like paintings of windows. She wasn't sure of the porches, where they went. People she didn't know moved behind the windows. Her chest hurt. It felt like wanting to cry; she wasn't sure. Maybe she was hungry. The purple air of the night blew into her head and made her dizzy. The family was small now, like puppets. They danced in the purple air in her head and they said things to her, but what did it matter? She was alone. Her skin shivered and wrinkled. Her heart beat like a toy that was wound too tight, but she smiled. Her feet wanted to run.

The glass door swung open. The handle was level with her nose. At the counter inside, an old man sat with a heavy beard like a blue shadow on his face. He wore scuffed black shoes and white socks. There was a hole in the heel of one sock, at the back. The sock-hole looked like gauze, like the gauze Carmolina wrapped around Grandma's feet, before the brown bandages. His eyes were red around the irises from his cigarette smoke and didn't seem to blink. There were no children in the restaurant.

The coffee cups were white with black cracks. Carmolina sat down behind one. The bottom of the cup was brown and gritty with the sugar stuck inside it. She asked for the menu. Chili cost fifty cents. She asked, where is the bathroom, please?

She held the door of the stall closed with her back. There was no toilet paper. She untied her tennis shoe, kicked it off. The money rolled onto the floor, next to the toilet bowl. The coins smelled like her feet. She had seventy-five cents and three pennies. She shoved the handkerchief into her panties, flushed the toilet, washed her hands.

"Chili, please," she said at the counter.

A phone call would cost a nickel.

She glanced sideways at the old man next to her. He had a cup of coffee in front of him. He slipped his teaspoon into the coffee cup slowly, as though the coffee had skin and he was breaking it. He slid it in sideways and half-filled the spoon with coffee. He tasted some of the coffee from the spoon, spilled the rest back into the cup.

The man behind the counter looked at her. He scooped the chili with a ladle out of a crusty brown pot, slapped it into a bowl.

The old man next to her picked up his paper napkin. He unfolded it slowly, he unfolded it as though he were afraid it would tear. He pulled it open the way Grandma would handle fabric for sewing, spread it carefully on his lap, then rested his hands exactly on each side of his coffee cup and didn't give Carmolina a look.

The man behind the counter slid the bowl in front of her.

"You live around here?" the man behind the counter said. He wore a white shirt and his hair poked through. Under his arms the circles were yellow and brown.

Carmolina looked at his brown teeth, the hard black lines in his flat fingernails.

She shoved the spoon into the chili.

"Hey, kid. I said did you live here?"

"Of course I live here," Carmolina said. The chili burned her tongue. She swallowed it; tears came to her eyes. She smiled. "I just love chili," she said. "Do you make it?" She felt a cough forming at the back of her throat. When she drank the water, the fire got worse. Grandma always said, eat the bread if it's too hot, the water she feed the fire in you mouth and melt you teeth.

"Do you think I could have a Saltine?" she said.

"OK, brat. Where do you live?"

The salt cellar had a little nick in the metal top, just a dent, as though a small animal had chewed it. The pepper shaker had one too.

"Down the street," Carmolina said.

The man was wiping the counter next to her. Someone on the next stool had eaten a bacon lettuce and tomato.

"Where down the street?" he said.

The chili spoon had somebody else's food left on it. It was hard and slick and white. She couldn't taste it.

She looked up at him.

"You're a dago kid, ain't you?"

She chewed the chili bean slowly. The skin of it slipped off, was separate and thick inside her mouth. Her stomach turned over like a man tossing in sleep.

"Ain't no dago kids live here." The man rubbed the back of his hands on his apron. "Ain't no dagos here anywhere."

"I really like this chili," Carmolina said.

He picked her bowl up slowly, pushed the white rag over the counter in front of her. She watched his fingers leave black prints on the bottom of the bowl.

He scooped the chili back into the pot with his fingers, spilled the water into the sink.

"Beat it, kid," he said.

The nickel dropped down the cold metal throat of the telephone. The cool plastic made her ear sweat. Inside the small holes of the receiver, Carmolina saw small shreds of tobacco, the phone was like a mouth, smelled like the mouth of an old man. The dial tone was slow and consistent, one flat sound inside her head. Her fingers pulled at the metal dial, pulled it forward to the little silver lever. Canal Six One Nine Six Six. The number clicked off inside her ear. The man was swiping his white rag over the counter; he turned off the lights overhead. Between the clicks of the dial turning, she listened to the silence of the cloth on the oily counter, of how quietly he cleaned it and watched her out of his blue eyes, through a curtain of cigarette smoke. There were heavy muscles inside his arms. The number rang at the other end of the line. The restaurant man flipped the cardboard sign on the glass door. The large black letters said "Open" inside the restaurant. Over the sink one light bulb was white and shrill over the dirty dishes. Carmolina watched the man's heavy arms in the water. He coughed. The cigarette fell out of his mouth, into the dish water. He lit another cigarette, threw the match into the water. The phone rang. The sound came out of the black telephone on her kitchen wall. Mama was sitting at the kitchen table, looking out the window. She had a cup of coffee in front of her, blue-black like her hair. She never put sugar into it. She was looking out across the alley, towards Grandma's house. Daddy was watching the television set in the playroom, the little pictures filled the room with blue-gray light, with its small moving pictures of small moving people, with gray faces and gray smiles. Daddy was lighting a cigarette. When the telephone rang, Mama was thinking about Doriana, about what it would be like for her in a home filled with children with broken brains. All the children there were packed in rows in their beds with pills in their mouths. All the pictures in their heads were splintered. They all looked at the ceilings of the rooms with the pills in their mouths. Even if they could move, they couldn't get out of the rooms because the doors were locked from the outside. Nuns sat in cold metal chairs by their doors and prayed for them with their rosaries. Doriana's face was the prettiest in the room because of her black eyes and blue lashes, but she was there anyway, being beautiful didn't stop anything. Her eyes watched the lights on the ceiling of the room but no one could fool Doriana, she wasn't home. Beside her was the wrinkled face of an old child having terrible dreams. Mama wanted a cigarette but she couldn't have one because Daddy hated it. He said women shouldn't smoke and if Mama really wanted one, she would have to sneak it in the bathroom, sit on the toilet seat and smoke it and then spray underarm deodorant in the bathroom, but Daddy would smell it anyway. He had an incredible nose. They would have a fight about it; Mama wouldn't yell. Mama called him Daddy too. Grandma called him Marco. Daddy was sitting in the dark room smoking his cigarettes and even watching the commercials. When the telephone rang, Mama thought it was Grandma calling to see if they had locked up Doriana safe now, and did anyone notice where Carmolina went with her groceries? What would they do with the lamb and the rabbit? The man behind the counter took off his apron, it had chili stains all over it, smashed beans and brown sauce. He was saying something to Carmolina through the glass door of the telephone booth. The phone rang. Mama got up from the kitchen table. She wasn't crying. Daddy was watching the commercial. When the show was over, he would read the newspaper in the bathroom where the cigarette smell was; that's when the fight would start. Mama wouldn't yell, she would just listen to him and then she would have her next cigarette on the back porch and watch the alley. Of course they would give the lamb away first. But everyone on the block knew that lamb belongs to Doriana, who would want it? They would keep the rabbit for awhile but when they knew Carmolina was gone for good they would say, "Let's get rid of the rabbit." The telephone rang again and Mama picked it up; she expected to hear Grandma's voice telling her how she had done the right thing and now that Carmolina stole the money and ran away, maybe they should think about making some new children. Mama would say, "yes, Ma," if Grandma was on the other end of the line, but it was her instead, it was Carmolina standing there and calling in the telephone booth when Mama picked up the phone in the kitchen and said, "Hello?"

Carmolina hung it up so quickly.

The man behind the counter didn't see her steal the paper napkin. She went back to the bathroom and used it.

"Gypsies are brave. They are a brave strong people," Carmolina said to herself as she walked out the restaurant door, out of the man's light, under the night's purple sky. Now she had a quarter and three cents.

2.

The light in a police station is always filtered.

The bars and iron mesh at the window impurify, so that if it is a day filled with sunshine, the sunlight that touches the station floor is its own residue. On gray days, there is no light at all, but a kind of muted definition of it. In a police station, light and all that accompanies it happens behind bars. A police station is life reduced to its simple elements, as though the molecules of the world were ball bearings.

Colors inside a police station are subdued; the feeling of the walls is clean and spare, like the bones of a dead bird.

There is also a kind of warmth in a police station, a desperate camaraderie created by the work of the men. There is a kind of shield that the police hold up around themselves, behind which they drink coffee in the mornings and eat sandwiches in the afternoons, their guns and billy clubs at their sides. The shield is not there to keep the others out; it is there to hold them in. They stand behind it and observe the workings of a world whose mutilated belly they see every day. They know the exact texture of a severed leg on a railroad track, how the tendons snapped, how far the blood in fantastic red spread itself, they know the precise curve of the white foot of a woman who hanged herself in a flop house from the iron mesh ceiling, the exact angle at which a body folded itself before impact on a pavement, how the belly tears open and spills, where the skin splits under the razor, with how much blood a naked female suicide fills the bathtub, where on the shower curtain the blood finally ends. Their badges have numbers on them, at night they go home and sit under lamps beside open windows with their wives and children.

Marco had been assigned to police headquarters since his second year as an officer of the force. He spent little time at headquarters. Most of it was passed cruising the silent night-time streets in the squad car with his partner, the two of them in the dark with their guns at their sides, the butts of the guns encased in wood. In the soft sweet dead of the night, the police car moved. Marco and his partner, having promised the safety of their lives to each other one more time in an endless string of night-time promises, spoke rarely to each other. Under their police caps, their brains thought of the lamps at home, how they were darkened now in the dead eye of night, how their wives and children were sleeping, under sheets, under certain safe roofs.

Marco had done the work of the police for ten years; it dried his throat.

His best friend at headquarters was Charlie King, a man much older than he who had survived more than twenty-five years on the streets and who now sat behind an old desk near a courtroom in headquarters, where he slowly, with his meticulous hand, copied out warrants for the arrests and searches and seizures. He had been copying for almost fifteen years. His hair was white and somehow out of control on his tight round skull; he required fine, silver-framed spectacles to see out of his blue eyes to the sheets of paper. The middle finger of his right hand had a bump on it from the fifteen years of writing, the skin of the bump shined, was flattened and purplish. The surface of his desk was covered with paper, engorged with paper, uncountable piles and sheets of paper demanded the appearance of one man in court, the search of a woman's apartment, the seizure if possible of a delinquent child.

He would never finish the paper work; it was piled up as high as the end of his own life; long after the scratch of his pen stopped and Charlie rested, another man would sit at his desk in the same wooden chair and have begun, again, the copying.

Charlie kept two books on his desk, in a small clearing in the right-hand corner. A dictionary because he was a poor speller, and a paper-back copy of *The Confessions of Saint Augustine* which he had purchased for thirty-five cents.

At lunchtime Charlie unwrapped from its waxed paper the salami on rye which in the early morning he had made for himself in his kitchen, wiped his glasses clean with a blue police handkerchief, and read the *Confessions*. When the oversized white-faced clock on the wall indicated that a half-hour had passed, he wrapped the waxed paper into neat squares, put it back into his paper sack, folded his paper sack into his pocket. Then he wandered downstairs to the squad room where he ex-changed stories with the young cops on the beat, where they grunted and shifted their heavy restless thighs and laughed easily or uneasily, where they handled lightly the pistols at their sides and rocked in a regular motion, like seamen swaggering a ship, where they crossed and uncrossed their arms against their blue-shirted chests, exchanged and amplified stories, placed one hand in the crotch of their legs and heaved up the heavy pants.

In his street clothes, Charlie thought, Marco looked very young. Standing in the squad room on his day off, Marco could be a kid asking for directions, confused in the big city. The curls of his black hair were matted against his forehead, in civilian clothes he was lean, taut as a cat. He stood and talked uneasily with the sergeant manning the desk while he filed an official Missing Person's Report on his daughter. Charlie threw his arm around Marco's shoulder, let it drop.

"Three days," Marco said in answer to Sergeant Cooper's ques-tion. He swung through the half-door of the desk, walked behind it, shuffled through the pink carbons of police reports filed by the night shift.

"There's nothin' in them," Cooper said. He wiped his forehead with the back of his hand; the day was a hot boil on his skin. He chewed hard on the green butt of his cigar.

He took the butt out of his mouth, looked back a minute at Marco, looked at the report, looked at Marco again. He hesitated, wrote down the information, turned to him again. Marco was carefully studying a pink report, he seemed to be memorizing it in case of a test.

"Marco," Cooper said, "she's been gone three days and you're just filing now?"

The skin around Marco's eyes was a slight yellow; for a moment the intense black of them flashed; the skin seemed yellower, the eye-lines deeper.

"She was wearing a red dress with red tennis shoes," Marco said. "Charlie. Hey. How's it going?"

Charlie waved, filled a paper cup with coffee at the oversized pot.

"That it, Coop? You got it all?" Marco shifted, adjusted the gun at his belt. The blue flame flickered a moment in his eyes. Charlie looked away.

Cooper nodded.

"Yeah," he said. "That's it. It'll go out over the wire."

Marco tapped the end of a cigarette on the desk, put it in his mouth, spit out the tobacco. "Right now," he said. "Don't wait to type it up."

"Sure," Cooper said. "Sure. Hey, Marc, hold your horses. I'll put it over the wire hot."

Cooper watched the two men walk away, bit down hard on his cigar.

"What the *shit* kind of guy waits three days to report his own damn kid missing?" he said to himself and sat down at the teletype.

*

"You look tired, kid," Charlie said. He pushed nine; the elevator doors shut.

"Yeah. I could use some sleep." Marco blinked at the numbers lighting up, swallowed hard, coughed deeply after inhaling the cigarette.

"What about Sarah?" Charlie said. "How is she?"

"Tired, Charlie," Marco said. "She's trying so damn hard, and she's tired." The coughing seized him like a trickster at his throat, his shirt creased with sweat.

"Hey, kid," Charlie said. "Lay off those things. They'll kill you."

"Here's our floor," Marco said.

In Charlie's office the sunlight shined in fierce bars and patches, mottled the papers on his desk. Marco ran the palm of one hand over a stack; his eyes were violently clear with the lack of sleep.

"You need an assistant, old man," Marco smiled. Charlie watched the black center of his eyes.

"I got half a salami on rye here. With mustard." Charlie pulled open the drawer of his desk; Marco shook his head.

"How about a pickle?" Charlie retrieved a jar of Koshers from the drawer of the desk, opened it. The room filled with the smell of garlic and dill.

Marco looked at him.

82

"Pickles?" he said. "You got pickles in your *desk?*"

"Want a Gerkin?" Charlie bent down to his desk drawer again.

"Pickles," Marco said. "The old man keeps pickles in his desk." The muscles of his face contracted until his features almost disappeared.

"Jesus, kid." Charlie slammed the office door shut.

The muscles of Marco's face refused to relax; it was as though his own eyes did not know he was crying.

Charlie drew the Venetian blinds on his office window shut; now the light was a sham. He looked at the face of the young policeman sitting behind his desk; his face maintained its strange contortion, as though the musculature had seized on that particular pattern and found it pleasing. It was inhuman, this grief, Charlie thought. Marco sat rigidly behind the desk, his hands held onto it as though a lion were trying to tear it away. Charlie left the room quietly, went to the water cooler in the hallway, half-filled a paper cone. The moisture of the water beaded in his warm hand; he searched his brain for something to say to Marco.

When he shut the door behind him again, he flinched at the sight of Marco's face.

"Marco?" Charlie said. He did not recognize his own voice. Charlie laid his hand on Marco's shoulder. He looked at the thin wedding band on his own finger; he might have taken it off fifteen years ago when Helen died. The brown spots of age on his skin told him that he was an old man who didn't know much.

"Hey, kid, I'll wait outside," Charlie said.

Marco watched the hand in which he had crushed the paper water cup; thin streams of water ran out of the cup and down his hand.

"You just sit here awhile and pull yourself together," Charlie said. "OK? I'm just going to go now." He slid out the door, shut it, opened it, peeked in again. "You just knock if you need me." He shut the door.

Marco looked at the piles of papers on Charlie's desk, rested one palm of one hand on them. He wished he were a priest, he wished he could absolve them all. He ran his hand across his eyes, the hands to him seemed helpless, lifeless, without power. They got wet when they touched his face. He looked at them, confused. He wondered if he would spend his whole life as a policeman. He wondered if he would die as one, with the thin metal star on his chest like some kind of artificial heart.

His hands were wet; he was confused. If he could look into the future, ah then. But the future had eyes of stone. And if you looked into the past, you saw the pictures. You could not turn from them. You wished you could change them, alter a word, a sentence, a year, maybe adjust your tie. You wished you could change the very first picture, if you could find it. But they were set there, the pictures, fixed and steady, they stared back at you; the past flashed them for you over and over again like a gambler with drunken eyes and a steady hand. One of the pictures was of her face: more beautiful than he could imagine any face, lit up with wonder and fear behind the veil of her wedding gown. He stood at the altar with his only brother, his sisters wore blue. He remembered thinking, while he stood at the altar, why blue?, and then the music began and the people turned in one direction as though the sun were entering the church and they were the flowers turning toward it. And so she had entered his life in white satin, the sleeves so long they ended in little points on the backs of her hands; she was entirely covered. From the altar he could not see her face; he might have been marrying anyone, a stranger. The white stranger floated down the aisle, she seemed to have no feet at all and the music to him so solemn and final was like the voice of God or His angels; thus she came to him. She would be his wife, this woman whose face he could not see. His mother sat in the front pew and the woman in white floated towards him, to claim him for herself. His body contracted with a shot of feeling. He would not call it fear, but it seized the muscles and bones of him and for a moment, he was a marionette, he could look outside himself and see the prepared face, the fixed wooden smile, the perfect pomaded hair of that ridiculous creature he was, holding in his hands a heart of ice. Then she was beside him, and he could almost make out her face behind the veil, could almost see the eyes, nose, mouth of the woman he had decided he loved. She was his own Sarah, she was a soft creature; her body was small and soft, rounded, the two of them made a contrast. She was much shorter than he; he, sometimes when he held her, rested his chin on top of her head and they laughed at the difference between them. When first he had seen her, he thought her more than beautiful, the word was so imprecise for her. There was something in the way she held herself in the world, the shyness of it, the quick graceful way she moved her eyes, the almost frightened way she entered a room, as though a ghost might be there. There was something in her so tentative, she seemed to hesitate in everything she did, as though she gave every movement she made a second thought. There was also in her a stiff core of something which he believed to be strength, or some kind of courage; it ran through the center of her like a glass rod. He saw it in the way she brought him food to the table; something fixed and determined. It was always there, that strange combination, as though two women lived in one body; he never knew which one he would see next. And always there was this beauty, which terrified and fascinated him, the severe pull of the jet hair away from the face, the fine features which looked up at him always somehow questioning, the small rhinestones stuck into her white ears, why did women do that? When the priest said the words which made them man and wife until the grave shall claim them, when the priest bequeathed to her his last name forever, she lifted the veil and again his body contracted, as though someone fired a gunshot into his spine. She turned to him to be kissed before the entire family, and it was as though her face were a mirror, and through the mirror passed all the faces of Sarah: laughing, crying, smiling, wondering, bewildered, content. After the wedding, they danced in the garden behind his mother's house. The band played from the porch. The players soon smelled of red peppers. The violinist had a shrunken body, with white hair and spectacles that kept slipping down his nose as he played. A fat man played an accordion with a red carnation in his striped lapel; the carnation soon wilted. The woman with the tambourine had black eyes. All the neighbors and children of the street poured into the garden, some of the children wore white dresses. The sunflowers bent their heads as people with wine in their bellies and music in their feet pushed past the flowers. A lot of wine disappeared. People began dancing in the street, outside the garden. Marco removed his tuxedo jacket, loosened his white tie, his face was speckled and red. Red paper lanterns were strung with lights around the garden; after a while they too began dancing. The yellow and blue lights and the red lanterns flew with the music; the violinist stuck his glasses on top of his white head and beat his feet like a madman so that everyone stared at the stars. Sarah removed her veil and placed it in the arms of Doria who watched from the porch, the sisters kicked off their shoes and the shoes landed in the flowers. Sarah kicked off her shoes, she moved in and out of the blue circle of sisters who held out their hands for the *tarantella*. Salvatore laughed loudly with the wine in his belly; he shoved a piece of wedding cake into his own face, then scraped off the cream with his fingers and ate the cream off his fingers. The sunflowers which could stop nothing bowed and bent under the red lanterns with the small bodies of children running in and out, stealing cookies and small glasses of wine. Someone broke a wine glass. There was laughter. The paper lanterns moved in the wind, the tambourine lady shook her breasts heavily. From blocks away the noise and the music could be heard; people came to complain "where is our sleep?", then they drank wine and soon they were dancing. Someone else broke another glass. The children fell into heaps in the flowers. Someone said, "take the wine away from the children." Marco looked up to the porch where his mother was sitting beside the band gone crazy; her hands were resting quietly above the folded wedding veil.

When he and Sarah went into the bedroom, they could still hear the music and dancing in the garden outside. Marco shut the door. This was his mother's bedroom. She had moved her things to the inner porch. On the dresser was the veil where his mother had placed it.

Sarah stood by the window and listened to the noise. The room was blue from the gas lamp on the street outside. He could hear the hiss of the gas. She was dressed in white with a wonderful face. Oh Marco I'm so happy she said, and when he held her in his arms, she felt him tremble. She was white in the blue street light. Hours later the noise had finally ceased. The blue light from the streetlamp was fainter, dimming in the light of the sun's rising. One by one, they had listened to the members of his family enter the house, laughing then whispering, then going off to their rooms. There was quiet talking and then there was silence. When Salvatore finally came in, he was completely drunk and singing as loudly as he could *O Sole Mio* of which he remembered few words; the wine had soaked them away. Marco had been able to smile at Sarah then; they both smiled for the first time. They heard Salvatore crash against the glass shelves in the bathroom; there was the sound of something broken. Marco wanted to go out to help him; Sarah said it would not look right. Much later, when Sarah had fallen asleep for a while, Marco listened to the fat padding of his mother's feet through the house, turning out lights. He heard her sit down on the couch in the living room. Now, with the sun rising a brilliant yellow, the blue of the room faded, the light turned its face towards day. The sound of his mother leaving the couch and going to her room on the porch wakened Sarah. He turned to her, touched her breasts shyly, she covered his hands with hers. He withdrew his hands. Sarah smiled. It's all right, she said; then she fell back to a gentle sleep like a child on the pillow. Lying there, with the hot summer air blowing gently the white curtains away from the window, he listened to the distant call down the street of the ice man whose horse's face was still covered in a feed bag. He heard the porch door slam where his mother was going out into the morning to feed the birds and for the first time in his life, he felt he was alone.

When Marco walked out of Charlie's office, his hair was combed precisely away from his face, subdued by the comb's plastic teeth. His face, Charlie thought, was like a baby's. There was no sign of crying in his eyes, on his skin. His features were so calm, Charlie wondered a moment. Charlie was a man of strong religious imagination. He believed heartily in the shower of rose petals which St. Thérèse de Lisieux promised to send to the world after her death. He would not have been surprised to see the stone statue of the Sacred Heart beat. It was an imagination which he took to bed with him, it climbed between the empty sheets with him at night. He followed it fervently to church each Sunday where he paid it homage in the crook of his white head.

"Let's go over to Pat's for coffee," Marco said.

Charlie nodded.

He went into his office, shut the door, removed his small straw hat from its nail, adjusted it on his white head, straightened his bow tie. He thought about it a minute, sniffed his nose, rubbed it, adjusted his tie again.

"Hmmph," he snorted and glanced at the chair into which Marco had slumped. He pulled at his nose thoughtfully, tugged with his fingers at the white hairs protruding, grabbed his suit jacket, opened the door.

The door was shut a minute.

Charlie opened it again, peeked in at his desk, shut it again.

*

Charlie and Marco swung through the glass doors at Pat's. Pat waved his fat red hand at them from behind his steam table. His face and hands were red from the steam, the skin of his fingers was permanently wrinkled with it. He smiled heavily with his mouth, and his strong white teeth showed in his Irish face. He wore a t-shirt over his hairy white chest; from a gold chain around his imposing neck swung the heavy medallion of the Virgin. His fingers were indelibly scarred from the frequent burnings of hot food. One patch on his left arm was irrevocably bald where a tureen of potato soup had spilled onto it. The soup left no scar; it simply balded his arm.

"Hey, Charlie. Hey, Marco," Pat waved at them again.

Charlie and Marco sat down at the table nearest the window; the sun shot through the naked glass. At the table behind them, a black prostitute was crossing her legs, reading the menu.

They listened to the clutter of Pat's. Police and their clientele ate side by side. A man arrested for burglary and just released on bond swallowed fat mouthfuls of pea soup at the side of a police captain. The police captain was keeping one eye on the white-faced restaurant clock so as not to miss the first call for uniform inspection. The man arrested for burglary was keeping one eye on the prostitute.

It was ceaseless clutter at Pat's, the clutter of policemen entering, sitting down starved at the spotless steel tables and bolting down a shank of beef, homemade soup, mashed potatoes, gravy and apple pie. In the mornings, Pat's filled with the fatty smell of heavy homemade sausage patties frying, potato hash browning on the grill, cups of coffee steaming, police and thieves standing in line with cigarettes in their mouths waiting to be served. The thick tough police in their heavy uniforms, with their wads of guns, stood beside lanky thieves in thin turtleneck sweaters and they all waited their turn, in the restaurant, just across the street from police headquarters.

"He looks good, don't he?" Charlie asked. He cupped the familiar bowl of his pipe as though it were the breast of a woman he loved; he lit the tobacco, squinted his eyes away from the breath of smoke.

Marco shifted in his chair, twisted his neck to glance back at Pat; his head was bent over a shank of beef, carving.

"He don't smile with his eyes," Marco said.

Pat looked up at them, said "I'll be right wichya," stabbed the weight of the knife into the meat.

Charlie picked up the menu. He didn't need to read it; he had been eating at Pat's now for almost forty years. If Pat ever changed the menu, Charlie would think he had died and gone to hell.

Pat rubbed his palms on his apron when he came over to their table, shook hands first with Charlie, then with Marco.

"Hey, Marco," Pat said. "I heard about your little girl. Sorry."

Marco drummed his fingers on the table, smiled into Charlie's eyes, looked up at Pat.

"Yeah, sure. Thanks, Pat."

"Can she have visitors?"

"No. No, the doctor said she should be left alone." He pushed the hair away from his face. "For a while."

"I'll send a card. To Sarah."

Pat slapped him on the back.

"Eh, kid. The coffee's on me. Apple pie too. That's all right, huh?"

Marco rubbed his hands over his eyes, lit a cigarette, his dark eyes watched the white paper slowly turn itself into ash. "Yeah," he smiled. "Yeah, old man, that's all right."

Pat rubbed Marco's head roughly with his large hand. "Eh, Charlie, you hear this dago? You hear this wop kid? He calls me old man just because I got a few lousy white hairs on my beautiful chest." He breathed expansively. "Victor Mature, he would die for this chest."

"OK, you mick," Marco laughed. "OK. The kid says OK." He drew hard on his cigarette. In the center of his chest, the small pain throbbed.

Pat laughed from an unreachable point in his belly, walked away.

"You see, Charlie?" Marco said. "It's in his eyes."

He lit one cigarette from another. "A woman is with you thirty years and then she's gone. Like God shitting on you." He pulled hard on his coffee, it made a sucking sound between his lips and the cup. He looked out the window, his face flinched in the light. "Why don't someone pull this damn shade down?"

Behind them, the black prostitute uncrossed her legs. The slit in her silver skirt cut up above her knees, deep into her thighs. She picked at the silver garter belt, pulled out a dollar bill, adjusted her stocking. She was hungry, it was in the pit of her stomach and made a noise. She scratched a painted fingernail across one breast, looked at the menu absent-mindedly, thought about apple pie. When she stirred the spoon in her coffee cup, it clinked metallically against the Buffalo china. Across the room, the police captain was looking at her.

3.

Carmolina sat on a curbstone.

Her legs were drawn up in front of her, she rested her chin on her knees. Before her ran the blue-black length of the street under a summer night. The lights were turned on, their electric faces stood between her face and the stars.

She squinted down the street. It felt so much like summer. It felt so much like summer because the warm air pushed itself against her like silk, then it moved away, went off to move the leaves of a tree, scare a scrap of paper down the street. It felt like summer because there was nothing she could do to stop it. The heat just beat down, even with the sun gone, and so it was all just a hint of magic, this black heat under the stars.

There was Grandma sticking her head out of the window, throwing her extra money. There was Daddy standing on the corner in a circle with all the other fathers. There was Mama washing dishes in the kitchen. They were all gone. They disappeared. She sat on the curbstone and watched the little pictures of them waving and smiling at her, Daddy turned his head and winked; she couldn't fold up any of the pictures and put them away.

It was night because the streetlamps blinked on. They burned their white eyes against the sky.

At the end of the street, a small white push cart turned the corner. It was a large box on wheels. An old man with yellow hair like sawdust pushed it from behind. He probably had a wife at home, or his wife died and he had a cat. The white box had large wooden wheels at the side, like the kind that are nailed to the sides of a barn; they rattled against the bricks of the street as though they would fall off. A ragged umbrella with red stripes ballooned out over the top of the cart. Underneath, the old man had built a glass box and under the glass box were dozens of red candy apples. He probably built the wagon at night, after the death of his wife, to save himself from loneliness, Grandma would say. The old man pushed his cloth cap back on his head, steered the cart's wheels past the rough stone curb. The red and white umbrella teetered a moment in the night's black air. The summer air might catch at the umbrella and fill it. It might float the cart and the apples away into the night and into the starred sky, and the old man would stand with his hands in his pockets, his cloth cap pushed back on his yellow fuzzy head that stared at the sky, and he would blink and watch the candy-apple cart float away into the sky like a new planet, and he would laugh with his hands in his pockets.

The wheels made it around the corner. The cart cracked and heaved in its wooden joinings. The umbrella righted itself, stuck its pointed head up again, and the cart stumbled on down the bricks towards Carmolina. She thought about a candy apple. She thought about it until it made itself a taste on her tongue. The apple was hard under the candy skin; she would have to lick the hard candy a long time before she got to the apple. Then she would know if the apple were sweet or green.

The cart moved down the bricks. The umbrella bobbed in the sweet air. Maybe it was all just a clown tripping down the street in a complicated dream.

The wheels swayed to the right, the cart swayed, the old man balanced slightly in that direction, all the candy apples shifted. The umbrella tilted and it all happened again in the other direction. The apple man straightened the hat on his head.

Carmolina shoved her index finger down between her heel and her shoe; she felt the quarter and three pennies. The cart stopped in front of her. There was an electric light in the little glass house filled with apples. The apple man had green eyes with a hundred wrinkles around them. When he smiled, his eyes disappeared. He stopped smiling so that he could see. He had perfect eyes for a candy apple man. He knew she wanted an apple. He knew if he stood there long enough, she would buy one.

Carmolina untied her shoelaces.

She heard the sound of the skooters, felt the sound through her feet. She squinted down the street and saw three boys on orange-crate skooters. There were skooters just like that, at home.

They came closer.

She ran down the street in one shoe. She held the other one in her hand, by its shoelaces. The money sweated in her palm, when they took it away from her. The street corner came up, she ran around it. She ran down the next street with her eyes like pools of water in her head that wanted to break; she wouldn't let them, she wasn't pigeon-hearted. Long behind her was the laughter of the boys who had forced her to run down this street. She scratched one of them good, right across his face, before he took Grandma's money away from her. The cement of the street bit into her foot. She looked over her shoulder, saw the naked street behind her. I'll bet that kick really hurt, she thought. She sat down on the steps of one of the houses, shoved her foot into the shoe, tied the shoelace, her head twisted towards the street corner, watching to see if they would follow her. They didn't; nobody followed her. On both sides of the street the houses were closed up and locked, with lamps burning in the windows. At one window she saw a woman sitting in a chair; her head was bent over something; probably a chicken. Her hair was tied in a clean bun, like Mama's. Inside the houses children were sleeping in pajamas next to their brothers or sisters. In one house, a man pushed the windowpane up, shoved a cat gently out onto the sill, pulled the curtains shut. The tobacco in his pipe smelled sweet.

Carmolina blinked her eyes fast, blinked them up above the roofs of the houses, blinked them past the chimneys; her lashes were soft. No one had ever taught her, in school, how many stars there were. There didn't seem to be many. When she was little, she lay under the Christmas tree in her yellow sleepers with her feet covered up, she hated that, and tried to count the ornaments. She was too stupid to do that, to count that high, and so she counted up to ten as many times as she could. Daddy picked her up and put her in bed. Grandma said all the stars were angels; so why weren't there more? She was too smart now, to think she could count the angels; she was confused that it seemed possible. The stars were the eyes of the angels, blinking. They blinked because they watched the small blue world spinning through the air with no one to hold it, and this made the angels blink. They blinked fast so that they wouldn't cry. That was the angels for you. One of the angels had green eyes.

She couldn't see the street sign from here. Even if she could read it, it wouldn't make any difference. She still wouldn't know anyone.

She got up, walked along the curbstone, whistled an Italian love song to herself, stopped, turned. There was no one on the street. She whistled again. Her feet were wearing red tennis shoes down there. One of the shoes had a hole in the toe. Above the tennis shoes were dirty knees under a red dress.

She looked across the street. In one of the windows, a young woman was sitting in a rocking chair, holding a baby high above her head. The baby's face was laughing, its eyes were open and startled, it kicked its small feet like a duck in the water. Of course the stars were the eyes of the angels. So many times people talked to her, told her things, important things she was supposed to remember now that she was eight years old. Carmolina, Sister Saint Virginia said, in order to get the volume you must multiply the length times the width times the height. Leave four empty bottles for the milkman in the morning, Carmolina, and don't forget to change the pan under the icebox. *Bambina,* Aunt Katerina she forget to write the peaches on the list, but you ask Augie anyway, no? She focused her dark eyes on the person who was talking, she concentrated her entire brain as best she could, but she always forgot something and the floor got wet and there was one too many bottles of milk in the morning. Then Grandma would take her face in her hands and laugh and say, *faccia bella,* you listen to the angels too much. Carmolina wasn't sure if that was true, it seemed to her that her mind just blinked away sometimes and forgot to listen, but it always came back, so no one could say it was gone for good.

Carmolina, she look at everything too hard, they said. She watched Mama when she was plucking the chicken, she waited for Mama to look up and smile. She just waited. She tried to look at things out of the corner of her eyes; it was making her eyes crooked. Grandma said it was because she listened too much to the angels.

Above her, the stars blinked.

She wished the name of this street made sense to her.

She breathed more slowly, whistled, shoved her hands into her pockets, humped her shoulders.

Night. A blink. An eye moving. Whose eye? A twist of the hand, fingers grip the dark, the dark has the hands of a skeleton. Hair falling into her eyes. Flash of red tennis shoes on hot pavement. This door is strange. That lamp is too bright. A head turning. Hair falling into place, out of place. Skin of rough objects. What was that? The hand of a dead man. The skin of a ghost reaching out to steal you. Fire hydrants shut, no water running out of them. Streetlamps are blue eyes, beating. A cat moving across the alley, silent, rubs against her leg. What was that? Gone. The eyes blink. Head jerks upwards. The sky is empty. The sky is black fabric, the devil will roll it away. The numbers are wrong. Here an alley holds a blank hand. There are murderers in the alley, they have knives in their mouths. A dog barks. It is no one's dog. It is the devil's dog. It will swallow you and you will live in the devil's belly. There are worms in the devil's belly. Chimneys jut. Smoke tangles. The eye shifts. Streets weave. No footsteps. Someone turned the world upside down and shook out all the people. Nowhere to go. Strange door, strange door, strange door. The lamp in a window snaps out. Hair falls. Dawn. The sun is an eye, staring through sun-blood. A cobweb moves in the air. The air is cold. Things change fast. It is a very fine cobweb. It breathes in the air like water. Slow. Things still. But the cobweb moves like water. The cobweb is sewn into a corner of the alley, between a wall and a garbage can. She is on her knees looking at the cobweb. It moves. Something is touching it. The cobweb falls apart under water. There is no spider. The rain slashes down like tiny knives and cuts apart the cobweb in her hands.

The drugstore door had a small metal bell above it, so that if someone walked into the store, the door hit the bell and it jangled, like a metal tongue. A woman came out, her hair twisted into cloth rags under a white hairnet. She looked past the high counter with the apothecary jars filled with red and green liquid. Carmolina stood on her toes, stared up at her own reflection in the apothecary jar. There was no sawdust on the floor; it was clean black and white tiles, little diamond shapes; if she looked at them long enough, she got dizzy.

The woman wiped the wet hair out of her face. She said something about the druggist her husband who was still asleep. She said something about Carmolina catching her death of cold, and who in the world was she? Why wasn't she home in bed? There was a telephone.

Carmolina followed her to the back of the counter. The woman adjusted the glasses on her face, peered at Carmolina, said my word, stay right here, and went to get her husband.

At home, in Mama's kitchen, the phone rang five times before Carmolina hung up.

She glanced sideways out of her eyes at the green rain spitting at the windows. It shivered her skin like slime.

4.

The green plant stood alone in the kitchen window. Its face was set small against the white curtain, against the silent gray fall of the city outside. Sarah stood by the window. She held a drinking glass filled with water in her hand. In her other hand, a long gray ash of cigarette cut into white paper towards the skin of her fingers. When she was young, she had seen a picture postcard of Miami. On the postcard the buildings were white, peach, pink; the palm trees were deep green, the sky looked lit by an artificial light. Someone had painted that picture. She tapped the cigarette against the windowsill, the ash fell to the linoleum floor. She poured half the water into the plant, dipped her fingers into the water, sprinkled the leaves. She lit another cigarette.

She closed her eyes. Pink buildings. That was a lie, of course. Nothing was written on the other side of the postcard. She didn't know anyone who had ever been to Miami, but she kept the card stuck into the wooden frame of her mirror above her dresser at home. One day it was gone. Her mother had probably thrown it away. Outside the sky threatened rain. She ran tap water over the cigarette.

On the back porch the clothes flapped in the wind like the hands of a madman. Sarah stood on the porch, listened. Behind her the clothes flapped wickedly, the sound was of a mouth saying nothing. The clothes would get wet.

She lit another cigarette, it burned from her lips, her fingers, her lips, the smoke curled white around her face. There had been no sleep for three days, three nights. The skin around the eyes was gray.

The first rain slammed at the porch.

The cotton sheets slapped angrily back, made a tough short sound like a shot.

She swept the hair away from her face. One gray strand, one black, then a whole fistful of hair blew loose from the soft bun at the back.

She yanked the wooden clothespins off the rope, dropped them into the clothespin bag. Sheets shirts blouses fell in a mound, missing the basket. Clothespins clutched at angry angles on the line, like broken teeth.

She lit one cigarette from another, ground out the dead one with the small leather heel of her slippers, watched the rain drench the clothes fallen outside the basket, watched the rain run in small green rivers down the hair of her arms. Fascinated, she watched her body drenched by the rain, the cigarette disintegrating between her fingers.

Her fingernails were wet.

The telephone rang.

She opened the back porch door, hesitated.

The phone rang again.

When she walked into the kitchen, her shoes were squeaking with the rain, rainwater squeezed out from the slippers onto the linoleum. The phone rang and rang.

There was no one on the other end. She replaced the receiver, looked round the kitchen. This was the second time in three days. Her clothes stuck to her like a thin coat of plaster.

She lit a cigarette, walked into the bedroom.

The bedclothes were entirely blue, and Doriana wore a blue night-gown. Next to the blue, Doriana's skin was like alabaster. There was something so perfect about her skin, it was untouched by her nine years, remained infant skin. Sarah brushed her wet hand against Doriana's forehead, feeling for the fever. It was there, her skin was a silk of fire. "I wish you were still a baby," Sarah whispered. Doriana slept under the pristine skin.

She peeled away one blanket from the bed, then another, slowly she peeled all the blankets away from the bed. She tried to lift Doriana from the bed; her body, asleep with pills, was dead weight. She squatted at the bed, slipped her arms under the child's body, lifted her out of the bed.

Doriana's eyes were squeezed shut, as though she were holding onto her sleep with her eyes.

Sarah stumbled to the rocking chair by the window, the full-grown child in her arms. "You have our eyes," she said. "We gave them to you. You have the eyes your father had the first day I saw him. I sup-pose I was young then. It all seemed to be night, and working, and running home to sleep, and sleeping, and waking up to work again. I kept waiting for it to change. I knew it would, finally. It had to." She touched Doriana's face. "My mama was always there. She washed dishes. We all worked so hard. At night I would fall asleep thinking, I would think it would have to change one day. Then it did. When your father walked into the restaurant, and I saw his eyes, everything changed. He smiled, he smiled just a little, and I saw it. I saw my life changing. He has the most gentle smile, Doriana. Have you ever noticed it?" She wrapped her wet arms around the burning body. "I was afraid at first. When he smiled, I was afraid of how I felt. Mama said he was a man, that I would always be afraid. I didn't believe that. I knew there would be something else, if I could stop being afraid, something like," she touched Doriana, held the small hand in her own, "something like you, Doriana. Now here you are." Doriana squirmed in her mother's lap; Sarah rocked more quickly. "Everything your father said made me laugh. There was so much laughter. Why was everything so funny, I wonder?" She lit another cigarette, turned her head to blow the smoke past the child's face. "There are things you must do for a man, things that confuse you, that you didn't expect. But you do them, and they make the man happy. Then one day, you do exactly the same thing, the same thing you've been doing for a long time, all along that made him happy, it made him laugh, and suddenly it doesn't work anymore." She glanced around the room, shook her head clear, looked up again as though she expected someone to walk in. "And you wonder if maybe you did it the wrong way this time, and you try doing it another way, then you try a whole new thing, but none of the things work. Then one day you look and see that there is nothing else left to do. You look into your pockets, and there is only a spool of thread and some needles."

She rocked the chair more quickly, Doriana in her drugged sleep held her fists tightly. "You've got it, the beauty, and when you grow up, you'll see. It will all happen to you." Doriana shivered, Sarah held her closer.

"That *will* happen to you when you grow up, when you grow up to be a beautiful woman." She looked down at the sleeping face, her eyes went suddenly confused, filled with tears. "Everything will happen the way it's supposed to? Doriana?"

The telephone rang again. Sarah's body jerked, she hesitated, settled back into her chair. "There's no one on the phone, Doriana. Someone is playing tricks on me." The phone rang again. She jumped.

She lugged Doriana into the kitchen like a doll. Again there was no one on the other end of the line. She sat down in the kitchen chair, watched the rain slam at the window.

"They thought I didn't hear them. They thought I was asleep in the next room. They gave me pills for the pain, and they thought I was sleeping. I heard them. '*Bello mio,*' your grandma said. 'Is Sarah better?' 'She's asleep,' your daddy said. 'It hard for one so young,' your grandma said. 'So soon a baby. She will not breast feed this one?' And your daddy said no. He understood, he is a very good man. When I took out my breast, he felt the same way. Your grandma said the pain would be too great. Daddy said the doctor would take care of it, and he did."

Doriana was absolutely still.

Sarah looked out the window. This rain would last all day, it was green and empty, hard and consistent like the ringing of a telephone when there is no one on the other end. The rain slamming, the phone ringing, nothing would leave her alone.

Sarah's eyes closed inside themselves, like a shutter of a camera about to take a picture. She watched Doriana in her newness, her new beauty just born into the world, how they protected her, protected her from everything, how she cried in the crib and tore her mouth into the toys, banged her fists against the mattress, got sick and disappeared. Sarah rose slightly, pulled the sheer curtains of the kitchen window closed. She hauled the weight of the sleeping child into her arms, moved across the floor like a cripple, locked the front door, pulled the chain across the door.

"I think we're alone," she said to Doriana.

In the chair, she unbuttoned the thin plastic buttons of her dress.

"This is a secret," she whispered to Doriana. "You are never to tell anyone."

One by one she undid the buttons, slipped the cotton dress down her shoulders, bent over the sleeping child to unsnap her bra.

Her breast fell out so unexpectedly, she had to catch it in her own hand. Doriana moved a little, the skin of her nose moved.

Sarah held the large breast in her hand, held the head of the child burning with fever against it.

"Baby," she said.

In her sleep, Doriana opened her mouth, closed it.

"Please, baby," Sarah said.

Doriana opened her mouth again, closed it over her mother's breast.

Sarah stroked the hot forehead.

In her sleep, Doriana sucked the dry breast.

5.

In the drugstore, on the other side of the counter, the druggist and his wife were arguing about what to do with the little girl who got lost in the rain. That was her. She supposed she was lost, she didn't know where she was, she didn't know what the druggist would do.

There was Mama on the other end of the line saying hello? hello? The sound of Mama's voice filled her like warm water. She looked at the telephone. There was Mama, quiet on the other end where

Carmolina hung up the phone in her face. She could never just hang up on Mama like that at home. There was no way to do it. There was always Mama's face, her eyes looking at her in that peculiar way.

One time when Carmolina was still little enough to play with dolls, she sat on the floor of the playroom with Maryalice. Maryalice was a stuffed doll; her face was a piece of fabric with the eyes and nose and mouth painted on. When Carmolina ran her hand over Maryalice's face, she could feel the paint. Maryalice's head thinned out to a point; on this point was painted a little blue bonnet.

Maryalice stared at Carmolina from her painted face.

Carmolina threw the doll high up over her head and squealed when she almost missed catching it on the way down. The painted face accused her and Carmolina felt strange. She repeated the toss, the doll flew higher, the light bulb in the ceiling burned into Carmolina's eyes as she watched Maryalice flying up.

She tossed Maryalice a hard toss.

Maryalice hit the ceiling.

Carmolina's whole body turned pink. She threw Maryalice again, hoping she could reach the ceiling on purpose. Maryalice hit the ceiling hard.

She was swept away with this strange feeling. When she tossed Maryalice again, she landed on the floor and a little stitch was gone in her face, like a cut.

Carmolina took Maryalice in her two hands and whacked her against the floor.

Maryalice looked at her out of her flat eyes.

A seam gave way in Maryalice's head and a bit of yellow stuffing fell out. Carmolina whacked her head again. She beat the doll wildly and tiny bits of stuffing shredded into the room. The room was filled with the stuffings of Maryalice.

Carmolina stopped a moment later and began hiccupping. She looked at Maryalice. Her face hung on by a thin white thread; behind the face was a mass of mangled stuffing.

Carmolina's eyes enlarged and she cried.

Her hands were filled with the stuffings; Maryalice's face hung like a little mask. Carmolina crumpled the face in her hand.

Mama stood in the doorway with a dishtowel in her hand.

Carmolina looked up and there were Mama's eyes.

She didn't understand why Mama wanted to slap her, she was crying already.

Mama didn't slap her. She raised her hand, and Carmolina saw she was about to be slapped, but then Mama did the strangest thing. She picked up Maryalice and took the face away from Carmolina. Give me that, she said, and Carmolina did, and Mama slowly on her hands and knees picked at the tiny bits of stuffing all over the floor. She moved around on her hands and knees looking for all the stuffing. Then Mama carefully folded Maryalice's face into her apron pocket. Carmolina looked at her and Mama just turned, on her knees, and looked at Carmolina with that question in her eyes.

Grandma had no questions in her eyes, because they were blue. Carmolina knew that Grandma was the only one in the family with blue eyes because she crossed the ocean to get to America. It took her so many weeks to cross the water, it turned her eyes blue. Grandma had blue eyes and always looked at Carmolina as though she were a pretty dish that could break. She touched Carmolina's face over and over and told her how pretty she was. In Italian Grandma always said *faccia bella* and sometimes when they were playing, she said *faccia buffone,* but Carmolina knew Grandma didn't mean monkey face; she was laughing. Grandma's house was filled with the Virgin Mary. On the radio was a Virgin Mary with a plant growing out of her back. On little shrines nailed to the walls all over the house were Virgin Marys. One time when Carmolina had to use the bathroom, she found a new Virgin Mary on the toilet tank. On that day she counted twenty-three Virgin Marys. She held it until she got home. In Grandma's bedroom was a picture of her mother, Great-Grandma Carmella who was a skeleton in Italy. Carmolina could not sleep in that room. Grandma told Carmolina that she had a magician watching over her.

"Carmolina," Grandma said, "you lucky. You have a magician."

Carmolina looked up from where she was shredding the dried red peppers between her fingers, turning them into dust.

"He watch over you. He bring you good luck like gold."

Carmolina listened the way she always listened when Grandma told her something important.

Grandma waved her hands in the sunshine, her hands were jewels.

"This magician, he watch over you."

"What does he look like, Grandma?"

"Ah," Grandma said, "Ah." Her blue eyes got bluer like the ocean. "He wear a gown. It soft, soft like. . .what you call it?" She looked at Carmolina.

"Velvet, Grandma?"

"Good. That right. Velvet. You like?"

"I like," Carmolina said.

"But this no story, little monkey. This is the true. You listen?"

The dust from the red peppers made Carmolina's skin warm.

"This magician, his mouth it skinny with yellow teeth, like you grandma, no? And on his head he carry," Grandma squinted a look into the summer sky, "he carry a little frog. A frog. Yes. The frog, he live on top the magician's head."

"Oh, Grandma."

"No. No joke. You listen." Grandma pulled another string of peppers down, wrapped them like ribbons in her lap, crushed them between her fingers for the Mason jars. "The magician, he perfect. But one thing, it is wrong." She looked at Carmolina with the star in her eyes. "His legs, they no good. One leg, she shorter than the other one."

Carmolina's eyes got big as onions.

"So you know what he do?"

"What, Grandma?"

"He carry a little white stool. And he hop. He hop on his good leg, and his bad leg, she land on the stool. Make a noise." She looked at Carmolina. "Make a thump. You no mind?"

"I no mind."

"So, wherever you go, you listen for thump thump thump. Like this." Grandma padded her fat hands against the arms of her wooden chair. "See? You hear? When you hear the thump thump thump, you know the magician he is with you. And he take care of you."

"Why, Grandma?"

"Because," Grandma leaned over the strings of red peppers, she twinkled her blue-star eyes at Carmolina, "because that magician he love you with all his heart."

Carmolina held her head still, to one side.

"You hear?"

"Grandma?"

"Yes, *bambina?*"

"Doriana has a magician too?" Carmolina looked quickly up at Grandma. "Doesn't she?"

Grandma's eyes got dark; she looked across the alley to the kitchen window of Carmolina's house.

"You no ask about Doriana."

Carmolina listened to Grandma breathing, Grandma shredded the peppers between her fingers and Carmolina listened to the sound of pepper dust.

"Doriana," Grandma said in the quiet, "Doriana she get lost in the forest."

Carmolina's hands stopped.

"Where, Grandma?"

Grandma held her white head high like a proud horse; she would not look at Carmolina. "We no know where. We try to find her. We still try to find her. We look. We never stop looking."

The sun shot down hard on them like the white hand of God. Carmolina held her breath still.

"She have such a beautiful face, so beautiful." Grandma's hands made the pepper dust.

"In the forest the birds are. Ah, such beautiful birds. White birds. Blue and pink. Doriana she go into the forest to look at the birds. The birds they sing in the trees, they sing, they turn into leaves. Doriana she have a key to the forest. It a secret. Only Doriana know where she keep the key. One day Doriana go into the forest. She forget the key. She get lost in the forest. She get scared. Her face it turn hot like a little peach and she scream and try to get out the forest."

Tears ran down Grandma's face like silk; God was pulling water silk across Grandma's face.

"She try to come home. From the forest. She no find her way."

Carmolina looked into the garden behind Grandma's house, where the sunflowers were. She listened to the movement of flowers, their swift rustling against the bees. "Where is the forest, Grandma?"

"Behind her eyes," Grandma whispered. She turned to Carmolina. "Doriana, she have a beautiful face, no?"

"Yes, Grandma."

"Her face, why you think it so beautiful?"

Something squeezed tight inside Carmolina. It was made of glass; it could break.

"I don't know, Grandma. Why?"

"Her face, she so beautiful," Grandma swiped at the tears, she was angry at them, "because Doriana fight so hard to come home. She look out her eyes every day and try to come home. When you fight to come home, you beautiful."

Carmolina sat in the center of the white silence with her grandmother. God was right there. If she turned around, God would put His hand on her shoulder, on Grandma's shoulder, He would hold them both in His arms, like Grandpa.

Grandma leaned over Carmolina. "You tell anyone you see you grandma cry and I take you little face and eat it up."

Grandma kissed her on the nose, shook her face in her hands. "The peppers, you think they make themself?"

In the center of the white sunlight, they began to crush the peppers. The magic net of God made a slight soft sound as He walked away from their porch; it sounded like the bees.

Carmolina blinked her eyes, shook her head clear, listened to the druggist yelling at his wife. She blinked and felt Grandma sitting in her eyes.

6.

Marco walked into the kitchen, his right hand set on the wooden butt of his gun, glanced at his wife, walked into the room next to the kitchen where the children played and where he locked up his guns in a desk drawer.

Sarah looked up from the board where she was cutting the lettuce leaves for salad, wiped the hair out of her eyes, looked out the window. It was still raining.

At his desk Marco unsnapped the holster, ripped the belt of bullets off with one swift pull of his hand. He emptied his pockets onto the desk, began to unbutton his shirt. He held his eyes the whole time steady on the window above his desk in the little room. The window faced the brick wall of a building four feet away.

"What happened at the station?" Sarah ran the water over the lettuce.

"I filed the report. I talked to Charlie."

Sarah looked up; her eyes had a blue smile in them.

"Charlie?" she said. "How is he?"

"The same. He asked about you. And Doriana."

"That's nice of him." She opened the icebox door, pulled out a white towel filled with vegetables. The smile in her eyes was bluer.

"How is Doriana?"

"The same, I think."

Marco picked up the newspaper, walked to the bathroom door.

"Did you talk to Ma today?"

"No." She unwrapped the towel. Inside there were half a green pepper, a tomato, four radishes. "No, it's strange how the phone kept ringing today, but there was never anyone on the other end."

Marco looked at her a minute, let it go. "Someone has the wrong number." He shut the bathroom door before he heard her say, "Yes, I suppose that's it."

Sarah looked at the food in her hands, looked at the torn lettuce. She wrapped it all back into the towel, put it into the icebox.

In the bedroom Doriana was packed again under three layers of blankets. The thermometer that morning had registered 103 degrees.

Her eyes were closed.

Sarah ran her hand over the child's forehead.

It was cool.

"Hi, baby," she whispered. "Daddy's home. He says hello."

Doriana lay still.

Sarah turned on the lamp.

"Doriana?" She leaned over her. "Doriana, Mama's here."

Doriana breathed heavily; her eyes opened slightly. Sarah could see the dark confused eyes under the white lids.

"Hi, baby," Sarah said and began to cry. "Hello there. It's about time you opened your eyes. You've been sick."

Doriana tried to move her hands; they were tight fists under the blankets.

"Nuh," she said.

"What, baby?" Sarah leaned closer. "What? Mama can't hear you."

"What is it?" Marco asked. He stood in the doorway naked to the waist.

Sarah looked at him. Her hands shook.

"Doriana woke up," she said. "I think the fever's down."

"Dear God," Marco said.

He knelt beside her.

"Doriana?" he said. "Dori?"

"I think she'd like to get up," Sarah whispered.

"She'd better stay in bed."

"Marco, it's been three days."

Marco stretched up like a cat. Sarah smelled him. "The doctor said to keep her there. We'd better give her another pill."

"I think she knows Carmolina's gone."

Marco turned at the doorway, looked at her.

"That's crazy."

"I think she's trying to say her name."

"This whole family has gone stark staring nuts," Marco yelled from the kitchen. "Where's the salad?"

"I'm sure the fever's broken," Sarah said over the chicken.

She took a bite of it, chewed it slowly, glanced hesitantly at Marco. "Maybe she doesn't need any more pills. Maybe she'd feel better at the table with us."

"Do you want another damn fork in your arm?" Marco said. He looked at Sarah's eyes. "God, I'm sorry. Hey honey, I'm sorry. Where's the anisette?"

Sarah looked at her plate. "Marco, I think she knows Carmolina is gone. I think that's why she got sick again."

Marco looked up. His eyes shattered like glass, like pieces of glass in front of her. She could pick them up and fold them into a napkin.

"We need more anisette. I'm going out to get some."

"Marco?"

He stopped at the door, his arm halfway into his shirt sleeve. He looked at her and the table empty of his family.

"Marco, I'm sorry. It's just that sometimes. . ." She glanced away from his eyes.

"Sometimes what? Go ahead, say it."

"It's just that sometimes I think we're making the same mistake. Doing it again."

He squeezed his hand over the doorknob.

"Sarah," he said quietly, "we didn't make a mistake. We did everything we could, remember?"

She looked at her hands on the kitchen table, at her dinner half-eaten on the plate.

"Now, I'm going out for some anisette and cigarettes. Then I'm stopping to see Ma. You give Doriana the pill."

He began to open the door, turned again.

"Hey." He held her face to his hands. "Hey honey I'm sorry. Everybody's so sorry. God is sorry. But there's nothing we can do for Doriana."

He kissed her cheek.

"We're a family," he said. "We've got to stick together."

"We're a family. I know."

"So give her the pill."

He walked over to the door again.

The deep pit of her stomach moved, the way it moved when on rare occasions he touched her.

"Marco?"

He turned to her. "What?" His face was so gentle; his eyes were so young, so bewildered, so closed.

"Nothing."

"See you later."

The telephone rang. Sarah's heart jumped like a bird's. She held one hand against the black plastic, could feel the vibrations ringing in her bones.

"Hello?"

"Hey, where were you? Asleep?"

"No, Marco. Where are you?"

"With Ma. She's in pretty bad shape. Look, we're all coming over. Make some food, ok?"

"Sure, Marco. What's wrong?"

"She keeps talking about Sabatina, how she saw black swans when Sabatina died. We're all coming over."

7.

It was raining. Her tennis shoes made no sound. Carmolina was not sure she was running down the street; she couldn't hear herself running. She bumped into a silver metal garbage pail. It had a cover on it that was fluted like a paper plate. The cover had a little handle on it.

The rain hit her skin like someone slapping warm hands against her face, but her face was cold. She wanted soup. She wanted barley soup, and she wanted Mama to make it.

She turned a street corner. The light from the streetlamp was green from the rain. The rain was green snakes falling out of the sky, they fell through the light of the streetlamp.

She stopped by a window. The curtain was white, was drawn

against the rain. Behind the window a family was sleeping.

Carmolina looked up at the window.

Mama? she called.

She would open the window now.

Mama? Carmolina called again.

There was a shadow at the window.

Mama!

The window opened.

A woman poked her face out between the curtains. She had yellow hair with cloth rags twisted into it.

She looked at Carmolina.

Mama? Carmolina said.

The mouth of the window snapped shut.

Always the lights, always the burning lights of the city shining down out of their glass eyes, casting hard light onto the city streets, burning hot glass. Always the row after row of glass city lights, naked bulbs hiding behind glass faces. Always the streets filled with houses, streets filled with windows with lamps behind them, and with families turning on and off the lamps. Her feet hurt. The small hole in her tennis shoe was ripped open. She thought about the music of her family, the music that her family made inside her. It was like the music in a music box, and it always surprised her. She could be washing dishes in the kitchen sink, or drying them if Mama wanted to wash, and feeling nothing in particular, when this music started, like the faraway music in a music box in another room. Her face would turn, and she would listen to see if anyone else heard the music. They didn't. But there would be Mama. There would be Mama just wiping off the kitchen table or stirring something in a pot on the stove. The kitchen walls would be so yellow; there would always be a chip in the white porcelain pot. Carmolina would stare at Mama, bewildered, and Mama would look up and smile and then go on with the wiping or stirring. Carmolina would stop what she was doing, and her mind would skip a little; she would stare at Mama until she no longer recognized her face. She would say to herself over and over, this is my mother, this is my mother, and suddenly, she didn't recognize Mama anymore, Mama could be anyone, it didn't mean anything that Mama was Mama. It was the same feeling that she got when she lay in bed at night and said her name over and over into the dark, until her name was just a sound. Then Mama would look up and say Carmolina, what are you staring at? That's when the music from the music box in the other room, the room that wasn't in the house, started. The music made her want to scream.

Her eyes got brittle from staring at strange things. Her face was a sheet of waxed paper. Her hands were clenched into fists that she

104

couldn't untie.

She walked down the street. Her feet hurt. She was hungry. She couldn't remember anymore how long it had been raining. The glass eyes of the city shined down on her. They wouldn't leave her alone.

She turned a corner. At the other end of the street was a police car. There was one policeman in the car. Another policeman was standing outside, leaning against the car door. He was writing something down on a pad of police paper.

The streetlight was a glass dome around him. The policeman turned and looked at her. He pushed his cap back on his head; the cap left a hard red line in his forehead.

Something snapped in Carmolina so hard, she thought she would cough it up. She looked at the policeman standing in the hard white circle of the streetlamp and his head was marked from his police cap. He stood inside the light's dome and looked at her in his police uniform.

Her feet went crazy. They started running down the street. They ran so fast, she could barely keep up with them. Her feet ran after each other so fast, it was as though her mouth were saying words over and over that she couldn't understand.

He stood inside the light and lit a cigarette. In the cold black lines of the rain, the smoke from the cigarette was blue.

She stopped and stared at the policeman. She looked up into his face and screamed, she listened to herself screaming something over and over. She coughed it up at him it hurt so much, her voice fell apart like a thousand stars and went flying into the glass faces of the streetlamps.

Someone picked her up and carried her into the front seat of the police car.

Someone said to please stop crying little girl.

Someone said what is your name?

Her voice fell apart like a thousand stars, she listened to the echoes inside her.

8.

She wanted to walk, she was perfectly fine, it was just that her legs wouldn't do it.

She looked out the window when the police car pulled up along the curbstone. She squinted through the hard light of the streetlamps, it was flat against her eyes. In front of her house was her father, he was standing in the rain with his arms folded across his chest. His face looked like he wanted to cry, like it might crack open in the rain. He stood there like a tree, with his arms crossed in front of him and there was Mama, under her umbrella, the white streetlight did something strange to her face.

Grandma held the umbrella over Mama, she stood with her arm

around her. The rain fell and didn't make a sound.

They all stood there like statues.

Something was wrong.

There were all their faces again finally and they were all wrong. The hard light from the street shined on them, and something was terribly wrong.

They weren't really her family at all. Her family went away and left all these strangers who just looked like them in their place, but these were pretenders. She would have to live with them and no one would ever tell her where her real family was.

They stood there with the rain running all around them, and the bright light confused everything. These people were all living in a house that looked just like hers, but not this house. Gustavo was there in the alley trying to fool her; he was standing under a black umbrella and it shone like snakeskin in the streetlight. He even had a blind horse. They thought of everything. Everyone was trying to fool her. They thought they could get away with it. But she could tell, no one could fool her. This was like looking in the mirror and the clock said ten after nine when it was really ten to three. It was that way.

The policeman carried her out of the car because her legs wouldn't work. That was part of the trick.

No one said a word, no one talked to her, they just stood in the rain and watched her. She kept her eyes on the man who was pretending to be her father. She never took her eyes off him. He was coming towards her, his mouth was open, he was saying something.

He was trying to say something so that she would believe him. They were all lying. Nothing would ever be the same again.

They took Doriana away and now there was probably someone upstairs pretending to be Doriana. Carmolina would always know that that wasn't the real Doriana at all; they had sent the real Doriana away a long time ago.

The man who looked like Daddy knew her name. He was saying it over and over.

Carmolina looked at the policeman.

What are you afraid of, the policeman said.

The policeman said, here comes your father.

No one will hurt you, the policeman said, this is your family.

I think she's delirious, the policeman said, she can't have eaten much.

She's been out in the rain, the other policeman said, I think she has a fever.

All the neighbors were lined up in the street in the rain, they were all watching her. The women were dressed in black as though everything was always a funeral.

They all watched, the women all talked to each other out of their mouths with no teeth.

They nodded their black heads towards each other. They whispered and the rain fell harder. Everyone knew the trick. The policemen were all in on it.

The man who knew her name walked up to her.

"You are never," he said, "going to leave us again."

The policemen walked back to the car, everyone smiled at each other.

All the women in black nodded their heads. They had her back.

I don't want to go home, Carmolina yelled.

The policemen hesitated at the door of the car.

She heard her voice yelling into the face of the man who looked just like Daddy, but that was a long time ago.

Maybe you ought to give her something to calm her down, the policeman said.

Daddy picked her up. We have something upstairs, he said.

Carmolina shrieked.

9.

Daddy sat her down on the bed. He slammed her down hard.

This, he said, is your bed.

He twisted her around by the neck to look at the room.

This, he said, is your bedroom.

This, he said, is where you live, and you are never going to leave us again.

She looked at him. When I grow up, she said, I'm going to go away forever.

Over my dead body, Daddy said.

10.

Mama was asleep in the bedroom. Carmolina stood at the kitchen window and the kitchen walls were perfectly yellow. She looked at the walls, squinted at them hard, blinked her eyes open and full again. Daddy was reading a newspaper in the bathroom. He would come out soon, with his newspaper rustling in his hands, all folded, the comics would be left on the bathroom floor for her to read, she would hear the soft shush of his pajamas. He would come out and turn off the light and say, go to bed now Carmolina, it's time to go to bed now. I am exactly eight and one half years old, she said to herself. In the kitchen sink the water dripped in separate drops over the dirty dishes. She looked at the dishes in the sink. There they were, with the blue flowers all around the edges. They were so faraway, she almost couldn't see them, it was like looking at them through the wrong end of binoculars. Daddy did come out like he was supposed to and he smelled clean from his bath. He smelled like warm water and soap. Turn out the light now kitten, Daddy would say. He said it. Then he said, if I turn out the light, you have to go to bed because you're afraid of the dark, aren't you. She nodded her head, yes. Daddy turned out the light, his feet walked into the bedroom. She shook her head no, and in a minute her eyes found everything in the dark. There was the white kitchen table, in the dark it was just a little white square and there were only the salt and pepper shakers on it. She walked into the bathroom, turned on the light. There were the comics, there were the cockroaches. She picked up the comics, folded them, smashed a cockroach. It stuck to the comics, one of its legs still moved a little, slowly. I hate cockroaches, she said to herself, and turned out the light in the bathroom. There was the icebox with the pan under it; the ice dripped. She opened the icebox, touched the towel wrapped around the vegetables, blinked something back behind her eyes. In the morning there would be bottles of milk at the door, in the morning she would wake up in bed next to Doriana and there would be milk bottles next to the door. She closed her eyes, tried to see the picture of her waking up next to Doriana tomorrow. Her eyes felt cold.

She looked out at the night. The night looked back in at her out of its glass eyes. From the window she heard the rush of the fire hydrant. She wanted to fall asleep by it, she wanted to get into bed next to Doriana and listen to the water that sounded like the tongue of a fish. She listened; it sounded like water. She shook her head. Behind the glass eyes of the night were the stars. Grandma said they were angels, she always said, Carmolina, the sky she full of angels to watch over us so we no get lost, but was it? Maybe they were just stars.

She looked across the alley to Grandma's house, the lamps were out there. In the dark, she could not see Grandma's old chair on the back porch, she could not see the red peppers on the clothesline. She squinted. Grandma's back porch was just a black square; it was empty. The peppers fell apart in her hands; when they got old they just turned to dust. Carmolina, Daddy called out, it's time to go to bed now. Grandma's lights were out. The whole family was asleep, only Carmolina was awake. Carmolina, Daddy called out again.

She squinted her eyes up at the confusing stars; there was no way to tell for sure. She was just a little girl with her face in the window. She reached up her hand to pull down the kitchen shade.

PART VI

SUMMER, 1958

The wooden chair was straight, it stood pointing towards the sun, though its back was torn into the fine hair of splinters. The chair was mahogany, the deep purple of its cushion was crushed and smoothed out flat, as though a giant had leaned on it. The sun did little harm to the chair, it was so old. The chair stood beside a bushel basket and a row of Mason jars on Doria's back porch.

Grandma Doria stood in front of the mirror in Katerina's bedroom. She was setting small rhinestones into her ears and her hands shook as she did it. She could not use her own bedroom mirror for the earrings. It was yellowed, the silver skin was peeling off. "The mirror, she like a fish," Doria said to herself, "and all the scales, they fall. I no want to look with my face into that mirror."

She wore her blue dress. She always wore her blue dress on best occasions. Rhinestones were sewn across the bodice. She placed her shaking hands on her breasts, looked at herself in the mirror. "Doria," she said to the mirror, "you an old lady, but you look nice. Today, you look nice." Her hair was dull gray, like pewter. She pulled a tortoise shell comb through it to part it; again her hands shook, and she asked the blue Virgin Mary on the dresser to help her comb her hair. With the comb, she pulled the pewter hair close to her face.

The chair waited for her on the back porch. In the mirror, Doria looked into her eyes and saw the old chair waiting for her. The chair waited in the sun, its old body shed wooden skin on its steady legs.

Below, in the streets, the entire neighborhood gathered, chattering. Old women in black cotton dresses with no teeth in their mouths, with gums honed like knives, their yellow hands shaking, their white laughter filling the spaces of their mouths, gathered. Around their necks hung the golden chains strung with golden crucifixes, golden medallions of the Sacred Heart eternally blessing, small silver medals of the slender Virgin, her hands raised sadly, golden chains hung with fire and with brown scapulars fading with their own bodies' sweat. Around their heads they tied black kerchiefs, their thin hair trapped beneath, their bony heads small skeletons moving with laughter and excitement.

Grandma Doria looked at her blue body in the mirror. Her legs worked poorly. She could no longer walk up stairs. Inside her body her final days chewed their black teeth upwards, towards the eyes which they would close. She bent closer to the mirror. She looked into her eyes, the stars were still there. "Ok, you old fat body," she said to the mirror. "Ok, you old eyes, you try to look sick. I know. I know." She pounded her hand over her heart, flattened the hand against her chest. "I know you all come for me." She glanced around the room, but the black swans were not there. She looked at the statue of the Virgin. "You want me, eh? Dominic, he calling for me, he say 'Where that old woman?' " She picked up the statue in her hands which were shaking. She looked again into the mirror. "You all think it time for me to die. Well, you just have to wait a little. First I go see Carmolina."

The voices of the women below drifted towards the bedroom window. Doria put one hand on top of the other to steady it, so that she would be able to put the earrings into her ears. The street voices drifted into the bedroom. Doria looked into the mirror, there was the face of her mother, there in the lines around her mouth was the face of her mother which hung in a picture in her own bedroom. It frightened Carmolina when she was a little girl. "Grandma, was she a nice lady?" Carmolina said once. "She a very nice lady," Doria answered. "Then why does she scare me?" Carmolina said. Doria shrugged her shoulders. "Because the pictures, they never the same." She looked into the mirror and behind her blue eyes with stars in them, and her mouth with the lines of her mother, she saw the reflections of the women dressed in black, standing in a long line behind her.

The women below stood on a hard, hot street; the cement slapped against their thin shoes and pained them. Near them, the men gathered in small black and white circles, the smoke from their cigars and cigarettes was blue in the white summer's air, the voices were deep and languid with the summer, their voices were molding the air with their sweet Italian.

Across the alley, Carmolina stood before a mirror placing pearl earrings in her intact ears. She was young and beautiful and dressed in white, in the gown of a bride, but she was not a bride. In the mirror's face, she saw reflected her own brown eyes, large, rimmed with blue. She pulled the black comb through her heavy hair, watched the hair spring out around her mirror-head, ruffled and disturbing. Her hair created light around itself, caught the day's light in it. Her eyes suffocated her face.

She watched the wash of brown light around her head, she held her eyes steady in the mirror. On her shoulders, her arms, the *peau de soie* of her dress was elegant. It had been made to fit her exactly, by a dressmaker. It was her first long dress, it skimmed the surface of the rug, it was like water around her small ankles. She leaned closer to the mirror, placed her hands on the mirror's cold face. There were her eyes, brown, filled with confusion and with the movement of something she could not quite name.

In the mirror's face, she watched her own hands lock the small strand of baby pearls around her neck. The string of seed pearls was begun when she was born seventeen years ago. They were meant for her to wear as a bride, they were strung each year one by one to make a full necklace for the marriage ceremony. Now Grandma was old. The old woman is dying, Mama and Daddy and the whole family said. Grandma would not live to see Carmolina marry. "I'm doing this for Grandma," Carmolina whispered to the mirror. She touched the pearls around her neck. "But they're wrong. Grandma's not going to die. We don't have to do this." She slid her feet into the white satin shoes, looked at her own mirror face. The mirror was soundless.

She opened the white satin purse, slipped the ring out. It was a cameo ring, it had belonged to Great-Grandma Carmella and her great-great-grandma. Some of the names were lost. The filigree was worn thin. Carmolina slipped the ring out of the purse, looked at the finely carved profile of the woman. She kissed the ring, dropped it back into the purse, locked its small golden lock. "They won't ever let us go, will they?" she asked of no one.

Mama's hand rested on her white back. She smiled at her mother through the mirror and her mother's black eyes smiled back at her, backwards.

Carmolina looked at her own mouth smiling, a hot blue line flashed across her eyes. Her hands shook.

"Mama?" Carmolina said. She felt the weight like heavy water behind her eyes, in her head somewhere.

Mama shrugged her shoulders, kissed her lightly on the back of her neck.

"Mama, I don't want to do this," Carmolina said.

"You have to," Mama said.

Carmolina held her fingers trembling like white birds before her own face in the mirror. No, she said to herself. In her wedding gown, Carmolina sat down at the kitchen window to watch the procession begin.

In the bedroom across the alley, Doria struggled into the shoes. Her large feet were purple under the brown-cloth bandages, under the heavy stockings. She rested on the bed a minute.

Last night, at her kitchen table, with her children around her, Doria said, "Carmolina, why she no come here instead?"

No one answered.

That night, Doria prayed to God. She asked Him her question. No one answered. She lay on the white pillow with her blue eyes seeing clearly into the night, there was the picture of her own mother on the wall, whose eyes saw nothing anymore.

Now the bedroom slowly filled with her children, with Katerina, Rosa, Josephina, Salvatore. Marco walked in last. He would not look directly into her eyes.

They walked her out to the back porch, where the wooden chair waited. The clothesline on the porch was strung with dried red peppers, her pantry was filled with shrunken figs and wrinkled black olives. Everything had always been this way.

Marco and Salvatore seated Doria on the chair, began to lift it. She forgot her purse, she said. They lowered the chair and watched her disappear into her kitchen. Grandma Doria stood a moment in her kitchen, looked at the old radio that played music for her in the mornings when she was alone, that played music for Carmolina when she was little and came home from school to have lunch with her Grandma.

She blinked, cleared her eyes, walked past Katerina's bedroom with the clean mirror into her own room. Now you look, she said to herself. Now you see why Carmolina turn her head. She walked up to the mirror whose face was worn away, whose silver skin was yellow and peeled. She closed her blue eyes a moment, whispered something, opened them into the ancient mirror. There was her face. She held her hands before her face, the fingers shook violently a minute, then stopped. She wiped her eyes, put the small white handkerchief back into her purse. She hesitated, looked at the purse, opened it; the stars in her eyes flashed. She walked slowly into her daughter Katerina's bedroom, opened the top drawer. There among the golden chains and strings of pearls which Katerina had bought for herself and kept in a blue velvet box were three coins. Doria picked them up, tied them into a knot in her handkerchief, slipped it into her purse.

From the kitchen window, Carmolina watched the line form behind her grandmother's chair, watched it squeeze itself into a small black and white parade with all the hands waving or shaking. Sitting by the kitchen window, Carmolina tried to stop her hands from trembling, tried to hold them steady in her lap.

The old women cackled around Doria being carried slowly down the street in her chair, the men killed their cigars and cigarettes out of respect. The women waved their white hankies into the evening, waved them back after the old woman in the chair like black birds with white beaks. Their old black voices stabbed the evening's air, filled it with white holes so that the evening was a bolt of poor lace. Doria, in her chair, smiled, nodded, smiled. Behind the chair her daughters followed, taking the withered hands of the women in black, taking the warm hands of the men in black slacks and white shirts who all murmured that *Gentildonna* BellaCasa was *bellissima* while her sons carried her.

112

Carmolina walked back to the mirror, looked into her own dark eyes. The skin of her throat burned as though she had been forced to swallow flame. She looked at the soft lines around her mouth. In a small corner of the mirror, near its beveled edge, she saw a purple shadow in the living room. She walked up to the shadow, knelt at the chair. Her white dress floated around her like silk water; she looked at Doriana in the chair. Doriana sat in the chair holding a doll. She was fat as a fat baby; she had the perfect skin of a baby, it was smooth and full as the overblown skin of an infant. Her beautiful features were lost in the fat of her face, so that when Carmolina looked into her sister's face she saw only the eyes she remembered from their childhood. She held in her fat hands a pink doll, held it up so that Carmolina could see it. The doll had black hair and a porcelain face.

Carmolina touched her sister's face, looked into the eyes that were locked into themselves.

"This is for Grandma," Carmolina said. "This is for the family." She laid her head to rest for a minute in Doriana's lap. Doriana stroked her thick fingers over Carmolina's hair. Her eyes filled with tears. She held the doll up again, shook it at Carmolina.

"Sometimes," Carmolina whispered, "sometimes, Doriana, I think it is you who has the luck." She adjusted the heavy plaid blanket over Doriana, watched her own hands shaking.

The sons carried their mother up the three flights of wooden stairs, three flights of wood that were dark and twisted and turned in unexpected places. Doria sat with her hands in her lap, over the blue purse precisely. The long sleeves of her dress were edged in blue lace; she held her hands still and the wedding band on her finger gleamed softly in the dark light of the hallway. They bumped her foot once; she said nothing as the pain made itself a snake in her leg. She smiled at Marco, at Salvatore, as they carried her up the stairs. In front of her, her three daughters walked to safeguard the way, calling out in Italian directions to the sons carrying her. Behind, the old women, all fallen now into silence, followed, and behind them walked the men in black and white whose dead cigarette butts filled their shirt pockets with ash.

At the landing of the third floor, Sarah stood at the closed door, her hands solid behind her.

Grandma's eyes smiled when they set the chair on the landing. She rose slowly, the rhinestones in her ears, on her dress and purse sparkling like rain.

On the other side of the door, before the mirror, Carmolina stared into her own face. Around her mouth, she saw the soft lines which she loved in her grandmother's face, the lines that were pronounced when she smiled. Her grandmother's eyes were blue, like the sea, they were clear and old as the sea. Her eyes were brown, the flame that burned the skin of her throat reached up behind the brown eyes. She looked down at the bodice of her dress, pressed her hands against the silk over the small breasts. In the mirror, Doriana was a small purple shadow, a shadow that fell asleep over a doll.

The door opened.

Carmolina was standing before the mirror and Grandma Doria saw not one but two brides in white dresses with heavy dark hair and heavy dark eyes.

Carmolina did not move.

Grandma shut the door behind her quiet as a whisper. She walked slowly towards Carmolina, her feet filling with pain like water. Her fat blue arms shook in the still space between them, her old mouth repeated, repeated in Italian, that Carmolina was beautiful, was beautiful.

Carmolina turned towards her grandmother. Grandma stood there in the confused light, her hands were reaching for her face, trying to touch Carmolina's face the way they did when Carmolina was a little girl and Grandma held her and told her *faccia bella*. Carmolina wiped her hands swiftly before her eyes, wiped hurriedly back at the burning behind them. She could not find the words for Grandma, she put on this wedding dress just so Grandma could see her dressed as a bride, and now she lost all her words, there were no words for Grandma, just a weight in her chest like gold.

Doria looked at Carmolina and remembered her. She saw her when she was three years old and went running on her small legs toward her, her small arms thrown open, her small voice singing in broken Italian the love songs Doria taught her. She saw her when she was five years old and washing her feet, and how her face turned pale but she did it anyway and once Doria heard her throw up in the bathroom and then flush the toilet. She saw Carmolina in her kitchen, her small face smiling, turned towards her grandmother, standing on her toes on the back porch trying to reach the peppers that flew up over her face and laughing, her round head shining in the sunlight, her small body in a red dress running up the stairs with the bags full of groceries. She watched the little hands, the head, the face, and then the little girl disappeared from the grandmother's eyes and in the mirror, the face of the child was gone, and there was the young woman Carmolina like a strong flower. You grow up, Carmolina, Grandma said to herself, you grow up and you little child face it gone forever from this world, but she in my heart where I watch her. Now you do this one last thing for you grandma in you bride's dress, now you do it even though it make you cry.

Grandma slipped the handkerchief with the coins knotted into it into Carmolina's hands. "My little gypsy," she whispered. "You remember?"

Carmolina untied the handkerchief, the thin coins sat in her hands. She looked up. "I remember, Grandma."

"This time," Grandma said, "I give them you on purpose."

Grandma sat in a chair next to the mirror. "You sit down next me, *bambina,*" Grandma said.

She held Carmolina's hands where she knelt before her grandmother.

In Grandma's eyes, a moment passed.

"Carmolina?" Grandma said, "you mad with me I'm dying?"

Carmolina moved her dark eyes away from her grandmother, tried to pull her hands away. Grandma held on hard. "You're not dying," Carmolina said. Grandma took her face in her hands the way she did when Carmolina was a little girl, forced Carmolina to look into her eyes. "Carmolina," she said softly, "the whole time you a little girl I never lie to you. I no lie to you now." She took Carmolina's hand, held it over her breast, let her feel the old heart beating under it. "I tell you the true, Carmolina. I dying."

Carmolina yanked her hand away, dropped her eyes. There were Grandma's arms around her, trying to stop her body from shaking. Grandma lifted her face, held Carmolina's face in her hands. "You forgive an old lady for dying?" she whispered. Grandma rocked her as though she were a little girl. "It all right you cry. You cry all you like. You think it break you heart. But you forgive me, and I tell you a secret." Grandma held her close to the blue dress where her own tears were burning into Carmolina's face. "I tell you a secret, little one. It break my heart too."

Grandma held her frail arms around her, then pushed her quietly away, touched her face with her old hands.

"Now," Grandma said, she wiped at her eyes behind her glasses. "Now I show you something, my Carmolina."

She lifted herself slowly out of the chair. Carmolina rose with her, held Grandma's hands steady and warm in hers.

Grandma pushed her gently from behind, forced her to look into the mirror.

In the mirror, Carmolina saw herself in the white dress, her grandmother behind her. There were Grandma's eyes, like a star, and a star was the face of an angel.

"You going there already," Grandma said, "you in a bride's dress."

Grandma held her hands on Carmolina's shoulders a moment, then sank slowly back into the chair next to the mirror.

Carmolina looked at her grandmother in the chair. One day when she looked, Grandma would be gone, she would blink her eyes for a moment and Grandma would be gone like a whisper, like something beautiful someone said once, a long time ago. The weight in her chest that was like gold shifted.

"Grandma?" Carmolina whispered.

She stood before the mirror; the mirror's face shined like a white jewel around her.

"Carmolina *mia*," Grandma said from her place in the chair. "*Bambina*," she said softly. "Now it you turn. You keep the fire inside you."

Carmolina looked into the mirror's silver face. It gave back to her her own face.

EPILOGUE

1.

Giovanni shuffled over to the seedman and bought three nickel bags of lubeans. The seedman used a dipper and the bottoms of the bags were wet straight through like diapers.

"No chi-chi nuts?" the seedman said. He wore a felt hat and red apron. His upper teeth were gone and his lower teeth were crooked and yellow like a broken fence; he spat out the shells of pistachio.

"No, lubeans," Giovanni said, "enough," and his fat hands searched for the pocket which lost itself always in the folds of his over-sized pants.

"The city, you think she do it?" the seedman asked. "You think she come tear us down like we a rotten building?" He spat into the street. "I think she do it. I think she make us all move."

Giovanni crossed himself. "Curse you mother's grave, you say a thing like that." He squinted his eyelids, fat like an oyster, down the street. "Eh, Carmella, Joanna, lubeans." He walked over to the hydrant, the thin soles of his shoes got wet, and he bent his fat body down like a sponge, cooling his feet. A yellow lubean fell out of its white bag, floated down the water by the curbstone. It was deep yellow, it floated, it disappeared.

No one snapped a picture.

2.

Underneath, the street is brick, brick that is no longer whole and red, but chipped and gray like the faces of dead people trapped under lava. The street heaves up bricks, the guts of the street spit up brick. The face of the street cracks open and reveals its belly of brick, the gray faces. Squads of men in white t-shirts and hard hats with pickaxes in their hands chew into the street's cement face and the face cracks and there is no body under the bricks, only the cracked cement face. Then the street explodes, explodes in the faces of the men with pick-axes who come to take the streetcar line away. They wrench the metal tracks of the streetcar line away from the face of the street, it is like peeling the wrinkles from an old woman's face. The streetcar tracks lie on the street like a skeleton and rust, the bones turn red in the sunlight, like the bones of a giant animal long since disappeared from the earth. First they gleam, then they are silent. The men with the pickaxes go away at night, and the gutted tracks are still.

The people of the neighborhood sit on wooden benches, eat lemon ice in fluted paper cups, their lips are wet from the ice. They look at the clean steel bones of the tracks.

At night the rats steal up. The water rats, disturbed in their sewers, surface and prowl the street on their padded feet.

Then the people stay in their houses.

In the dark, the yellow eyes of the rats glisten, glisten with the light of sewer water, with the light of the streetlamps reflected in their pupils. The sound of their feet is a hissing sound. They run along the street, along the steel skeleton of tracks.

The children catch one.

Augie the grocer finds a drowned rat floating in a barrel of green olives.

The sound of the pickaxes chews at the day.

Alone at night, the tracks lay on the surface of the street's cracked face, pointing at nothing.

3.

"Eh, Stephanzo, you no move. The city, she change her mind, then you be sorry. Where you go?" Giovanni's eyes filled with the shadows of Stephanzo and Sophia piling full the truck with their pictures, the couch, the lamps, the children.

"Everybody here turn crazy?" Giovanni shouted.

Stephanzo looked at the yelling man, his mouth was filled with spit, his eyes burned.

"You the one crazy, Giovanni. The city she run over you children and smash them flat, like this." Stephanzo rammed his hand into his crooked arm. "They call us wops. They say these streets have to go. Open you damn eyes."

The two men faced each other in the dark street. The fire in their eyes burned, they did not see each other, then Giovanni felt his anger go soft.

"You give *me* the arm, Stephanzo? *Me?*"

In the night street the two men were still, embraced each other.

"What you do, Stephanzo? Where you go?"

Stephanzo shrugged his shoulders. "What you do, Giovanni?"

"Me?" Giovanni laughed.

4.

The water of the fire hydrant spits vigorously, it is a white waterfall, it is spitting its enormous vital life into the street, it is water, it is blessing the street, it is holy water blessing the street. A secret pipe runs from the church where the blessed Father Anthony died, it connects to the delicate throat of his holy water font, the pipe runs secretly to the thick metal mouth of the fire hydrant and the fire hydrant is spitting blessed water into the street, covering the children. The old women who go into the church in the mornings reach their dry hands into the fonts and the fonts are also dry. The gypsies have stolen the holy water, the women say, and bless themselves with parched hands. But the water is pumping out of the fire hydrant onto the children who play in it. Hundreds of children play in the water. They come from all the streets, children who have been hiding in closets, children who played hide and seek and were never found come running out of their hiding places and play in the water of the hydrant. There are hundreds of children, no one can count them. Mrs. Consuelo, Mrs. Schiavone, Mrs. Giorgino stand like confused chickens in a circle and try to count the children, but no one can count them, where did they all come from?, whose children are these? The children come falling down out of the trees, they fall from the trees like the leaves in autumn, and they all run into the fire hydrant. They splash at each other and laugh, their voices become the voice of the water, they are singing, they throw the water above their heads, they throw each other above their own heads, they are singing in the water and the women shake and nod their heads and can not count the children.

The voice of the water slows.

The children grow sleepy.

One by one the children grow sleepy and begin to stumble out of the water.

They have water in their eyes. They can not see straight for the water, for the laughter.

The bigger children pick up the littler children and carry them out. The big children want pajamas for the little children.

The voice of the water slows.

It is disappearing.

The thrust of the water's song becomes softer.

The singing of the children is stopping.

The singing of the water is stopping.

The water stops.

The secret pipe which runs from the holy water font of the blessed Father Anthony, may he rest in peace, is empty.

5.

"You put them back, you hear. Put them back."

Giovanni on one side of his living room hung the pictures of his mother and father back onto the nails still in the walls, Mrs. Giovanni on the other side of the room took down the wooden crucifix, the small grotto with the blue candle.

"You leave the mother *alone!*" Giovanni shouted and Mrs. Giovanni wept in the kitchen. At night, Mrs. Giovanni silently packed away the small cotton and wooden and iron possessions of her family into boxes, into scrub buckets, into paper sacks. In the morning, Giovanni unpacked them, so that now the wooden spoons were stuffed into a vase in the bedroom, the madonna was on the back porch next to the washboard and clothespins, the soup pot was in the window of the living room next to a Mason jar filled with rosaries.

Giovanni went to sit alone on the concrete stoop of his house. Berrywood Street had disappeared as though it were a picture someone wiped away. The city said the Italian ghetto should go, and before the people could drop their forks next to their plates and say, pardon me?, the streets were cleared.

The houses of the families with their tongues of rugs sticking out were smashed down, the houses filled with soup pots and quick anger, filled with forks and knives and recipes written in the heads of the women, were struck in their sides with the ball of the wrecking crane and the knives and bedclothes and plaster spilled out. The women laughed and waved to each other, they raised their hands in the early sun and called out to one another sleepily, and the hands and the women and the rugs fell through the air, the toys and the voices landed on the ground.

Next to Giovanni's house, where the little wooden home of Mrs. Consuelo had been, a dark wooden fence made a perfect square around nothing. The sunflowers still grew in Doria's garden, behind the house that wasn't there. Across the street, all the buildings were gone, so that Giovanni could sit on his stoop and look into Quincy Street a block away. Augie's grocery store was an empty frame, like a stage prop someone forgot to move. The butcher shop stood empty of its chickens. Mrs. Schiavone's butcher block shone under the sun in the alley, the blood congealed on the wood like skin.

6.

The clown at the circus stands in a ring filled with light. His face is painted with sad paint, his mouth is a white line that droops down. He dances. He does funny movements with his great clown shoes. He pulls a string and the daisy in his lapel squirts water. The audience laughs. The clown is startled.

He bows. His red nose bumps into his shoes.

The light in the ring gets smaller.

He shivers, moves to the center of the light.

The light gets smaller still.

The clown leaves the circle of light.

The audience is uneasy.

The clown returns, smiles, bows, holds up his broom.

Sadness runs like silk through the audience.

The clown bends seriously over his broom, begins to sweep the edges of the light. The light gets smaller and smaller. The clown sweeps furiously, he is trying to get all the light-edges.

The circus music slows.

The clown looks up out of his face.

He is standing in the middle of a tiny circle of light.

It barely covers his feet.

One more sweep and the light will be gone.

Carmolina sits in the audience with her grandmother.

Grandma is frightened.

The light she go away, Grandma says.

Nothing goes away, Carmolina says.

Carmolina puts her hands over her grandmother's hands.

Do your feet hurt, Grandma? she asks.

My feet, they fine.

The clown picks up the broom again.

Carmolina, Grandma whispers, you hear the magician? He still there?

He's there, Grandma.

Faccia bella, Grandma says.

The clown sweeps the light away.

The music stops.

It's only a trick, Grandma, Carmolina says. Don't let it fool you.

AFTERWORD

"A SONG FROM THE GHETTO"

Paper Fish represents a landmark in Italian/American literature, though few critics have ever heard of the book.[1] It was first published in 1980 by a now-defunct publishing house. Only one thousand copies were printed and it went out of print within months of its publication. Yet *Paper Fish* was saluted by its first readers as a masterpiece. A pre-published portion of the manuscript received the Illinois Arts Council Literary Award, and the novel was nominated for the Carl Sandburg Award. Jerre Mangione read the manuscript and praised De Rosa's extraordinary literary debut.[2] Fred Gardaphé, who reviewed the book for the *American Italian Historical Association Newsletter,* recalls thinking of *Paper Fish* as "one of the greatest works" he "had ever read" ("Breaking and Entering" 12).[3] In 1985 Helen Barolini reprinted an excerpt from the novel in *The Dream Book: An Anthology of Writings by Italian American Women,* while Mary Jo Bona analyzed its interweaving of issues of gender, ethnicity, and illness in an article published in *MELUS* in 1987.

Despite these unyielding efforts, *Paper Fish* and its author remained in the shadows for fifteen years. Apart from a handful of academics who occasionally taught the book in Italian/American culture courses by giving their students photocopies, *Paper Fish* was excluded from literary history. This reprint of De Rosa's book, then, represents a discovery as well as a recovery. As with other works that were published long after their composition, such as H.D.'s *HERmione* (1981), or that received late recognition, such as Zora Neale Hurston's *Their Eyes Were Watching God* (1937), this reprint of *Paper Fish* urges readers and scholars to interrogate the long silence surrounding the book and its author.[4] Ironically, silence enveloped De Rosa's novel in the midst of debates about the canon, minority literatures, ethnicity, and gender—that is, in a climate that ought to have welcomed *Paper Fish*. It becomes imperative, then, to consider the politics of publication and distribution as they influence the construction of literary history and the emergence of a writer and a tradition—in this case, an Italian/American female literary tradition.

*

Tina De Rosa was born in Chicago, where she still lives. Her maternal grandparents were Lithuanian, but as a child De Rosa identified primarily with her paternal grandmother, Della, whom she describes as the most influential person in her life.[5] Born in Boscoreale, near Naples, probably in 1888, Della came to the United States when she was about seventeen years old. She died in 1963, when the author was nineteen years old, leaving a void that De Rosa would try to fill through her writing. De Rosa's work thus became a "home" in which she could take refuge, a site of soothing memories, where even tragedy and ugliness could be incorporated into her life and made the source of magical storytelling.

Until she was seventeen, De Rosa lived with her family in the Taylor Street area on the West Side of Chicago. One of the few people in her neighborhood to go to college, she attended Mundelein College of Loyola, a Catholic university in Chicago. After working at various jobs and gaining some writing experience, she earned a master's degree in English from the University of Illinois, where she studied under Michael Anania, who read early drafts of *Paper Fish* and encouraged her to cut and revise the manuscript. In 1977 Jim Ramholz of the Wine Press became interested in publishing the book.[6] In 1978, while trying to finish *Paper Fish*, holding two jobs, and struggling through economic hardship, De Rosa received a writer's residency from the Ragdale Foundation that enabled her to complete the book (Gardaphé, "Interview" 23). Paper Fish was thus written in stages: begun around 1975, it was completed in 1979, though the author put it away for over a year in between.[7]

Cross-cultural marriages such as that of De Rosa's parents, though not frequent among first- and second-generation immigrants, did occur in the ethnically diverse Chicago of De Rosa's childhood, where different ethnic groups coexisted in the same neighborhood. This was the case on the West Side, which, although regarded as primarily Italian by "outsiders," was home to many ethnicities, including Irish, German, Mexican, Greek, Jewish, Polish, and Czech (Pacyga 606).[8] While growing up, and as she started writing, De Rosa defined her ethnicity as primarily Italian/American.[9] De Rosa's silence about her Lithuanian ancestry depends not only on the fact that her paternal grandmother kept alive her *italianità* in the family, but also on the seeming reluctance of her maternal relatives to discuss their origins and the reasons for the family's emigration. Her mother's family lore, which fascinated the young De Rosa, remained vague, almost mysterious. By contrast, she was exposed in her daily life to the Italian language and customs, both in her household and in the Little Italy where she grew up. *Paper Fish* dramatizes the author's relationship to her dual heritage. Grandma Doria, whose mind knows "only Italian" (43), is the wise and benevolent matriarch to whom everyone, including her "foreign" daughter-in-law Sarah, turns for guidance and comfort. She is also the one who tells Carmolina of a distant, mythical Italy, "the land that got lost across the sea, the land that was hidden on the other side of the world" (15). Unlike Grandma Doria, Carmolina's maternal grandmother remains a distant, unresponsive, "stiff" (46) figure. While privileging Italian culture, *Paper Fish* gives voice to the disorienting experience of cultural dislocation, which Sarah suffers repeatedly. Once married, Sarah must leave behind "the small white houses of the south side of the city," with their "picket fences between the yards" (49), and move into the little cold-water flat on Taylor Street, where "the guttural and minced Lithuanian in the throats of her family, her neighbors, was stilled" (49) while the "sweet" and "musical" Italian spoken by her husband's family "fell" "meaningless" on her ears (50). The pregnant Sarah wonders "which language the baby would speak" (50) as she listens to the Italian that remains incomprehensible to her. Although not central to the story, the author's Lithuanian background emerges in fragments such as these, shedding light on the experience of cross-cultural identity, which De Rosa also examines when she focuses on the predicament of third-generation Italian Americans like herself.

In "My Father's Lesson," an autobiographical essay published in 1986, De Rosa reflects on the expectations that her family, especially her father, had about her future, and describes her philosophy of work—a philosophy that is in harmony with her aesthetic vision:

> For a long while, I expected to find satisfaction, fulfillment, in my employment. I was the new generation, the one my father tended as carefully as my grandmother had tended her garden. My work, it was promised to me, would be, unlike my father's, fulfilling. So off I went to college, where I studied sociology, and then to graduate school, where I lost myself in literature and poetry. For a long time, I believed my father's promise, and wondered why I kept changing jobs. I suppose that I was seeking perfect employment, the kind my father always said I would have. But I was also discovering that I am a writer, and that, for me, an indestructible distinction exists between my employment and my work. Always, I would be wanting to run home. (15)

Through the distinction she draws between "employment" and "work," De Rosa both rejects the paternal promise of success and pays tribute to the father who unwittingly taught her "how to be a writer" (15). Like her father, who "spent his whole life doing the sad and hidden work of society, then came home and hid his face in the little world" of his family,[10] De Rosa finds refuge in her books, her "silent children" ("My Father's Lesson" 15).

A comparison can be drawn between De Rosa's aesthetics of work, rooted in her father's experience, and Pietro di Donato's representations of the laborer's relationship to a demonized "Job," a powerful force that "loomed up, damp, shivery gray," waiting to swallow the workers with its "giant members" (*Christ in Concrete*, 8). In his novel *Christ in Concrete* (1939), di Donato simultaneously illustrates the dehumanization of the workers—"The men were transformed into single, silent beasts" (9)—and infuses labor with the humanity of the workers themselves. Like other Italian/American and working-class authors, di Donato "elevates the common worker to the status of a deity...as a way of dignifying the plight of the worker" (Gardaphé, "Continuity in Concrete" 5). In "An Italian-American Woman Speaks Out" (1980), De Rosa expresses similar concerns, and questions capitalist ethics by asking:

> What happens to a person who is raised in this environment full of color, loud music, loud voices, and genuine crying at funerals and then finds herself in a world where the highest emotional charge comes from the falling of the Dow Jones average, or yet another rise in the price of gold? (38)

To fight alienation, De Rosa forges for herself an uncontaminated space, a home where her work becomes possible, where she can put to good use her father's lesson. In a self-conscious manner, De Rosa acknowledges the worker's need to sell her labor; yet she manages to create a space that is, as much as possible, immune from the ill effects of capitalist exploitation. In a quasi-utopian fashion, De Rosa envisions her home as separate from the alienating world of the modern laborer.

"My Father's Lesson" and "An Italian-American Woman Speaks Out" are two of the essays that De Rosa published during the 1980s. These essays constitute a disjointed, fragmentary autobiography, one that could be called, to borrow Gardaphé's description of Barolini's work, an "autobiography as piecework." They document the writer's journey towards authorial self-fashioning. It is a journey that requires negotiation between Italy and America, between the myth of the tightly knit family and the myth of the individual.[11] The emphasis on a self-contained and self-sufficient individual, predominant in mainstream Anglo-American culture, is at odds with the central place of the family in the pre-capitalist, predominantly agrarian culture of late–nineteenth-century Southern Italy. It was this Italian cultural heritage, caught in a time capsule, that the immigrants passed on to new

126

generations of Italian Americans. These new generations were thus torn between the culture of descent, epitomized by the family, and the culture of consent, with its self-sufficient, even ruthless individualism.[12] From this perspective, *Paper Fish* develops De Rosa's autobiographical narrative in a fictional text that, while documenting the disappearance of the world of the author's childhood, testifies to the struggle between conflicting cultural values sustained by Italian/American women.[13]

For women writers, who entered a world that stood in contrast to the domestic sanctum of Italian womanhood, the struggle was indeed arduous.[14] In "Becoming a Literary Person Out of Context," Barolini writes that her aspiration to become a writer was "outlandish" in her Italian/American milieu. For her, an inextricable link exists between writing and class:

> [Frances Winwar's] story is not typical because she was born in Italy of educated parents who understood and abetted her career, as is true for women writers in Italy in general.... One can cite names of Renaissance court women who wrote, but again this was a function of class and privilege. And since it was primarily the uneducated masses who migrated to America, they did not carry with them, to transmit to their progeny, a tradition of literacy, much less the concept of being writers of literature. (266)

Yet these "uneducated masses" carried with them oral traditions that, through storytelling and song, would be passed on to the new generations. A deeply internalized self-hatred—characteristic of the works of many Italian/American writers, but also of working-class writers—has at times stood in the way of the development of a literary tradition, even after literacy became available to the children of immigrants.[15] "I no longer belong to the Italian-American working class," De Rosa wrote in 1980. "My parents were successful in moving me out of it. After I moved far enough, I wanted to leave, and went as far as I could. But sometimes I try to go home, and that is where the heartache lies. You find out that you really can't go home again, no matter how much you might want to" ("Italian-American Woman" 39). *Paper Fish* represents De Rosa's attempt to "go home again" and soothe "the heartache." An analogy can be drawn between the separation experienced by the immigrant, and the separation from the family that moving into the middle class entails for the working-class person. Like many other working-class writers, De Rosa views the family as a homeland that can be revisited only through writing.[16]

*

Written after the deaths of De Rosa's grandmother and father, *Paper Fish* represents an attempt to make the absent present: "I wanted them to be eternal," she writes, remembering her family. "I wanted the brief, daily lives they lived never to end" ("Career Choices" 9). Struggling with her sorrow, De Rosa kept trying to tell her family's story; overwhelmed by the intensity of her own remembering and the awareness of her loss, she would temporarily abandon the writing and take it up again later, each time beginning a new section of the work. As she wrote, her family members "would die over and over again," to be reborn in her fiction.[17] The result is a prismatic text, whose pieces cohere into a fragmentary narrative reminiscent of the fiction of high modernism. The complex structure aptly portrays—just as it emerges out of—the emotional turmoil that triggered the author's creative process. De Rosa's modernist strategy becomes the means by which she captures her memories and translates them into poetry. Her experimental, highly lyrical prose is reminiscent of H.D.'s high modernist fiction (although literary antecedence must be excluded because H.D.'s fiction was published posthumously, in the last fifteen years, and has received critical recognition only more recently.)[18]

De Rosa writes poetry that tells stories and creates scenes familiar to the Italian Americans from Chicago (Gardaphé, "Breaking and Entering" 12). The impressionistic style of *Paper Fish* evokes a surreal atmosphere: the writer paints her characters with light, almost unfinished strokes, more concerned with evoking a feeling than completing a portrait. The story of Carmolina BellaCasa, a third-generation Italian/American child, unfolds as a series of overlapping layers in which past, present, and future interweave in a complex temporal dimension that, disregarding linearity, creates a mythical time. Yet in this mythical time the author inscribes the lives of Carmolina and her family with the scrupulous precision of a realist writer. The eight parts into which the book is divided, including a prelude and an epilogue, fit together like the pieces of a puzzle that keeps undoing itself.[19] The opening words of the first section, "This is my mother," which appear set apart from the rest of the text under the title "Prelude" (1), stand almost as a subtitle, suggesting that the writing that follows is itself the "mother," the locus of creativity that brings the past, through memory, back to life, incorporating it in a continuum in which past, present, and future are inseparable. The clash of tenses soothes the sorrow that accompanies loss, and the unobtrusive authorial voice takes everything in, returning all the memories to the reader as a feast of voices, blending them into one harmonious song. The prelude thus opens with the vision of the unborn, unconceived Carmolina observing her mother and father:

My mother's skin brushes strawberries, her skin will brush my father's, that night their skin will make me, but I know none of this. I am less than the strawberries, I am less than the carving my father is making with his hands, less than the brown intent of his eyes over wood, less. (2)

Yet this "less" than life represents an all-knowing voice that seeps through the walls of houses, through the consciousness of each character, seeing and knowing everything through the creative power of its imaginative storytelling.

While Tina De Rosa lacks literary foremothers, her character, Carmolina, finds sustenance in the voice of her grandmother. A vehicle of cultural transmission and a source of emotional nourishment, Grandma Doria provides Carmolina with the material out of which the author forges the book's poetry. As Bona puts it, Carmolina "uses her grandmother's memories of the homeland as the subjective topography for her own fertile imagination" ("Broken Images" 92). The domestic detail takes on a mystical aura as the storyteller's touch uncovers the spiritual in the most mundane objects and details. Thus Carmolina's reversed writing on a bakery bag suggests her "access to literary creativity in the midst of everyday reality" ("Broken Images" 98).[20] Indeed, it is this "everyday reality" that provides the poetic subject matter of the book. In her essay, "Career Choices Come From Listening to the Heart," De Rosa writes:

> In our cold water flat, my father, who was a policeman, constantly played classical music, and operas. My grandmother, an immigrant from Bosca Royale [sic] near Naples, sang all the time. She sang while she cooked, while she cleaned, while she made the beds. I listened to their music. I could see that the lives they were living were simple, ordinary lives, lives that no one would ever notice, but that there was a beauty there that must be understood in the eyes of God. Even as a child, I knew this. Even as a child, I listened to them, watched them, and knew that they were extraordinarily beautiful, and temporary. (9)

De Rosa's pantheistic vision endows everything it comes across with life. The rugs that hung out of the houses resembled "great tongues" that "dry in the sun," that "panted out of the clutter of the tight rooms into the sunshine above the head of the horse who watched the children" (*Paper Fish* 34). In the description of the first encounter between Carmolina's parents, Sarah and Marco, which takes place in Sarah's parents' restaurant where she works as a waitress, a spiritual aura equally envelopes Sarah *and* the pots in the kitchen: as "the sunlight through the windows banged the pots hard and metallic, the silver light bounced off them and into her eyes" (4). The kitchen glows with the light of Sarah and Marco's newly born love, and the reader is transported into a universe in which the ecstasy of love is a miracle that happens inside the small restaurant, which "filled with light," to the delight of the children looking upon the scene and also to the delight of God (5).

The unorthodox religiosity of the book has its origin in Grandmother Doria, who is variously associated with God in the novel. The spiritual aura that pervades the narrative draws upon Doria's Southern Italian roots and the distinct brand of Catholicism practiced in Southern Italy. Blending folklore and Christian beliefs, Doria manufactures tales to explain the world to Carmolina, to teach her about sorrow and joy, life and death:

> There is a mountain in Italy filled with candles. . . . Each person has his own candle. When he is born the candle is lit; when the candle goes out, he dies. You can see this mountain, Carmolina, only in your dreams, but God will not let you see your own candle, even in a dream. If there is a mistake, and you see your own candle, you will die. This is how people die in their sleep. (24)

Doria's God is not infallible. The story of the mountain of candles, like all of Doria's fables, draws upon a mythology rooted in the storytelling of peasants who, while timorous of God and intimidated into subjection by a Church complicitous with the landlords, were undaunted in their transformation of Christian dogmas. In her travel memoir *No Pictures in My Grave: A Spiritual Journey in Sicily* (1992), Susan Caperna Lloyd documents the blending of Christian and pre-Christian elements in the Easter procession, a ritual central to Catholicism. Searching for the matriarchal roots of the procession in Trapani, Sicily—which she believes can be traced to the cult of Demeter and Persephone—the author paints a portrait of a popular and subversive Catholicism that, while seemingly bowing down to the Church, maintains its own integrity and a distinctly antiauthoritarian quality. It is this peculiar kind of Catholicism that one recognizes in the pages of De Rosa's book. In his discussion of part VI of the novel, Gardaphé points out that Grandma Doria "is carried on a chair up to Carmolina's room in a scene that recreates the traditional procession of the Madonna" to see her granddaughter dressed as a bride:

> In Italian tradition, the daughter (and quite often the son) does not leave home until she is married. Marriage is the ritual through which a young woman establishes her independence from her family. However, it also means shifting from an identification with family to

an identification with a male who then becomes her new patriarch. De Rosa's presentation of this scene signifies a defiance of the Italian tradition. Carmolina achieves her adult identity, not by attaching herself to a man, but by taking it from her grandmother who acknowledges it through the blessing she gives her granddaughter.

> In preparation for the visit Grandma Doria dons her blue dress. . . . Blue is the color traditionally associated with the Madonna, and it is fitting that the blue-eyed matriarch of the BellaCasa family wears it as she is carried up to see her granddaughter. (*Italian Signs* 137)

This humanizing of religion—a recognition of the divine in the human—which, after all, is intrinsic to the origins of Christian theology, is creatively incorporated into the domestic rituals of the BellaCasa family.[21] The appreciation for the small objects of creation that prevails in Grandma Doria's fables and throughout the narrative draws upon a Catholicism linked to the people and to the earth, reminiscent of Franciscan mysticism and its rejection of the authoritarian practices of the Church. The poetry of the book lies in its capacity to uncover, through language, the sacred in the mundane; this capacity is a gift that Carmolina receives from her grandmother. While "breaking the red peppers" for the sausages that will make Carmolina laugh as she eats them, Doria is simultaneously "making the world" for her granddaughter (15). Her "shabby old fingers" perform miracles (15). It is significant that the working title of *Paper Fish* was "Saintmakers": to De Rosa, the faces of her family members and "the tiny, ordinary lives they had led," are indeed "holy, and of great value" ("Career Choices" 9).[22]

Asked by Gardaphé about the title of her book, De Rosa said that she had chosen it because "the people in the book were as beautiful and as fragile as a Japanese kite" ("Interview" 23). But the fish carries other associations as well.[23] A few pages into the book, the fish emerges through the nauseating "smell of dead fish burning"—an odor unbearable to Sarah, who is pregnant with Carmolina, and screens herself with her hand from the smell while "the smoke rested outside the window like a serpent; it stared out of its white eyes" (10). Throughout the book, death and birth intertwine in the fish imagery, replete with analogous associations in Christian symbolism, in which the fish stands for Jesus. Water imagery is endowed with similarly contradictory associations. In the opening pages, the first encounter between Marco and Sarah is described as a falling "into the sea":

> He fell beneath the surface of the sea. He floated into the blue water, his head showing like a rose that has a face, like a silent animal filled

with anguish, filled with joy, and his heart, his life, was liquid, fluid like a fine fish, and he fell far beneath the sea. He was a marionette without strings, the sea was his string, his ribbon, holding him gently. His life dallied below him, below the water, his life was magnificent and his smile was small, above the liquid line of the sea. He was a doll, floating, with a marvelous secret just under the water. (10–11)

The fluidity of the language in this passage exemplifies De Rosa's style: her prose is dense, sensual, musical, and evocative of surrealistic images and sounds. The ambivalence of the fish (both beautiful and revolting, delicate and offensive) and the water (nurturing and threatening, liberating and suffocating) establish from the very beginning a clash of imageries and themes which is sustained throughout the novel, consistent with its function as both celebratory song and dirge.

Accordingly, Carmolina's beautiful sister Doriana is afflicted by a mysterious illness: she is a "swan, a black swan that flew into the incorrect night, followed the wrong moon," leaving her family "with glass eyes" (2). "Broken" early in her life, Doriana is the child so beautiful that she "frightened" her own mother (2). She represents the unknown, the mystery that the author never tries to solve, but only contemplates in awe, resigned to the fact that "It is all leaves, leaves falling out of a tree, with no hands to catch them" (2). Doriana's origin remains a mystery even to Grandmother Doria, although she is the one who weaves the tale that makes the unfathomable accessible, describing Doriana as "lost in the forest":

In the forest the birds are. Ah, such beautiful birds. White birds. Blue and pink. Doriana she go into the forest to look at the birds. The birds they sing in the trees, they sing, they turn into leaves. Doriana she have a key to the forest. It a secret. Only Doriana know where she keep the key. One day Doriana go into the forest. She forget the key. She get lost in the forest. She get scared. Her face it turn hot like a little peach and she scream and try to get out of the forest. . . . She try to come home. From the forest. She no find her way. (100)

De Rosa's exquisite language turns "broken" English into poetry. *Paper Fish* thus confers literary dignity upon the speech of those first-generation immigrants who struggled to express themselves in a language that often felt hostile and unconquerable. Writers such as Diana Cavallo and Maria Mazziotti Gillan have articulated the linguistic tribulations of immigrants. The speaker of Gillan's "Public School No. 18/Paterson, New Jersey," contrasts her "words smooth" in her "mouth" "at home," where she "chatter[s]" and is "proud," to her silence in school, where she "grope[s] for the right English/word," fearing "the Italian word/will sprout from...[her] mouth like a rose" (12). The protagonist of Cavallo's *A Bridge of Leaves* describes his grandmother "stammering the brittle sounds of a new tongue that flushed waves of Mediterranean homesickness through her with each rough syllable" (14). Legitimizing orality—and *Paper Fish* is indeed a "speakerly" text, with its own distinct accents[24]—the novel stands as a tribute to the unrecorded beauty and poetry of the voices of women immigrants, exemplified by Grandmother Doria.[25]

Like Grandma Doria, Doriana is instrumental in what Fred Gardaphè calls Carmolina's "lyrical self-awakening" (*Italian Signs* 131). Doriana's consciousness represents a hidden self to which the narrative longs to gain access, though her direct perspective emerges only briefly. Throughout the novel Doriana and Carmolina mirror each other. From the very first encounter between the baby Carmolina and the "small person" Doriana, they recognize a mysterious sameness as they look into "each other's eyes" (*Paper Fish* 11).[26] Frightened after overhearing her family discuss the possibility of institutionalizing Doriana, Carmolina runs away and is swallowed by the streets of Chicago. Thus Carmolina replicates her sister's dislocation: she also cannot find her way home.[27] De Rosa plunges the reader into the mental and emotional universe of the young girl and, in doing so, endows the grim urban landscape with fantastic traits and a poetic aura.[28] "Streetlamps are blue eyes, beating. . . . The sky is black fabric. The devil will roll it away. . . . A dog barks. It is no one's dog. It is the devil's dog. It will swallow you and you will live in the devil's belly" (92). Carmolina wanders for three days through this frightening world which "someone turned . . . upside down," having "nowhere to go" (92). Her journey and subsequent illness bring all the conflicts of the novel into focus. If Doriana cannot heal, Carmolina will recover from her illness to develop an identity outside the symbiotic relationship with her sister. Unlike Doriana, Carmolina finds the "key" to exploring the forest. After three days, in a symbolic resurrection, she comes back "home"—both to the home of the past and to a new home that she will construct for herself. She ominously tells her father, "When I grow up . . . I'm going to go away forever" (107). Analyzing the final scene, in which Carmolina, as a young woman, faces her own mirror image, Bona argues;

> The fact that Carmolina's own face is reflected in the mirror (without the shadow of Doriana or the reflection of her grandmother, who had stood next to her) reinforces Carmolina's acceptance of death and her role as a young, ethnic, American woman who will keep the fire inside of her, however difficult and demanding that may be for her. ("Broken Images" 103)

While both Doriana and Carmolina represent sacrificial, Christ-like figures, Grandma Doria's symbolic system empowers Carmolina to save herself.

Doriana's instability reflects the dislocation of the Italian family in America: "She seemed always to be moving towards another place, different from this" ("Broken Images" 13). Linking the displacement of immigration and mental illness, Bona argues that, like other Italian/American women writers, De Rosa "uses the topic of illness both as a realistic comment on the prevalence of sickness in underprivileged communities and as a metaphor for the immigrant experience of living in a world that does not readily welcome outsiders" (94).[29] Indeed, Grandma Doria employs the dichotomy of home and forest to explain to Carmolina both Doriana's beauty and her illness:

> "Where is the forest, Grandma?"
> "Behind her eyes," Grandma whispered. She turned to Carmolina. "Doriana, she have a beautiful face, no?"
> "Yes, Grandma."
> "Her face, why you think it so beautiful?"
> Something squeezed tight inside Carmolina. It was made of glass; it could break.
> "I don't know, Grandma. Why?"
> "Her face, she so beautiful," Grandma swiped at the tears, she was angry at them, "because Doriana fight so hard to come home. She look out her eyes every day and try to come home. When you fight to come home, you beautiful." (100)

Grandma Doria holds "the city" responsible for the illness that consumes Doriana. The city is "like a spider sucking the blood of the wonderful child," and "the child bled out her brains, her smiles, her own words into the empty grey light of the city and there was nothing to feed her" (64). "[L]ike a giant" (40), the city destroys the little family; its buildings are described as "bones crushing against little Doriana" (64). Through the use of body imagery, De Rosa represents the urban monster as driven by a deliberate and ineluctable force, greedily devouring the fragile Doriana, reducing the family to "little pieces" (63). If the city crushes the immigrants like a giant, De Rosa defies its destructive power and puts back together the little pieces through the redemptive force of her vision and her language.

*

Paper Fish depicts a world few readers have encountered before in fiction or in the stereotypical film versions of Italian/American lives.

Chicago's Little Italy constitutes the setting in which Carmolina witnesses the disintegration of her ethnicity. In De Rosa's *bildungsroman*, Carmolina's growth is juxtaposed to the vanishing of the culture that nourishes her.[30] Berrywood Street disappears "as though it were a picture someone had snapped away":

> The city said the Italian ghetto should go, and before the people could drop their forks next to their plates and say, pardon me?, the streets were cleared.
>
> The houses of the families with their tongues of rugs sticking out were smashed down, the houses filled with soup pots and quick anger, filled with forks and knives and recipes written in the heads of the women, were struck in their sides with the ball of the wrecking crane and the knives and bedclothes and plaster spilled out. (136)[31]

The demolition of the Italian ghetto resembles a carnage, and *Paper Fish* becomes the means by which the author attempts to rescue the memory of what is inexorably gone. The choral narrative in this passage, as elsewhere in the book, takes on the characteristics that Janet Zandy identifies as typical of working-class literature:

> [A]lthough it relies heavily on autobiography as a genre, its subject is rarely isolated or romanticized individualism. Rather, its *raison d'être* is to recall the fragile filaments and necessary bonds of human relationships, as well as to critique those economic and societal forces that blunt or block human development. (*Women's Studies Quarterly* 5)

While De Rosa painstakingly recovers a history that otherwise would be lost, the nostalgia that pervades *Paper Fish* never becomes a pathetic longing for the stereotypical tokens of a stultified, one-dimensional Italian/American culture.[32] The imaginative and deeply personal story of Carmolina remains rooted in the collective history of Italian immigrants in Chicago, though, as Zandy writes, "Liberating this kind of [working-class] memory involves the reconstruction of a set of relationships, not the exactitude of specific events" (*Liberating Memory* 3). De Rosa's book stands as an elegiac reminiscence drenched with the sounds, colors, and smells of the quotidian life of an Italian/American family living in a cold-water flat on the West Side of Chicago in the late 1940s and 1950s.

While the first Italians had arrived in Chicago a century earlier, in the 1850s, from Northern Italy, the largest migration of Southern Italians occurred between 1880 and 1914 (Candeloro 229). The Italian population in Chicago, which never reached the numerical proportions of New York's Italian community, settled in several ethnically diverse Little Italys rather than in one large all-Italian neighborhood. If in the first half of this century Italians were not fully accepted or integrated members of the community, with the rise of Mussolini to power and the outbreak of World War II, the situation only worsened for Italians in the United States—regardless of their political beliefs. *Paper Fish,* set in the aftermath of the war, illustrates the sometimes subtle prejudice suffered by Italian Americans. Introducing Marco at the very opening of "The Memory," the narrative describes Carmolina's father as "a young man tall and thin, still not comfortable in his policeman's uniform. . . . He was, in the eyes of the department, still a rookie, Italian and stupid. He was treated politely, but with little respect" (4). Rather than indicating trouble-free assimilation into the mainstream, Marco's position in the low ranks of the police department may represent the attempt of local authorities to send ethnic policemen back into their own neighborhoods to deal with the "locals." But it is when Carmolina is ostracized for being a "dago kid" (77) that one recognizes De Rosa's awareness of cultural tensions and feels the full impact of her condemnation of bigotry. Imprinting itself indelibly on the reader's memory, De Rosa's portrayal of the Italian/American working-class world establishes a powerful critique of prejudice. *Paper Fish* forces one to come to terms with an American culture that simultaneously celebrated Shirley Temple and Dorothy of *The Wizard of Oz* and ghettoized "dago kids" such as Carmolina, as well as other racial and ethnic minorities.

In an essay on ethnicity and class, Rudolph Vecoli rejects the classification of Italians as "white (or persons of non-color) sans ethnicity," and argues that such a classification overlooks the "significance of class in human society" (296). Vecoli thus addresses the overly simplistic dichotomy between European and non-European cultures, a dichotomy that oftentimes ignores specific historical and social circumstances—in this case, issues of emigration and assimilation. The history of Italians in the United States is a multifaceted one: They came from different regions, speaking a "jigsaw puzzle of . . . Italian dialects" (*Paper Fish* 40), driven by dreams of success, and, for the most part, by extreme poverty. A vast number of immigrants, specifically in Chicago, were involved in labor activities, and contributed in a significant manner to the history of the American working class (Vecoli 299–300).[33] Mocking and rejecting facile racial, ethnic, and class labels, the poet Rose Romano writes: "I'm not/ oppressed enough. I/haven't been conquered/enough. I'm not Olive/ enough. I may as well be Italian." Romano's cutting verse expresses her outrage at an American culture that at best infantilizes Italians, at worst criminalizes them. In "Mutt Bitch," Romano proceeds "to take inventory" of herself:

> I'm a woman.
> I'm a contessa
> on my father's side,
> contadina on my
> mother's side.
> I've got a
> high school equivalency diploma
> and an associate's degree
> in liberal arts.
> I'm a skilled blue collar worker.
> I'm a published poet.
> I've got a Brooklyn accent
> with Italian gestures.
> I'm a dyke.
> I'm a single working mother.
> All this stuff doesn't add up to
> just
> one
> person.
>
> Fuck it. (*Vendetta* 38–9)

Through her seemingly anachronistic juxtaposition of titles indicating radically different levels of social status, Romano rejects a simple definition of social identity and class. At the same time, she claims validation for her personhood, a personhood that explodes the strict boundaries of identity implied by the notion of a singular self. In "An Italian-American Woman Speaks Out," De Rosa voices her exasperation at the sense of displacement that she experiences as the "educated" granddaughter of Italian immigrants, "an educated lady who came from the streets of a ghetto, who didn't blink twice at fistfights, or horse shit—or the word" (38). In *Miss Giardino* (1978), Italian/American novelist Dorothy Bryant explores an analogous sense of displacement through her character Anna Giardino, another "educated lady" from the ghetto. These writers have poured into their works an awareness of the conditions of displacement and cultural marginalization that afflict Italian/American writers, particularly those of working-class origin.

If the social and cultural status of a group is linked with that group's capacity to produce a literature that will tell its stories and record its past, then the status of Italian/American literature bespeaks the tangled history of Italian Americans. Because of their problematic status as "white ethnics," Italian/American writers do not easily fit within the paradigm of "minority writers," although they have not gained acceptance into the mainstream as the members of northern European groups have.[34] Assimilation in itself—and the ethnic self-silencing that it entails—poses questions concerning the repression of a group's cultural identity.[35] Victims, along with other Southern and Eastern European groups, of the harshest forms of prejudice and persecution in the early stages of their immigration, Italian Americans quickly learned that "whiteness" was the key to assimilation in Anglo-America.[36] More importantly, they learned that by suppressing their ethnic identity they could "pass"—especially if they were women, who could relinquish their surnames in marriage.[37] *Paper Fish* rejects the notion of a monolithic "white ethnicity" and brings to the forefront the marginalization suffered by a particular group of "white ethnics."[38]

Popular cultural representations of Italians in Chicago have focused on the mafia wars and on such notorious figures as Al Capone. These figures, like Mario Puzo's and Francis Ford Coppola's Don Vito Corleone, appeal to the fantastic vision of Italians that mainstream America has cultivated—and that critics have not, for the most part, scrutinized.[39] After all, the gangster is an American hero: he is defiant of the law, a warped descendant of the American colonist, with whom he shares the fearless determination to explore and expand his territory.[40] De Rosa defies stereotypical representations of Chicago Italian Americans as mobsters by portraying the very neighborhood ruled by Al Capone in a completely different light: "It was Al Capone's neighborhood," she recalls, "we were always in fear of that. . . . We were so denigrated. People were afraid to come to my neighborhood." Thus she turned to writing to show what was "beautiful" about the world she grew up in: "I wanted to tell people that they couldn't trash us like that."[41] The Italian Americans in Chicago, De Rosa demonstrates, have other stories to tell, like the lyrical and moving story of Carmolina and her family.[42]

Excluded from both the literary mainstream and the margin, Italian Americans occupy an ambivalent position, complicated by their connection with a humanistic tradition to which the majority of Italian immigrants had no access.[43] Nor could they count on an already established literary tradition to articulate their issues and conflicts, or legitimize their cultural identity.[44] Yet Italian/American literature exists and has flourished. Scholars such as Olga Peragallo, Rose Basile Green, Fred Gardaphé, Anthony Tamburri, and Mary Jo Bona have documented the existence of this tradition. Literary journals such as *VIA: Voices in Italian Americana, Italian Americana,*

MELUS and *Differentia* have created a forum for Italian/American writers and critics.[45] *la bella figura,* a journal that Rose Romano published and edited from 1988 to 1992, and malafemmina press, Romano's valorous publishing enterprise, published exclusively writings devoted to Italian/American women, while Guernica, a Canadian publishing house, consistently brings forth the works of Italian/Canadian and Italian/American writers. But while forums do exist, barriers still prevent most Italian/American writers from achieving recognition, both in the academic world and in the publishing market at large.[46] An Italian/American classic such as *Christ in Concrete,* after a brief moment of notoriety, suffered from years neglect, remaining, like di Donato's other works, out of print for years.[47] On the other hand, Mario Puzo's *The Godfather,* mistaken by mainstream America as the authoritative text on Italian Americans, became a best-seller and the basis for three enormously popular films. Other mafia best-sellers have included Nicholas Pileggi's *Wiseguys,* followed more recently by *Casino,* which Martin Scorsese adapted, like *Wiseguys* (retitled *Goodfellas*), into yet another motion picture on the mob.[48] Yet the literature produced by such writers as Gilbert Sorrentino, John Fante, Felix Stefanile, Joseph Tusiani, and Anthony Valerio disputes such reductive and bigoted views of Italian Americans. And when an author like Giose Rimanelli turns to the mafia as a subject matter, it is from quite a different angle, and the result can be a daring literary experiment such as *Benedetta in Guysterland: A Liquid Novel.*

If Italian/American male authors have been struggling to achieve recognition, the problems of invisibility and legitimization are magnified for Italian/American women. What Barolini has called "The Historical and Social Context of Silence" (*Dream Book* 3) lies at the core of the literary production of many Italian/American women.[49] Writers such as De Rosa have written with little knowledge of the community of writers and readers at work forging literary spaces for the representation of Italian Americans.[50] From Frances Winwar, born Francesca Vinciguerra, who anglicized her name at her publisher's request, to Rita Ciresi and Agnes Rossi, two contemporary writers who inscribe an internalized sense of cultural invisibility in narratives that both expose and suppress ethnic identity, Italian/American women have for the last fifty years waged a war against silence, a war fought through written words that rarely have reached a large audience.[51] It is only when voices are heard, and when other voices reply, that a literary tradition can be formed.[52]

Paper Fish was published a year after *Umbertina* (1979), a female immigration narrative by Helen Barolini.[53] With the combative purpose of demonstrating the existence of an Italian/American female literary tradition, in *The Dream Book* (1985) Barolini gathered under the same umbrella authors as diverse as Sister Blandina Segale, Frances Winwar, Antonia Pola, Mary Gordon, Dorothy Bryant, Sandra Mortola Gilbert, Leslie Scalapino, Louise DeSalvo, Anna Monardo, Daniela Gioseffi, Diane di Prima, and Tina De Rosa. In an interview, Barolini lamented the general exclusion of Italian/American women authors and described The Dream Book as her "literary manifesto," through which she wanted to ensure that "some acknowledgment be given to Italian American women writers, that their names be part of the literary record, that redress be made for having neglected and overlooked a whole segment of writers" (Bonomo Ahearn 47).[54]

Before Barolini, other authors had written about Italian America between the 1940s and the 1960s in narratives filtered through the lens of their gender: Mari Tomasi in *Deep Grow the Roots* (1940) and *Like Lesser Gods* (1949), Julia Savarese in *The Weak and the Strong* (1952), Antonia Pola in *Who Can Buy the Stars?* (1957), Diana Cavallo in *A Bridge of Leaves* (1961), Octavia Waldo in *A Cup of the Sun* (1961), and Marion Benasutti in *No Steady Job for Papa* (1966).[55] All of these works, with the exception of *Like Lesser Gods,* are currently out of print. The fact that many of these authors told in their books of the struggle for survival of Italian/American workers—be it in the city, as in *The Weak and the Strong,* or in the granite mines of Vermont, as in Tomasi's fiction—suggests the extent to which the combination of working-class consciousness and ethnicity in literature has not seemed palatable to mainstream publishing. The fact that many of these authors never published a second novel signals the fragility of a tradition that lacked a community to sustain and nurture its growth.[56] To this day, the most established and prolific Italian/American woman writer (in terms of publications) is Helen Barolini who, while well known by scholars of Italian/American culture and some scholars of ethnic literature, remains virtually unknown in most academic circles.[57] Authors such as Dorothy Bryant, Rose Romano, Mary Russo Demetrick, and Maria Famà have resorted to self-publishing, which helps to keep one's books in print; but even this becomes an increasingly difficult task in the corporate publishing world.[58]

While *Umbertina* has by no means reached the popularity or critical recognition of such feminist novels as Sandra Cisneros's *The House on Mango Street* (1984), Alice Walker's *The Color Purple* (1982), Bharati Mukherjee's *Jasmine* (1989), or Amy Tan's *The Joy Luck Club* (1991), Barolini's work has received at least some critical recognition.[59] *Paper Fish,* on the other hand, was swallowed by a void even darker than that from which it emerged.[60] This lyrical novel can indeed be described, in the author's own words, as "a song from the ghetto":[61] for her, literary isolation replaced urban marginalization. De Rosa's "individual talent" surfaced without a tradition to support and facilitate its emergence. The author's claim that her novel has more in common with a book like Anne Frank's *The Diary of a Young Girl* (1952) than with an Italian/ American tradition sheds light on the writer's fear of the consequences of racial hatred and clarifies the multiple links that *Paper Fish* establishes with autobiography, *bildungsroman,* and the literatures of various ethnic and racial minorities. It also signals the distance between the author and other Italian/American writers created by the lack of any recognized tradition. If one thinks of the importance of Zora Neale Hurston for Alice Walker and other African/American women writers, one can begin to appreciate the courage necessary to write in isolation. Walker claims that she realized her "need" for Zora Neale Hurston even before she knew Hurston's work "existed" (*In Search* 83). Indeed, Hurston's relatively recent canonization has consolidated the sense of a tradition for African/American women authors.

Writing about the marginalization she experienced as an Asian/ American woman, Amy Ling remarks that she found solace in reading such texts as Helen Barolini's *The Dream Book,* Alice Walker's *In Search of Our Mothers' Gardens,* Audre Lorde's prose and poetry, and Virginia Woolf's *A Room of One's Own.* Arguing that "Italian American women have suffered similar oppression from the men of their own culture, a similar sense of alienation from the dominant Anglo-American tradition, and the same affinity with black women writers that Chinese American women feel," Ling writes that she "fear[s] that the Italian American woman's perspective may have been overlooked, again" (740). Ling's observation seems accurate when we think that *The Dream Book* is currently out of print, and that *Umbertina* is available only in the few surviving copies of a small print edition, making Barolini's efforts, if not vain, then largely unrecognized by the mainstream press, academe, and the general reading audience. With its commitment to publishing and reprinting women's, and especially working-class, literature, The Feminist Press has opened an important door for *Paper Fish* and for Italian/American women's literature in general.[62]

In a compelling essay on ethnic discrimination, Rose Romano denounces the silencing of Italian/American voices and asserts that "censorship doesn't always have to be censorship in order to be effective" ("Where is Nella Sorellanza?" 152). This reprint of *Paper Fish* puts an end to fifteen years of "effective" censorship and claims a place in literary history for Italian/American women. Yet such a victory does not come easy. Explaining that "the immigrant genre presents readers with the repeated coalescence of wonder and shame in relation to one's place in a given culture," Frances Bartkowski argues:

> What speaks to the victory of wonder over shame is the ethno-autobiographical text itself as a document of having claimed a place, culturally speaking. Yet the narratives of this coming-into-place are replete with the brutal lessons of shame, even as they recount the exultation of instants of shamelessness. (88)

The history of *Paper Fish* is the history of a journey towards cultural recognition. Recognizing the shame that lies at the core of her writing, De Rosa triumphantly affirms the power of "wonder" to transcend shame. "Though I grew up in what the world would call a ghetto," she writes, "I was surrounded constantly by beauty" ("Career Choices" 9). Finally claiming a place in the history of American literature, *Paper Fish* overcomes the isolation of both urban and literary ghettoes, and transforms "the disempowered experience of an unshared tongue" (Bartkowski 86) into a poetic feast of words that enables the tradition personified by Grandma Doria to sing.

ACKNOWLEDGMENTS: Thanks to Tina De Rosa for generously sharing information that was crucial to the writing of this afterword. My gratitude to the Feminist Press, especially Florence Howe and Kim Mallett, for believing in Tina's book, and in my own work. A special thank you to my copyeditor, Jean Casella. I want to express my debt to Fred Gardaphé for his helpful insights and for his unfailing support of Italian/American writers and critics. Josh Fausty and Emily Giunta Cutts helped in more ways than I can say. This essay is dedicated to the women in my family—*per le donne della mia famiglia*.

E. G.

NOTES

1. On the use of the slash (solidus) rather than the hyphen in the adjective form of Italian/American and other similar terms see Tamburri, *To Hyphenate or Not To Hyphenate*. Tamburri argues that the slash avoids privileging one of the two cultures and signals a relationship in which Italian and American engage in a dialectical exchange.

2. Mangione's statement, which appeared on the back cover of the book, reads: "*Paper Fish* is an outstanding literary event, a first novel that breaks through the barriers of conventional fiction to achieve a dazzling union of narrative and poetry. . . . Hers is a delightfully fresh voice, filled with ancient wisdom which is new and probing, miraculously translating the most ineffable nuances of human existence in a language that is consistently beautiful and vital."

3. Gardaphé, who was the first critic to write about *Paper Fish*, thus sums up the particular significance that this book held for him: "Through writers like DeRosa, I learned that Italian-American culture was multi-dimensional and could never be simply categorized" ("Breaking and Entering" 12).

4. *A roman à clef, HERmione* was written in 1927, but was published posthumously, not only because of its overt autobiographical elements, but because of the centrality of lesbian love in the novel. See Friedman and Du Plessis. The late recognition of *Their Eyes Were Watching God* has received much critical attention. See Mary Helen Washington's foreword (vii–xiv) and Henry Louis Gates Jr.'s afterword to the book (185–95), and Alice Walker's "Zora Neale Hurston: A Cautionary Tale and a Partisan View" and "Looking for Zora" (*In Search* 83–116).

5. In "An Italian-American Woman Speaks Out," De Rosa writes that the "ghost of one's grandmother" is "as real as the food on one's plate" (38).

6. Ramholz received a grant from the National Endowment for the Arts to publish *Paper Fish.*

7. The biographical information is based primarily on Gardaphé's interview with the author and on my conversations with her.

8. This multiethnicity is reflected in *Paper Fish;* a Mexican-American family lives on the floor below the BellaCasa family (*Paper Fish* 10).

9. De Rosa's self-identification as an Italian American is testified to by her essay "An Italian-American Woman Speaks Out" (1980) and by her other published works: *Paper Fish*, a biography of Bishop Scalabrini (1987), and a handful of essays she wrote in the 1980.

10. "BellaCasa," the last name of the family in *Paper Fish*, means "beautiful home."

11. The struggle between the family and the individual in Italian/American culture has

been examined in various disciplines. See Boyd et al.; De Rosa, "An Italian-American Woman Speaks Out"; Barolini's introduction to *The Dream Book;* and Bona's dissertation, "Claiming a Tradition."

12. See Werner Sollors's classic distinction in *Beyond Ethnicity.* Although this distinction has undergone much criticism (see Brenkman 98–99), it nevertheless maintains a broad epistemological validity.

13. Grandmother Doria's storytelling enables Carmolina to "make her inevitable journey away from the family and into her self," Gardaphé argues. "To help her reach this goal, Grandma Doria teaches Carmolina to turn memory into strength" (*Italian Signs* 133). In "Feminism, Family and Community," Jeanne Bethke Elshtain sheds light on the creative and radical potential within the family which, she contends, stands in opposition to "the 'needs' of capitalism" and the "market images of human beings" created by capitalism (260). The collection of essays edited by Penny A. Weiss and Marilyn Friedman in which Elshtain's essay appears, *Feminism and Community,* provides a multiplicity of perspectives on the function of various kinds of communities in shaping women's self-definition. The question of whether or not ethnicity, race, and nation define one's identity is one De Rosa indirectly takes up in *Paper Fish,* a book that emphasizes the instrumental role of ethnic heritage in forging the author's artistic talent. In her poem "Ethnic Woman," Rose Romano rejects the view of "ethnicity" as something she "drag[s] out/of the closet to celebrate quaint holidays," and eloquently explains the connection between self and ethnicity: "I could write my life/ story with different shapes in/ various sizes in limitless patterns of/ pasta laid out to dry on a thick, white/ tablecloth on my bed." She asks her imaginary interlocutor, "Must I teach you/ to read?" Yet this is not an ethnicity that "define[s]" you, rather "you define it" (*Wop Factor* 57).

14. For studies of the historical and social conditions of Italian/American women see Boyd et al. and Gabaccia. In the opening poems of *Italian Women and Other Tragedies,* entitled "Italian Women," "My Birth," and "Daughters," Gianna Patriarca, an Italian/ Canadian writer, powerfully inscribes the experience of womanhood in the patriarchal Italian family.

15. Torgovnick, "On Being White, Female and Born in Bensonhurst" (*Crossing* 1–18). Many Italian/American writers, male and female, have lamented the lack of support within the family for fledgling writers. See Ciresi, "Paradise Below the Stairs." The literate children and descendants of Italian/American immigrants, thrown into a world in which their culture does not receive recognition, have often camouflaged their ethnic and class identities. Writers like Rose Romano, Maria Mazziotti Gillan, and Tina De Rosa reclaim, through their writings, those very identities. In "Reclaiming Our Working Class Identities: Teaching Working Class Studies in a Blue-Collar Community," Linda Strom writes of the painful gap that her "education" had created between her and her family, though her family had encouraged her in her pursuits (131–32).

16. On working-class literature see "Working-Class Studies," an issue of *Women's Studies Quarterly* edited by Janet Zandy, and *Calling Home* and *Liberating Memory,* also edited by Zandy.

17. Information on the composition of *Paper Fish* was given to me by De Rosa during telephone conversations that took place in 1995.

18. Interestingly enough, H. D.'s experimental fiction is represented primarily by a number of *roman à clef,* a category that can be used to describe *Paper Fish. HERmione,* written in 1927, was published in 1981, a year after the publication of *Paper Fish,* while other novels by H.D were published later: *Bid Me To Live* in 1983, *The Gift* in 1984, and *Asphodel* in 1992. *The Gift* is especially akin to the child's perspective of *Paper Fish,* with its focus on the memories of Hilda Doolittle's childhood in her hometown of Bethlehem, Pennsylvania.

19. On the structure of *Paper Fish* see Bona, "Broken Images" and Gardaphé, "The Later Mythic Mode" in *Italian Signs* (131–41). For a discussion of time in *Paper Fish* see Bensoussan.

20. Other authors endow the quotidian and monotonous domestic activities with a creative function. In the poetry of Sandra M. Gilbert, domestic chores become poetical subject matter, as in "Doing Laundry" (Barolini, *Dream Book* 349). Helen, one of the two female protagonists of Louise DeSalvo's novel *Casting Off,* thinks of how "one could read the progress of her life in the spills of mysterious substances that now nearly obliterated her favorite recipes. . . . this dripping and this dribbling had been Helen's way of making history, and she had been reluctant to give it up in favor of the pristine page with no splotches and no spills. . . . Sometimes she wondered why she always remembered events in terms of the things that she had eaten" (28–30).

21. For a feminist analysis of Catholicism, and specifically the Marian cult, see Hamington. See also Torjesen. Martin Scorsese's *The Last Temptation of Christ* (based on the novel by Alikos Kazantzakis), a film that attempted to capture the paradox of the divine in the human (or vice versa), caused one of the most explosive controversies in film history due to the virulent responses of many Christian groups.

22. "Doriana's face was the ivory-white face of the Virgin Mary, praise God. Grandma Doria watched the sleeping face of the child on the pillow. The eyelids closed perfectly, like the lines in a saint's statue; the eyelids seemed carved by the hands of a saint-maker" (*Paper Fish* 63).

23. The sleeping Doriana, "Stuffed in under all the sheets and blankets," is compared to a "dead fish." The skin of Sarah's hand is described as "puckered and scaly like a fish flat and dead on a beach where the ocean tossed it away" (53).

24. According to Henry Louis Gates, Jr.'s definition, the "speakerly text" is "a text whose rhetorical strategy is designed to represent an oral literary tradition . . . . the narrative strategy signals attention to its own importance, an importance which would seem to be the privileging of oral speech and its inherent linguistic features" (181). See also Gardaphé, "From Oral Tradition to Written Word: Toward an Ethnographically Based Criticism" in Tamburri, Giordano and Gardaphé eds., 294-315.

25. On ethnic women's voices see Krause ed.

26. On the relationships between sisters see Foster ed.

27. *Alice's Adventures in Wonderland* and *The Wizard of Oz* come to mind as possible—though distant—literary antecedents, especially because of their combination of enchantment and darkness.

28. The stream of consciousness of De Rosa's prose and the crucial function of topography in the novel recalls the experiments and the representation of urban setting by modernist authors such as James Joyce, Virginia Woolf, and Jean Rhys. Sandra Cisneros's critically acclaimed novel *The House on Mango Street* (1984) places Esperanza Cordero, a girl growing up in the Latino section of Chicago, at the center of the narrative. A comparative study of *Paper Fish* and *The House on Mango Street*, including a reception study, might shed light both on ethnic self-representation and on the cultural construction of ethnicities in American culture.

29. "It is truly no secret that life for ethnic groups in America has been equated to a Dantean hell; that alongside the usual hardships of poverty and hunger come serious and debilitating mental illnesses that arise in America and cannot be cured there; that the family, however much loved and passionately honored by men, is often unrelentingly painful for women" (Bona, *Voices* 13).

30. For a discussion of *Paper Fish* as a *bildungsroman* see Bona, "Broken Images" and Gardaphé, "The Later Mythic Mode" in *Italian Signs* (131–41).

31. See Candeloro 244. Ironically, the neighborhood was destroyed to make room for the University of Illinois, where De Rosa would receive her M.A. in English and where she would begin to outline *Paper Fish*. To this day the few surviving residents blame the university for the destruction of the community and the uprooting of its members.

32. In 1987 the Academy Award for best film was given to such a misguided and misleading portrayal of Italian/American culture as *Moonstruck*. Despite their artistic value, Coppola's *The Godfather* and Scorsese's *Goodfellas*—possibly the most popular Italian/American films of the last twenty-five years—propose images of Italian Americans that perpetuate stereotypical views. See Sautman.

33. For an account of Italian/American working-class history see Vecoli.

34. Candeloro notes that the Italian Americans in Chicago, for example, have achieved better economic status, but they have not yet reached a much sought after "respect" (247–48).

35. See Rose Romano's controversial essay on her relationship to the lesbian community, "Where is Nella Sorellanza?" and her poem "This is Real" (*Wop Factor* 12–13).

36. The trial of the Italian anarchists Nicola Sacco and Bartolomeo Vanzetti, and the lynching of Italian Americans in New Orleans in 1891, represent two chapters in the history of Italian Americans in the United States. In "Dago Street," Rose Romano remembers, as if she had witnessed it, the 1891 lynching. Bona points out that the interweaving of past and present "allows Romano to reinforce the insidious persistence of ethnic prejudice in America" ("Learning to Speak Doubly" 165). Also see Nazzaro.

37. In a review essay of Romano's *The Wop Factor* (1994), Bona argues that "the poet who talks back . . . compels the reader to recognize the potential cultural genocide inherent

in...passing." She quotes Romano: "Most Italians escape by hiding,/don't teach the children Italian,/use Italian to tell the old stories,/and never complain./Now most Italians pass/and don't know it" (*Wop Factor* 22). Scholars such as Sandra M. Gilbert and Marianna De Marco Torgovnick have only recently begun using their Italian family names. Gilbert wrote to Helen Barolini: "I am really Sandra Mortola Gilbert...and my mother's name was Caruso, so I always feel oddly falsified with this Waspish-sounding American name, which I adopted as a 20-year old bride who had never considered the implications of her actions!" (*Dream Book* 22). Gilbert's Italian/American voice emerges, significantly, in her poetry, which she seems to consider as unrecognized, somewhat clandestine writing: "As for my poetry...I don't feel myself to be a tremendously established poet. In fact, I'm always interested when people even know that I write poetry" (Hongo 99). See Gilbert's book of poems, *The Summer Kitchen* (1984), and also "Piacere Conoscerla: On Being an Italian American," in Tamburri, Giordano and Gardaphé eds., 116–20. In *Crossing Ocean Parkway: Readings by an Italian American Daughter* (1994), Torgovnick considers her marriage to a Jewish man, which enabled her to "cross," as epitomizing the self-silencing of the *"paesani"* who "often sport last names that aren't Italian" (viii). For a discussion of white ethnicity see di Leonardo.

38. For a discussion of white ethnicity and race see Ignatiev.

39. In her poem "Mafioso," Sandra Mortola Gilbert questions mainstream views of Italian Americans: "Frank Costello eating spaghetti in a cell at San Quentin,/Lucky Luciano mixing up a mess of bullets and/calling for parmesan cheese,/Al Capone baking a sawed-off shotgun into a/huge lasagna—/are you my uncles, my/only uncles?" (Barolini, *Dream Book* 348).

40. "Turning to crime," argues Humbert Nelli, "was not a denial of the American way of life, but rather comprised an effort by common laborers who lacked skills to find 'success'" (quoted in Candeloro 241).

41. Telephone conversation with the author, 26 September 1995. Referring to Humbert Nelli's research, Candeloro points out that during the Capone era, "the members of the corrupt syndicates were *American*-born practitioners of the *American*-ethic of success" (241).

42. *Paper Fish* is the first novel about Italians in Chicago, although several sociological studies about Italians in Chicago exist. See Nelli, *Italians in Chicago* and *Role of the "Colonial" Press*. Candeloro's essay, "Chicago Italians: A Survey of the Ethnic Factor, 1850–1990," provides much information about the history and changing status of the Italians in Chicago.

43. See Lucia Chiavola Birnbaum in Tamburri, Giordano, and Gardaphé eds., 282–93.

44. In 1994 the *New York Times Book Review* published an article by Gay Talese entitled, "Where Are the Italian American Novelists?" See the responses of some Italian/American scholars and writers in *Italian Americana* to Talese's article (Gioia et al.).

45. Most scholarship on Italian/American literature has been published in these journals as well as in the proceedings of Conferences of the American Italian Historical Association. Gardaphé's book, *Italian Signs, American Streets,* is the first comprehensive study of Italian/American literature to be published in twenty years. See also the special issue of *VIA:*

Voices in Italian Americana, devoted to women writers, which I guest-edited.

46. On the questions of recognition and identity in a multicultural society see Gutman ed.

47. See Gardaphé's introduction to the 1993 reprint of *Christ in Concrete*, x–xviii.

48. Other Italian/American male writers who have achieved success, such as Don De Lillo, have for the most part avoided Italian/American subjects. On De Lillo as an Italian/American writer see Gardaphé, "Visibility or Invisibility."

49. For a discussion of the connections between gender and authorial emergence see Barolini's introduction to *The Dream Book*.

50. See Barolini, "Becoming a Literary Person." See also Bona's introduction to her dissertation, "Claiming a Tradition," and Giunta, "Blending 'Literary' Discourses."

51. See Louise DeSalvo's essay, "A Portrait of the *Puttana* as a Middle-Aged Woolf Scholar" (Barolini, *Dream Book* 93–99). On Frances Winwar see Barolini's introduction to *The Dream Book*, 6. For a discussion of the question of ethnic self-representation in Rossi, see Giunta, "Narratives of Loss" and "Reinventing the Authorial/Ethnic Space." On Ciresi see Fausty, "Masquerading Narratives" and his review of *Mother Rocket*. In DeSalvo's *Casting Off*, a novel published only in England and currently out of print, the characters are Italian/Irish/American working-class women, but their Italian/American identity emerges obliquely, expressing a position common among individuals of Italian and Irish ancestry. Because of the more socially accepted status of the Irish, in intermarriages the Italian element was often subsumed, even concealed. Such a conflicting position emerges powerfully in *Casting Off* and in the writings of Italian/Irish/American writers such as Agnes Rossi. (See my essay "Reinventing the Authorial/Ethnic Space.") Louise DeSalvo encodes the Italianness of her characters in their Irishness, though their Italian identity also emerges powerfully in other ways. Her novel thus explores questions of ethnic identity—and identification—on many different levels. For an analysis of ethnic invisibility, see Gardaphé, "Visibility and Invisibility" and "(In)visibility: Cultural Representation." See also Romano's autobiographical essay "Where is Nella Sorellanza?"

52. In an unpublished interview, referring to her response to reading Carole Maso's *Ghost Dance* (1986), De Rosa commented, "After calling for so long, I finally hear an echo" (Fausty and Giunta).

53. In 1978, Dorothy Calvetti Bryant published *Miss Giardino*, a novel that explores issues of gender, age, ethnicity, and class.

54. The question of an aesthetic value that would determine inclusion in, or exclusion from, the canon is inseparable from the social and cultural contexts in which these works were produced. Virginia Woolf's question comes to mind: "What conditions are necessary for the creation of works of art?" (*Room* 25).

55. In her dissertation, Mary Jo Bona traces the history of an Italian/American literary tradition from the 1940s through 1980. Mary Frances Pipino, a graduate student at the University of Cincinnati, is completing a dissertation on Italian/American women that also examines the development of an Italian/American female literary tradition.

56. Virtually all traces of some of these writers are seemingly lost, as in the case of

Antonia Pola, author of *Who Can Buy the Stars?* (1957), a book that gives "an account of an Italian immigrant woman which is forceful, unsentimentalized, and sharply different from the portraits of submissive women which seemed to be the standard for her time" (*Dream Book* 161). The book's exploration of issues of gender, class, age, and sexuality makes it a particularly intriguing text.

57. For a discussion of Barolini's career see Gardaphé's "Autobiography as Piecework" and my essay "Blending 'Literary' Discourses." For a study of the field, see my article "Crossing Critical Borders."

58. Hale Mary Press was "founded to commemorate all women who lost their ethnic, given names at Ellis Island and who were renamed 'Mary' in legal, immigration papers" (back cover of Demetrick and Famá, *Italian Notebook*).

59. For a discussion of *Umbertina* see Gardaphé, "The Later Mythic Mode," in *Italian Signs, American Streets* (123–31); Giunta, "Blending Literary Discourses"; and Tamburri, "Helen Barolini's Umbertina" and "Umbertina: The Italian/American Woman's Experience" in Tamburri, Giordano and Gardaphé eds. 357–73.

60. Mary Jo Bona argues that, "separated from their literary foremothers in Italy, Italian women in America have perceived themselves to be writing in a void, without support from early models or from contemporary writers similarly concerned to legitimate the connection between ethnicity and literary creation" ("Broken Images" 90). The relationship between Italian/American women and their Italian "foremothers" is a complex one. Who are such foremothers? Can Italian/American women writers claim a connection with other writers by virtue of their national origins? This is a topic that has not yet been explored in criticism.

61. During a telephone conversation with the author that took place in August 1995, she described *Paper Fish* as a "song from the ghetto," akin to Anne Frank's Diary.

62. In 1997 The Feminist press will reprint three works by another Italian/American woman, Dorothy Bryant: *Miss Giardino, The Confessions of Madame Psyche*, and *Ella Price's Journal*.

TINA DE ROSA:

A BIBLIOGRAPHY

"An Italian American Woman Speaks Out." *Attenzione* (May 1980): 38–39.

Bishop John Baptist Scalabrini, *Father to the Migrants*. Darien, CT: Insider Publications, 1987. An excerpt was published in *Fra Noi* (October 1987).

"Career Choices Come From Listening to the Heart." *Fra Noi* (October 1985): 9.

"My Father's Lesson." *Fra Noi* (September 1986): 15.

Paper Fish. Chicago: The Wine Press, 1980. Reprint. New York: The Feminist Press, 1996. An excerpt was published in *Rhino* in 1979.

An excerpt also appeared in *The Dream Book: An Anthology of Writings by Italian American Women*. Ed. Helen Barolini. New York: Shocken, 1985. 250–59.

"Psalm of the Eucharist." Eds. Tamburri, Anthony Julian, Paolo A. Giordano and Fred L. Gardaphé. *From the Margin: Writings in Italian Americana*. West Lafayette: Purdue University Press, 1991. 193–201.

"Silent Night, Homeless Night." *Fra Noi* (January 1986): 1, 8. A revised version appeared in *Volunteer News*, a publication of the Chicago Emergency Volunteer Organization, 2.2 (Fall 1987): 3–8.

WORKS CITED

Barolini, Helen. "Becoming a Literary Person Out of Context." *Massachusetts Review* 27.2 (1986): 262–74.

———. ed. *The Dream Book: An Anthology of Writings by Italian American Women*. 1985. New York: Shocken, 1987.

———. *Umbertina*. 1979. Salem, NH: Ayer, 1989.

Bartkowski, Frances. *Travelers, Immigrants, Inmates: Essays in Estrangement*. Minneapolis: University of Minnesota Press, 1995.

Benasutti, Marion. *No Steady Job for Papa*. New York: Vanguard, 1966.

Bensoussan, Nicole. "Paper Fish: Une esthetique du temps." *L'Esthetique de la representation*. Annales du C.R.A.A..

Bona, Mary Jo. "Broken Images, Broken Lives: Carmolina's Journey in Tina De Rosa's Paper Fish." *MELUS* 14.3–4 (Fall/Winter 1987): 87–106.

———. "Claiming a Tradition: Italian American Women Writers." *Dissertation*. University of Wisconsin, Madison, 1989.

———. "Learning To Speak Doubly: New Poems by Gianna Patriarca and Rose Romano." *VIA: Voices in Italian Americana* 6.1 (Spring 1995): 161–68.

———. *The Voices We Carry: Recent Italian/American Women's Fiction*. Montreal: Guernica, 1994.

Bonomo Ahearn, Carol. "Interview: Helen Barolini." *Fra Noi* (September 1986): 47.

Boyd, Betty Caroli, Robert F. Hearney and Lydio F. Tomasi. *The Italian Immigrant Woman in North America*. Proceedings of the Tenth Annual Conference of the American Italian Historical Association. Toronto: The Multicultural History Society of Ontario, 1978.

Brenkman, John. "Multiculturalism and Criticism." *English Inside and Out: The Places of Literary Criticism*. Eds. Susan Gubar and Jonathan Kamholtz. New York: Routledge, 1993. 87–101.

Bryant, Dorothy. *Miss Giardino*. Berkeley, CA: Ata Books, 1978. Reprint. New York: The Feminist Press, forthcoming 1997.

Candeloro, Dominic. "Chicago's Italians: A Survey of the Ethnic Factor, 1850–1990." Eds. Melvin G. Holli and Peter d'A. Jones. *Ethnic Chicago: A Multicultural Portrait*. 1977. Revised and expanded ed. Grand Rapids, MI: William B. Eerdmans, 1995. 229–59.

Cavallo, Diana. *A Bridge of Leaves*. New York: Atheneum, 1961.

Ciresi, Rita. *Mother Rocket: Stories*. Athens: University of Georgia, 1993.

————. "Paradise Below the Stairs." *Italian Americana* 12.1 (Fall/Winter 1993): 17–22.

Cisneros, Sandra. *The House on Mango Street.* 1984. New York: Random House, 1991.

Demetrick, Mary Russo and Maria Famà. *Italian Notebook.* Syracuse: Hale Mary Press, 1995.

DeSalvo, Louise. *Casting Off.* Brighton, U.K.: Harvester, 1987.

di Donato, Pietro. *Christ in Concrete.* 1939. Preface by Studs Terkel. Intro. by Fred Gardaphé. New York: Signet, 1993.

di Leonardo, Micaela. "White Ethnicities, Identity Politics, and Baby Bear's Chair." *Social Text* 41 (Winter 1994): 165–91.

Fausty, Joshua. "Masquerading Narratives: 'Passing' in Rita Ciresi's Mother Rocket." Paper presented at the conference, "The Situation of Contemporary U.S. Fiction: Fiction at the Turn of the Century." John F. Kennedy Library. Boston, April 1995.

————. Review of *Mother Rocket: Stories. VIA: Voices in Italian Americana* 6.2 (Fall 1995): 204–7.

———— and Edvige Giunta. Unpublished interview with Tina De Rosa. North Brunswick, NJ: October 1995.

Foster, Patricia ed. *Sister to Sister: Women Write About the Unbreakable Bond.* New York: Doubleday, 1995.

Friedman, Susan and Rachel Blau Du Plessis. "'I Had Two Loves Separate': The Sexualities of H.D.'s 'Her.'" *Montemora* 8 (1981): 7–30.

Gabaccia, Donna. *From the Other Side: Women, Gender, and Immigrant Life in the U.S. 1820–1990.* Bloomington: Indiana University Press, 1994.

————."Italian American Women: A Review Essay." *Italian Americana* 12.1 (Fall/Winter 1993): 38–61.

Gardaphé, Fred L. "Autobiography as Piecework: The Writings of Helen Barolini." *Italian Americans Celebrate Life, the Arts and Popular Culture: Selected Essays from the 22nd Conference of the American Italian Historical Association.* Eds. Paola A. Sensi Isolani and Anthony Julian Tamburri. Staten Island: American Italian Historical Association, 1990. 19–27.

————. "Breaking and Entering: An Italian American's Literary Odyssey." *Forkroads: A Journal of Ethnic American Literature* 1.1 (Fall 1995): 5–14.

————. "Continuity in Concrete: (Re)Constructing Italian/American Writers." Unpublished paper.

————. "An Interview with Tina De Rosa." *Fra Noi* (May 1985): 23.

————. "(In)visibility: Cultural Representation in the Criticism of Frank Lentricchia." *Differentia: Review of Italian Thought.* Special Issue on Italian American Culture. 6–7 (Spring/Autumn 1994): 201–18.

————. *Italian Signs, American Streets: Reading Italian/American Literature.* Durham: Duke University Press, 1996.

————. "Visibility and Invisibility: The Postmodern Prerogative in the Italian/American

Narrative." *Almanacco: Studi di Italianistica* 2.1 (Spring 1992): 24–33.

Gates, Henry Louis, Jr. *The Signifying Monkey: A Theory of African-American Literary Criticism.* New York: Oxford University Press, 1988.

Gilbert, Sandra M. *Emily's Bread.* New York: Norton, 1984.

Gillan, Maria Mazziotti. *Where I Come From: Selected and New Poems.* Toronto: Guernica, 1995.

Gioia, Dana et al. "Where Are the Italian American Novelists?" *Italian Americana* 12.1 (Fall/Winter 1993): 7–37.

Giunta, Edvige. "Blending 'Literary' Discourses: Helen Barolini's Italian/American Narratives." *Romance Languages Annual* 1994 Vol. 6. West Lafayette: Purdue Research Foundation, 1995. 261–66.

———. *Crossing Critical Borders in Italian/American Women's Studies.* Proceedings of the National Conference of Italian American Studies. New York, April 1995. New York: John D. Calandra Italian American Institute. Forthcoming.

———. "Narratives of Loss: Voices of Ethnicity in Agnes Rossi and Nancy Savoca." *Canadian Journal of Italian Studies.* Special Issue on Italian American Culture. Forthcoming.

———. Reinventing the Authorial/Ethnic Space: Communal Narratives in Agnes Rossi's Split Skirt." *Literary Studies East and West. Constructions and Confrontations: Changing Representations of Women and Feminism East and West.* Vol. 13 (1996). Forthcoming.

———. ed. *VIA: Voices in Italian Americana.* Special Issue on Women. 7.2 (Fall 1996).

Green, Rose Basile. *The Italian-American Novel: A Document of the Interaction of Two Cultures.* New Jersey: Farleigh Dickinson Press, 1974.

Gutman, Amy ed. *Multiculturalism: Examining the Politics of Recognition.* Princeton: Princeton University Press, 1994.

Hamington, Maurice. *Hail Mary? The Struggle for Ultimate Womanhood in Catholicism.* New York: Routledge, 1995.

H. D. *Asphodel.* Introduction by Robert Spoo. Durham: Duke University Press, 1994.

———. *Bid Me To Live* (A Madrigal). New York: Dial, 1984.

———. *The Gift.* New York: New Directions, 1982.

———. *HERmione.* Introduction by Perdita Schaffner. New York: New Directions, 1981.

Holli, Melvin G. and Peter d'A. Jones eds. *Ethnic Chicago: A Multicultural Portrait.* 1977. Revised and expanded ed. Grand Rapids, MI: William B. Eerdmans, 1995.

Hongo, Garrett and Catherine Parke. "A Conversation with Sandra M. Gilbert." *The Missouri Review* 9.1 (1985–86): 89–109.

Hurston, Zora Neale. *Their Eyes Were Watching God.* 1937. New York: Harper & Row, 1990.

Ignatiev, Noel. *How the Irish Became White.* New York: Routledge, 1995.

Kazantzakis, Nikos. *The Last Temptation of Christ.* Trans. P. A. Bien. New York: Simon and Schuster, 1960.

Krause, Corinne Azen ed. *Grandmothers, Mothers, and Daughters: Oral Histories of Three Generations of Ethnic American Women*. Boston: Twayne, 1991.

Ling, Amy. "I'm Here: An Asian American Woman's Response." *Feminisms: An Anthology of Literary Theory and Criticism*. Eds. Robyn R. Warhol and Diane Price Herndl. New Brunswick: Rutgers University Press, 1991. 738–45.

Lloyd, Susan Caperna. *No Pictures in My Grave: A Spiritual Journey in Sicily*. San Francisco: Mercury, 1992.

Maso, Carole. *Ghost Dance*. 1986. Hopewell, NJ: Ecco, 1995.

Nazzaro, Pellegrino. "L'Immigration Quota Act del 1921, la crisi del sistema liberale e l'avvento del fascismo in Italia." *Gli Italiani negli Stati Uniti: L'emigrazione e l'opera degli italiani negli Stati Uniti d'America*. Atti del III Symposium di Studi Americani. Firenze, 27–29 maggio 1969. New York: Arno, 1975. 323–64.

Nelli, Humbert Steven. *The Role of the "Colonial" Press in the Italian-American Community of Chicago, 1886–1921. Dissertation*. Chicago: University of Chicago, 1965

———. Italians in Chicago, 1880–1930. *A Study in Ethnic Mobility*. New York: Oxford University Press, 1970.

Pacyga, Dominic A. "Chicago's Ethnic Neighborhoods: The Myth of Stability and the Reality of Chicago." Eds. Melvin G. Holli and Peter d'A. Jones. *Ethnic Chicago: A Multicultural Portrait*. 1977. Revised and expanded ed. Grand Rapids, MI: William B. Eerdmans, 1995. 604–18.

Patriarca, Gianna. *Italian Women and Other Tragedies*. Toronto: Guernica, 1994.

Peragallo, Olga. *Italian-American Authors and Their Contribution to American Literature*. New York: S.F. Vanni, 1949.

Pola, Antonia. *Who Can Buy the Stars?* New York: Vantage, 1957.

Rimanelli, Giose. *Benedetta in Guysterland: A Liquid Novel*. Montreal: Guernica, 1993.

Romano, Rose. "Where Is Nella Sorellanza When You Really Need Her?" *New Explorations in Italian American Studies*. Proceedings of the 25th Annual Conference of the American Italian Historical Association. Washington, D.C., 12–14 November 1992. Eds. Richard N. Juliani and Sandra P. Julani. Staten Island, NY: American Italian Historical Association, 1994. 147–54.

———. *Vendetta*. San Francisco: malafemmina press, 1990.

———. *The Wop Factor*. Brooklyn/Palermo: malafemmina press, 1994.

Rossi, Agnes. *The Quick: A Novella and Stories*. New York: Norton, 1992.

———. *Split Skirt*. New York: Random House, 1994.

Sautman, Francesca Canadé. "Women of the Shadows: Italian American Women, Ethnicity and Racism in American Cinema." *Differentia: Review of Italian Thought*. Special Issue on Italian American Culture. 6–7 (Spring/Autumn 1994): 218–46.

Savarese, Julia. *The Weak and the Strong*. New York: G.E. Putnam's Sons, 1952.

Sollors, Werner. *Beyond Ethnicity: Consent and Descent in American Culture*. New York: Oxford

University Press, 1986.

Strom, Linda. "Reclaiming Our Working-Class Identity: Teaching Working-Class Studies in a Blue Collar Community." *Women's Studies Quarterly.* Issue on Working-Class Studies. 23.1–2 (Spring/Summer 1995): 131–41.

Talese, Gay. "Where Are the Italian American Novelists?" *The New York Times Book Review* (14 March 1993): 1, 23, 25, 29.

Tamburri, Anthony Julian, Paolo A. Giordano and Fred L. Gardaphé, eds. *From theMargin: Writings in Italian Americana.* West Lafayette: Purdue University Press, 1991.

———. "Helen Barolini's Umbertina: The Gender/Ethnic Dilemma." *Italian Americans Celebrate Life, the Arts and Popular Culture: Selected Essays from the 22nd Conference of the American Italian Historical Association.* Eds. Paola A. Sensi Isolani and Anthony Julian Tamburri. Staten Island: American Italian Historical Association, 1990. 29–44.

———. *To Hyphenate or Not to Hyphenate. The Italian/American Writer: An "Other" American.* Montreal: Guernica, 1991.

Tamburri, Anthony Julian. "Umbertina: The Italian/American Woman's Experience." Tamburri, Giordano and Gardaphé eds., *From the Margin: Writings in Italian Americana.* West Lafayette: Purdue University Press, 1991. 357–73.

Tomasi, Mari. *Deep Grow the Roots.* Philadelphia: Lippincott, 1940

———. *Like Lesser Gods.* Milwaukee: Bruce Miller, 1949.

Torgovnick, Marianna De Marco. *Crossing Ocean Parkway: Readings by an Italian American Daughter.* Chicago: University of Chicago Press, 1994.

Torjesen, Karen Jo. *When Women Were Priests: Women's Leadership in the Early Church and the Scandal of Their Subordination in the Rise of Christianity.* San Francisco: Harper, 1995.

Vecoli, Rudolph J. "Italian Immigrants and Working-Class Movements in the United States: A Personal Reflection on Class and Ethnicity." *Journal of the Canadian Historical Association* (1993): 293–305.

Waldo, Octavia. *A Cup of the Sun.* New York: Harcourt, Brace & World, 1961

Walker, Alice. *In Search of Our Mothers' Gardens.* 1967. New York: Harcourt Brace Jovanovich, 1983.

Weiss, Penny A. and Marilyn Friedman eds. *Feminism and Community.* Philadelphia, Temple University Press, 1995.

Woolf, Virginia. *A Room of One's Own.* 1929. Foreword by Mary Gordon. London: Harcourt Brace Jovanovich, 1981.

Zandy, Janet ed. *Calling Home: Working-Class Women's Writings.* New Brunswick: Rutgers University Press, 1990.

———. ed. *Liberating Memory: Our Work and Our Working-Class Consciousness.* New Brunswick: Rutgers University Press, 1995.

———. ed. *Women's Studies Quarterly.* Issue on Working-Class Studies. 23.1–2 (Spring/ Summer 1995).